Stay with Me

Stay with Me

Me

Eleanor Green

Stay with Me

Contact information: contact@authoreleanorgreen.com

Cover Art by: Kiley Murphy

www.authoreleanorgreen.com

Eleanor Green

Indie Chicks Rock, this is for you. #FYW

Acknowledgements

First, the readers. Without your reviews, comments, emails, and support, this book would be stuck in a journal. I love connecting with you and hearing your perspective.

My family deserves a major shout-out for letting me hide and escape in the words. Kiley, my husband, is the greatest man I know, supporting my dreams, encouraging me to continue when I want to delete all the words, and not throwing things at me when I mistakenly call him a character from the book.

A special thank you to my daughter for making graphics, my son for bringing me a fresh cup of hot tea—knowing I'll leave it untouched and need another—and bringing me back to reality when I desperately need it.

Thank you to my father-in-law for letting me take over his RV and call it my writing cabin!

My editor, Meghan Hand, and Jennifer Sing of *Proof This,* for finding the errors and laughing with me instead of at me. Behind every good book are a great editor & proofreader with amazing suggestions.

My girls—I wouldn't be here without you! Faith, Livia, Celeste, Ruthie, Elisabeth, B.A., and Niecey. I love you HAM! #StartedFromTheBottom

Quos amor verus tenuit, tenebit.

~Those who true love has held, it will go on holding.

—Seneca

Stay with Me

One

Cooper

Love—such a small word for a feeling that took over my entire being.

Briley had fallen asleep easily in the master bed of her family's vacation home, while I lay awake watching her breathe. The moon was full and lit up the condo bedroom as if a lamp was on. With the sliders open, it was too warm for covers, but she insisted on having the white sheet pulled up over her body. Still, I could make out every curve of her figure as she lay on her stomach, her back rising and falling with each breath.

I'd loved Briley my entire life—that wasn't news. But the closest she'd ever come to telling me she loved me was our silly one-four-three code. Deep down I knew she'd tell me she loved me one day, and I had been willing to wait forever to hear it.

When she finally whispered the words—three stupid words that somehow brought a man to his knees—my heart was healed, made whole. I swear I could actually feel it pumping stronger with more life than it ever had before. You know the saying, so good it hurts? Truth. My heart pumped so furiously, it was uncomfortable, but a pain you'd pay money to feel over and over again.

I knew at that moment I'd do anything for her. It was my job to protect her, keep her safe, and I knew without a doubt that I would lay down my life for her.

I let my eyes take in the marvelous making of Briley. Her hot pink panties visible through the silky sheet caught my eye. Unable to move my gaze from her delectable body, I let it roam over her firm ass to the dip of her lower back. The sheet hugged the curves of her waist and stopped, her back and arms bare. Finally, I couldn't stand it. I had to touch her. My hand instinctively stroked her arm, causing her to stir and wiggle to my side.

I fell asleep with her in my arms, snuggled up to me like I was her lifeline. She was mine, no doubt. Then Mother Nature sang us to sleep, using the sound of the waves crashing onto the shoreline, just outside the sliders. Nothing and no one could intrude on us here in our own little slice of heaven.

Sometime in the middle of the night, I felt her body jerk and she let out a muffled cry. She was still asleep, but her body was shaking and tears rolled down her cheeks into her hair.

Nudging her shoulder, I woke her up. "It's okay. Just a nightmare." Pulling her closer to me, I rubbed her arms, trying to calm her. She swiped at her tears, but they kept falling, her body still shaking. "You're safe. I've got you," I whispered over and over again, until she began to settle. "Want to talk about it?"

She sat up, crossing her legs Indian style, and swiped more tears away with the back of her hand. Reaching for the sheet, she pulled it up to her chin. I couldn't tell if she needed it for security, or if she was trying to hide her bare breasts from me in her vulnerable state.

Short bursts of arrested breaths made me worry she might hyperventilate. Drawing in a deep breath, she began retelling the dream in short, choppy sentences. "It was awful, Coop. Just awful." She chewed on her bottom lip, eyebrows drawn together as she tried to shake the images from her mind.

I didn't know what to say or what else to do besides pull her into my lap and hold her until she cried it out.

"It was just a bad dream." I pressed my lips to the side of her head.

"It has something to do with that birth certificate. My parents . . . they're not who they say they are, or I'm not who *I* think I am. Whatever it is, something is wrong . . . very wrong."

Stroking her back, I made promises I didn't know anything about. "No, no. It was just a dream. I promise."

"But the look on everyone's faces . . . like I didn't belong," she cried. "Even you. You were there, standing next to my dad. He was alive, and you knew it all along, it was all a game . . . a freaking game."

I stroked her hair some more, trying to bring her comfort while a chill walked up my spine. "It was your mind playing tricks. None of it was real."

"I know," she finally sighed, resting her head against my chest, her breath becoming steadier. "But it seemed real. And the worst part was the hate in your eyes. I ran . . . I kept running, but I wasn't going anywhere. You were right on my heels, laughing and taunting me."

"Oh, baby, I'm sorry. Look at me." I lifted her chin and stroked her cheek with a thumb. "I'm right here, as serious as I've ever been, and I'm not going anywhere." Not when I just got her. No fucking way. I kissed the top of her head, her tear-soaked cheeks, and eyes. "I'll always love you, Briley. Even when you don't want me anymore, I'll still be there for you, watching over and protecting what I love most in this world, my girl."

She sniffed, took in a cleansing breath, and looked at me for a long time. Her eyes, glassy with tears, studied mine, searching for the assurance she needed, and I desperately needed her to believe. She was mine, for as long as she'd have me, and I was hers until the day I died. Most likely even after.

"I'll always want you." Her fragile hands, still shaking, cupped my face. "You've always been my rock, Cooper Sterling. I trust you and I love you, so much. I know that I'm safe in your arms. It's where I belong; it's where I always want to be." She kissed me, seeming to savor every slow second. Despite the careful pace, a growing passion quickened and pulsed within me.

Torn between wanting to comfort her and the raw lust developing, I pulled away. "Baby—"

"Please, Coop . . . please." Her lips crashed back into mine, ravenous and impatient.

Peeling the sheet from her body, I cupped her breast, manipulating a nipple between my fingers until it was stiff. She groaned and moved to straddle my lap, my arousal twitching beneath her in anticipation. Before I had the chance to get her ready, my erection was in her hand. Fuck, she did things to me. I groaned, enjoying the feel of her soft hand. Moving her panties to the side, she centered my tip at her entrance and worked her way down my length, moving slowly. The only sound in the room was our heavy breathing mingled with the collision of waves against the shoreline.

I gripped her hips to hasten her movements, but she needed the control and took it. Head buried in my shoulder and fingers gripping my back, we rocked to a leisurely tempo. And breathing through it, trying to hold off, only intensified the sensations. *You're killing me, baby.* Trusting her with control provided a powerful moment, and we both reaped the rewards. Fuck, I loved this girl. She rested her head on my chest, her breath coming out in puffs against my chest as we rode the aftershocks together.

With bodies tangled together, I knew this would be a special place for us. I'd bring her back here someday. Maybe an anniversary. Not our honeymoon, that would be special and I'd love to take her somewhere more secluded where I could watch her splash around for days in crystal blue waters and a tiny bikini. Maybe for a weekend when the stress of everyday life proved to be too much. I envisioned our children one day playing on that beach out there, while we sat on the lanai, watching.

On second thought, we'd be out there with them, jumping waves and making sand sculptures. It was too soon to think about kids, but indulging in a few internal thoughts about the future couldn't hurt. Right now I had exactly what I'd always wanted, nestled into my side.

Yes, love was too weak a word. But knowing Briley, she'd come up with something stronger.

Two
Briley

Sweet, salty air blew in from the open sliders and dragged a strand of hair over my nose. Blinking my eyes, I realized it was still dark outside—the sun just barely casting a faint glimmer across the glass of the sliders—and the space next to me was empty. But before I could worry, the smell of coffee wafted through air, arousing my senses and easing my mind.

Cooper, I thought with a lazy smile.

Normally I liked to snuggle deep under the covers, petitioning for another five—or twenty—minutes of sleep, but since it was our last day on the island, the sunrise was begging for my audience. Letting one eye enjoy sleep while the other remained barely open, I located the object of my dreams.

The soft glow of hallway light invaded the darkness, illuminating Cooper's large frame. Even in the shadows I could see that he didn't bother covering his nakedness. He sauntered toward me, all male and muscle and a cocky grin.

"Coffee?"

"Please," I answered, my voice thick with sleep. "How much time have I got?"

"Not much. We can take the coffee with us, or skip out if you'd rather stay in bed." He waggled his brows and sat beside me, holding both our cups.

I was way too sleepy for *that,* not being a morning person. Cooper, on the other hand, was full throttle as soon as his feet hit the ground. Until I'd been up for at least twenty minutes, a full cup of java in my system, I was groggy and moody. Even then, I wasn't fully human until I showered. However, there was a new excitement in the air. Not only did I have the sunrise to look forward to and another day on my favorite island, I got to share it with my best friend and the man I loved.

Worry and doubt over unanswered mysteries tried to seep in, attempting to poison my mood, but I shook the thoughts away and concentrated on sipping the hot coffee without spilling it.

"We can always go back to *bed,*" I declared, trying to waggle my too-tired-to-obey brows. I sat up, taking the mug in my hands and sipping the hot brew carefully. "This is our last shot watching the sun rise."

He presented the best look of feigned shock I'd ever seen. "Were you thinking I wanted to . . . good grief, woman, get your head out of the gutter! I was only thinking about your beauty sleep." His eyes rolled dramatically, eliciting a giggle from me. "Besides, you've worn me out. I need a break." He huffed and leaned back on the bed frame.

I glanced between his legs, noticing how easily he was affected. "Obviously." I smirked before climbing out of bed. "Sunrise, sex, and scooters."

Fighting the temptation to look at his reaction, I set my mug on the nightstand, walked across the room to the bathroom, and shut the door. When I was finished and came back out, his expression, exactly as I had pictured it—lips twisted into a smirk, eyebrows knitted together—was waiting for me.

"Is that the name of a new band? Sunrise, sex, and scooters?"

I knew he was teasing, knowing full well what I meant. "In that order, too."

"I can't make any promises. We'll do all three before we leave this afternoon, but there might be a few more S's in that equation." He gripped me at the waist and pulled me toward him, leaning in for a kiss.

"I couldn't possibly guess which one." I giggled and then jumped when he smacked me playfully on the ass.

Eager to see the sun rise over the ocean, I slipped a tank top over my head and pulled on a pair of shorts.

"For chrissakes, B, seriously?"

"What?" I glanced back to see what I'd done and where I'd kicked off my flip flops.

"I can see your nipples through that tank and you're not wearing panties. Not only am I gonna have to fight off every man on the fucking beach, but I'll have to do it with a raging hard on."

"Oh, stop." My fist punched his shoulder without fazing him. "No one's ever out there this early except a few shellers, and they'll be looking down the whole time."

He stood, arms stubbornly planted over his chest and watched me intently as I searched for my flip flops.

I threw my hair behind my shoulder and narrowed my eyes at him. "How many women will *I* have to fight off of my very hot, very naked lover? At least *I'm* covered!"

I expected him to tease me back, or chase me. But he simply set his mug down and kept his eyes locked on mine as he crossed the room in a few easy steps. He took my hand and wrapped it around his waist while taking my chin in his palm.

"Boyfriend," he corrected me. "Lover sounds cheap." A simple brush of his lips against mine caused my eyes to flutter and my skin to pebble—or maybe it was the way he said *boyfriend.* "This," he waved his hand down the front of his body, "is for your eyes only." Then he flashed a casual wink before releasing me. "Your flip flops are by the front door."

***

I adjusted the water temperature, letting the steam fill the space as we undressed. Our coming together was the perfect example of an oxymoron—two people more comfortable with each other than siblings, since birth, filled with such uncertainty and fear they had almost thrown any potential of a relationship away. Now, standing before each other, naked and exposed in every way possible, there was no question he was my chaotic peace, my irresistible uncertainty.

As we stared at each other, love oozing from both of us, I wanted to be playful, make a joke to lighten the serious mood around us. Something about how we hadn't bathed together in nineteen years. But my mouth wouldn't open, and I couldn't have formed words if I had tried.

I'd had this man over and over again in the past two days, but each time it felt like the first.

My blood began to simmer as I looked at his incredible body, the hours spent in the gym evident in his muscular arms and broad shoulders.

Reaching out, I trailed my fingers down his abs, over each ripple of muscle. His body tensed, and he drew in a deep breath, causing me to look up from my worshipful sketch across his stomach. His lids were heavy with lust, a knowing smile pulling at the corners of his mouth, ruining me for every other smile in the world.

He stepped into the shower, pulled me in behind him, and shut the glass door. Not a word was spoken as he eased me back into the water, saturating my hair. He filled his palm with shampoo and worked my strands gently until they were thick with suds.

"I think you used too much shampoo." I smirked as he continued to rinse the massive amount of bubbles.

"What's next? Conditioner?" He looked to me for guidance as he eyed the bottles.

"Hold out your hand." I lifted the conditioner and poured the right amount into his open palm. "Just the ends."

He worked it in, using the extra on his hands to massage my shoulders.

"You're too tense, B. I thought you'd be more relaxed by now."

I let myself enjoy his fingers plying my tense muscles. "I guess I've got a lot on my mind." My eyes closed when he worked his thumb into a stubborn knot on the right side of my neck.

Maybe if you bite down on it . . .

A flutter of butterflies lit up inside me. Last night he had bitten a spot between my neck and shoulder—not hard enough to break the skin—and it sent me over the edge. I'd never experienced that before and was surprised by the erotic sensation. Not surprisingly, the left side was absent of those stubborn knots he was trying to work out.

"Worried about the birth certificate?" he asked, digging until I grimaced. "Almost got it."

"I've gone over it again and again, and I can't come up with a legitimate reason for my parents to have someone else's birth certificate. I mean, if my life was a soap opera, I could imagine that maybe I was stolen. Or switched at birth. But my parents are good people. They're normal folks with average lives. You know my mom, and you knew my dad. My father wouldn't have died with a secret like that."

"Of course not," Cooper whispered, turning me and pulling me into his arms. "It's nothing like that. There has to be a simple explanation. When your mom gives you the details, you'll see it was all a misunderstanding. In fact, we'll have a good laugh at your vivid writer's imagination." He chuckled, but I wasn't buying it. I picked up on the subtle worry in his voice.

Wanting to change the subject, I backed out of his arms and picked up the shampoo. "Your turn." I squeezed a nickel-sized dollop into my palm. "This is our last day on Sanibel, and I'd like to enjoy it outdoors." Flashing him a wink, I pushed him under the spray, massaging the shampoo into his head and giggling every time he moaned. Cooper had always loved having his head massaged, but he was putting on a show that would've given any Hollywood actor a run for his money.

"Does it really feel that good?" The pads of my fingers tingled as I pressed into his scalp.

"Yesss," he dragged out the word.

"You still have that weird head massager with all the metal tines?"

"No." His voice was muted, and it sounded like he was deep in thought. "I bet they still make them. I should get another one."

"Your own version of a sex toy," I teased. "Don't take it to work with you, everyone'll think you're a perv."

He leaned back and rinsed the suds from his hair. "Everyone already knows I'm a perv." He raised one eyebrow and halted me with his grin.

His eyes roamed down my body, his gaze becoming intense. Everything was intense—the way he looked at me, like he'd never seen me naked before, and the way his hands worshipped my flesh with slow, methodical movements.

Time stood still as steam billowed around us. So still, I was sure the water from the shower head was flowing slower—a seductive dance, enticing us further. Every sensation was extreme and concentrated. Every flutter of my heartbeat felt against my ribs.

God, this man was stunning—his massive, sculpted physique inked with beautiful designs that only added to his bad boy persona. Our eyes met and locked, his expression a mix of warmth and hunger. He leaned down, pressed his mouth to mine, and kissed me so deeply I could've easily turned to liquid and slipped down the drain. He had a way of melting me to the core, and I couldn't get enough. When he pulled away, a bemoaned sigh slipped from my lips, then he nuzzled into my neck, kissing and sucking as I panted in response.

I leaned my head back and to the side, giving him more access to the spot that drove me wild. The stubble on his face scratched against my skin, burning a trail from shoulder to ear. It was what I'd craved. Instinctively, I reached my arms up and crossed them loosely around the back of his neck. Standing on tiptoes, I pushed into him, feeling his hard length jump against my belly. I couldn't wait another second for him to be buried inside of me.

"I need you," I breathed, my head lolling to the side as he skillfully worked my neck and ear.

He had me so heated, I was ready to detonate on the spot. I was ready to beg if necessary.

There was no hesitation in his movements. Lifting my left leg, he set my foot on the tiled corner wall seat. Our eyes met and something passed between us as he positioned himself at my entrance. I'd never seen or experienced the depth of emotion that radiated through both of us in this moment.

We both gasped when he pushed into me, my eyes sliding shut as a wave of ecstasy overtook me, tickling my flesh with trails of goose bumps. He moved slow, making love to my body and soul as he whispered praises in my ear.

Besides whimpering and irregular heavy breathing, the only word that spilled from my lips was his name. And if I hadn't known before, I knew without a doubt now that I was inexorably in love with Cooper Sterling, and I never wanted to know what it felt like to live without him.

Three

Cooper

Briley had twisted my heart so many times over the years, shaping it into whatever form fit in the moment. She broke it, pieced it back together, and sometimes left it in my chest, hollow and barely beating. Don't get me wrong, she had no idea what she was doing, or when it was happening. She was the kindest, most compassionate person I knew. Always sacrificing, making peace no matter the cost to her, and caring for others.

As busted up as I was on the inside, she mended my heart right there in the shower stall, beneath the spray of warm water. Speaking with her eyes alone, she gave me everything. All I needed was her love, but what I got instead was complete trust. With raw vulnerability, she gave me her heart, trusting me to be the guardian of such a rare gift. Surely she knew by now I would protect it with my life.

It felt so good to be inside of her. Fucking amazing. I rocked in and out of her, watching the expression on her face. I was putting that look on her face, making her moan with every thrust. She dug her fingers into my shoulders when I started to move at a faster pace. I wouldn't be able to hold on much longer, and I wanted her to let go first. Needed her to.

Sliding my hands under her ass, I hoisted her up and leaned her back against the wall. She wrapped her legs around me as I lifted her hips slightly, in order to hit the spot that seemed to drive her wild.

"Oh God, oh God!" she screamed.

Let go, baby, I silently begged. My efforts to hold my release were now out of my control. She felt so damn good. I watched her face in awe as her core tightened around me. It was fascinating seeing her consumed by something so powerful she couldn't even keep her eyes open. When she breathed out my name, it began. Sensory overload. My focus settled on this exact point in time, like my entire life had built to this moment. Like there was nothing before this and would never be anything after. Everything was black then white. Light shimmered around me, its warmth easing me back together until I was in the present again.

There was no sense in screwing up the moment with words. Instead, I eased her down and held her in my arms until our bodies stopped quaking. A few times I had to adjust the water temperature as it started to cool.

When the handle wouldn't turn any further, we exited the shower and dried off. I didn't know how in the hell I was going to recover from that, get on scooters, and play hard the rest of the day. All I wanted to do was climb under the covers and hold her. For hours.

She must've read my mind, or the look in my droopy eyes. "You look tired." She pushed her bottom lip into a pout. "Quick nap?"

I wasted no time climbing under the covers and pulling her close. The last thing I remember is her snuggling into my side, then I was out, the girl of my dreams snuggled into me.

***

After a too-short nap, Briley was up and raring to go. I was still lagging, but she threw a protein bar at me, and we headed out to the rental shop. Briley looked fucking adorable in a white swimsuit cover that tied around her neck, and I couldn't stop staring at her. She was happy and playful. It'd been a long time since I'd seen her like this.

We pulled out of the rental shop and hopped on a red 49-cc scooter, Briley's arms around my waist as I sped down the road toward Captiva. I looked like a fool on the tiny thing, but I felt like a king.

Briley pointed things out and had us stopping every ten minutes or so as she showed me things that were hidden to the rest of the tourists. She knew where to find manatees, and pointed out a certain tree that was covered in little black crabs. I hoped she didn't see the shiver run down my spine as I watched the creepy little things crawl over each other, coating the tree like thick, black bark.

She spoke animatedly about the foliage, naming each tree and plant as I drove at a casual pace. When we crossed over Blind Pass onto Captiva, she made me slow down so we could read all of the signs. Each house had a clever name.

"Pair-a-dice!" she squealed. "That's my favorite."

We ate lunch at a screened-in place overlooking the water. It didn't look like much from the outside, but the food was great and I was starved, as usual. I finished my plate and half of hers after she pushed it away.

"Last stop," Briley said as I pulled the scooter into a parking space at the tip of Captiva Island. "The waves are great here."

"Have we missed any?"

"Missed any?" She scrunched her face in the cutest way.

"I'm sure we've dipped our toes in every beach on both islands. I just wanted to make sure we didn't miss one." I tossed the scooter key in the air, caught it, and flashed her a wink.

"You're not having fun?" She frowned.

16

I untied her sarong and set it on the seat of the scooter. She adjusted her white bikini bottoms and shifted her weight to one side, her right foot pointed as she drew shapes in the sand.

"I'm having a blast. Why do you ask?" I gripped her waist, slippery from the mixture of sweat and sunscreen. Her skin was hot from the sun, and the way her bikini hugged the parts of her I wished my hands could touch . . . I was in need of water, now.

"Hop on." I turned my back to her and lowered myself so she could climb up.

"You're crazy!" She wrapped her arms around my shoulders, her breasts pressing against me and her body sliding across my back as I walked.

Shit. Bad idea.

I squeezed my eyes shut and blew out a breath to gain control. The beach wasn't crowded, thank God, so I made my way to the water at a fast pace, Briley clinging to me even after I'd gotten waist high.

"You staying back there all day?" I tried to wriggle her loose.

"I like it here. You're giant muscles are like hard pillows," she cooed, resting her head on my shoulder. "And you're so warm." I felt her smiling against my neck.

"You're killing me here," I chuckled. Why the fuck couldn't the water be colder? Glaciers would've been appreciated.

Finally, she pushed off of me and into the water. "Sorry." A giggle. "You're so easily turned—" Just then, a wave rolled over her head, smothering her words. She pushed her sea-soaked hair off her face and wiped her eyes. "Thanks for the warning," she said sarcastically, but still smiling.

"Thanks for taking one for the team." My raging hard on had eased after watching her being bowled over by that wave.

For the next hour, we jumped the waves, rode them to the shoreline on our stomachs, and found sand dollars with our toes. Briley was in charge of placing them back down on the ocean floor, her touch more gentle than mine. We only found one that wasn't alive, and she insisted on giving it to a little girl collecting shells along the shore.

"Would you like to have this?" She set the sand dollar in the little girl's hand.

"You found a whole one! Thanks!" The girl beamed.

By the time we returned the scooter around three, we were both beat.

"Let's get dessert on the way out," I suggested, offering one more thing for her to look forward to before we left her island. I hated seeing the sadness already building in her eyes. Maybe one day, when my business was established and funds were flowing more freely, I'd buy a place down here for us. She had her mother's condo, and could visit anytime, but a place of our own sounded like heaven.

"Okay." She perked up. "I know the perfect spot."

Key lime pie was her choice, of course. I had chocolate cake, but I admit she'd chosen more wisely. She would've fed me the entire thing if I'd let her, so I had to pretend I couldn't eat another bite. I loved watching her eyes close with every mouthful as she savored the flavors.

"You make it difficult for a guy to be in public when you do that, B."

Her eyes shot up at me, wide with question. "What am I doing?"

"Eating that pie like it's the best sex you've ever had." I closed my eyes for an instant and added discreetly, "Moaning as you suck every last morsel off that fucking fork."

Something flashed in her eyes, but she let it die and took the final bite, scraping her fork against the plate to get every last bit. We ordered coffee to get us through the drive ahead, and to extend our time together. Driving home separately was going to suck.

"You know what's weird?" Briley asked.

"These tiny cups?" I tried to lift the dainty white cup to my lips.

She chuckled, then shook her head. "No. We know everything about each other. What do we talk about now? I mean, I can't ask you what your favorite color is or if you played sports in school. I know all the answers."

"You don't know *everything*," I argued teasingly.

Briley's eyebrows perked up. "No? Tell me, secret agent, what don't I know?"

Maybe I shouldn't have gone there. This could get ugly if I didn't think carefully about each question.

"Let's do this on the drive," I suggested. "It'll be fun and keep us awake for the drive back to Tampa."

***

Briley followed behind me as we drove off the Causeway, exiting the island. Once we pulled onto I-75, I dialed her cell and waited for her voice to come through the Bluetooth speakers in my truck.

"Hello?" she answered, her voice so sweet.

"So, here's how it's going to go," I started, drumming my fingers against the steering wheel. "Since we've known each other all our lives, courting will be different. So let's pretend we've just met and play the twenty questions game anyway."

"We're courting?" She giggled. "We so should've had a chaperone this past weekend." Her voice transformed into something from the early eighteen hundreds with a thick southern drawl. "Mr. Sterling, you're much more wise to the ways of this world than little ole me."

I played along. "Nicely played, Miss Sheffield. So, you're an actress?"

"I dabble." I could picture one of her shoulders shrugging casually as held onto the steering wheel. "And what do you do for a living, kind sir?"

"I'm a stripper." I deadpanned.

"A stripper?" she asked, southern accent gone, and the inflection in her voice giving away a hint of shock.

"Yeah. I prefer to call myself an artist and dancer." As hard as I tried, I couldn't keep the laughter at bay.

"You must bring home some cash, shakin' that fine ass on stage."

"I do okay."

We both shared a laugh before we got back to the truer questions and answers. All through our conversation, I kept going back to the "fine ass" phrase. That felt good to hear.

"So, Cooper Sterling, tell me about your friends."

"Well, I've got a few buddies that I like to have a beer with. But my best friend—don't laugh when I tell you this—she's a girl. We've been close since we were babies, and she's not like other girls." Nostalgia got the best of me and the words come out unfiltered. "I mean, she's got all the parts, but she's not all fluffy and hard to read. She gets me and I get her. We shoot straight with each other and skip those games people play. She likes to watch sports . . . basketball especially, and she can shoot a three-pointer like no one's fucking business. Of course, she's not as good as me."

I heard her huff over the line. "She sounds ugly. A girl that can kick your ass in basketball must be seven feet tall and butchy."

"I never said she could kick my ass in any sport," I corrected, feeling her smirk through the phone. I glanced in my rear view mirror to catch it, but the sun had set, and all I could see were head lights. "And she's nothing like you described. I remember when we were kids, thinking she was the most beautiful girl in the world. Now that she's all grown up, she takes my breath away."

Cheese ball, I thought, grimacing. Hopefully she was eating it up.

I went on, my voice soft. I couldn't help it. "Her name is Briley, but I call her B for short. Wanna hear something funny? She's obsessed with bees so her mom calls her Bee. You know, B-e-e, like the honey bee."

"That's ridiculous! Poor girl." She snickered. "So, have you made the moves on this ugly duckling?"

I knew she was being funny, but her words irked me. "I told you, she's gorgeous," I said sternly. Would she never know how beautiful she was? Then I laughed, trying to bring the mood back. "And I didn't have to make the moves. She did. The woman was all over me, couldn't get enough. I have to take long showers just to get a break from—"

"That's not true, you big oaf!" She sounded mad, but I could hear the laughter in her voice.

"You're right, you follow me into the shower, too." I laughed so hard, the truck swerved and I had to pull myself together.

"Be careful, Cooper." The worry and sincerity in her voice sobered me in a flash. "I just found you, I can't lose you."

"Sorry, babe. We're almost home. Your turn, whad'ya wanna know?"

"How many women . . . Nevermind, don't answer that. Hmm, if things don't work out between us . . . Damn it! Let me think. Okay, if you could travel anywhere in the world, where would you go?"

If things didn't work out?

My fingers tightened around the steering wheel, mimicking the feeling of my heart clenching in my chest. "B, why are you so insecure? You know me. You know you can trust me. I've been in love with you my entire life. I'm not going to hurt you. I'm not him."

"I know, I'm sorry. Old ghosts and all." Her voice was soft, almost a whisper. "So, favorite color?"

"Blue. What's your favorite candy?" *Lemon heads.*

"Lemon heads. Favorite season?" she asked.

"Fall. Favorite movie?" *An Affair To Remember.*

"*An Affair To Remember.* Hey, we're coming up on your exit."

"I thought I'd make sure you got inside, help you with your bags and all." Plus, the idea of leaving her for the night was making me ache already, and I wanted to make sure her house was safe. Blake had been dealt with, but that didn't mean shit with that crazy bastard. He was unstable and unpredictable.

Ten minutes later, we pulled into her driveway. I rolled her suitcase inside and checked the house over, making sure no one—Blake—had gotten in.

"Coop," she said. "Can you stay?" Her eyes were soft and pleading.

My heart melted. The idea of leaving her seemed impossible anyway—*whipped!*—so of course I wanted to stay.

"Are you scared, B?" I asked, the hair on the back of my neck rising in anger. I hated the thought of her lying in bed night after night, worried about that asswipe breaking in.

"No." She shook her head and lowered her gaze. When she spoke again, her voice was quiet, almost a whisper. "I'm just not ready to say goodbye."

"Me either. I never like leaving you." I gripped her waist with my hands, my fingers overlapping. "I can stay. I'll have to get up early and go home before work, though."

"I'll get up with you, and we'll have coffee together." Her face lit up, those big brown eyes sparkling. She wasn't much of a morning person, but I'd take what I could get.

"Deal."

Briley locked the front door and checked it twice before she was satisfied. She shuffled her feet down the hallway, covering her mouth with the back of her hand as she yawned. Exhaustion must've gotten the best of her as she stripped down to her panties, leaving her clothes wherever they landed. I stripped as well, leaving my clothes in a pile on her bedroom floor. Then, skin on skin, I pulled us down to the bed, draped the covers over us, and breathed in her scent—clean with a hint of coconut—before kissing her shoulder.

"G'night, B."

She took a deep, satisfied breath and exhaled, "Night, Coop."

I felt her body relax almost immediately, her breathing finding a slow, peaceful rhythm. Physically, I was exhausted, but my mind refused to settle. I couldn't stop thinking about how perfectly this trip had ended, and how lucky I was that my plans had worked. The look on her face when she realized it was me behind her playing our song. Thank God she told her mother everything and I was able to get the bartender's help.

She was finally mine now, and I didn't want to waste a moment of our time on sleep. But my body betrayed me after a while, taking me into a deep, tranquil slumber. With the woman I loved in my arms trusting me to protect her and keep her safe.

Four

Briley

I was hot, like I'd been wrapped in an electric blanket in the middle of summer. An arm wrapped around my torso while a massive, heavy leg was draped over my lower half. Cooper was sound asleep, his thick, dark lashes splayed across the flesh beneath his eyes like a feather duster.

I knew he had to go home to get ready for work, otherwise I would've endured the sweat-inducing heat of his body half-covering mine, just so I could watch him sleep. He was beautiful like this, his strong jaw relaxed. Allowing another moment to study him, I let my fingers roam over his warm skin, tracing the curve of each muscle like a sculptor admiring new clay. My hand cupped his cheek, savoring the feel of his morning scruff. Before waking him, I indulged in a daydream about watching him shave. Maybe helping . . .

Running my fingers through his hair, I whispered, "Coop." He didn't stir, so I nudged his shoulder. "Time to get up." Nothing. Suddenly I felt claustrophobic, trapped beneath his weight and heat. "Cooper." I wiggled, trying to free myself. "Get—" More squirming and pushing. "Up!"

At the same time I freed myself from his leg, he stirred.

"I'm up." He sat up and scrubbed his hands over his face. "What time is it?"

I reached for my phone on the nightstand. "A little after seven."

"Shit, I must've been tired. I haven't slept that hard in a long time."

25

"Yeah, you were out."

He turned on his side, propped himself up on an elbow, and looked at me. "How do you do it?"

"Do what?" I pulled the covers up to my chin, feeling bashful suddenly as he watched me.

"Wake up looking so beautiful."

I pulled the sheet up further to cover my face. "You're still half asleep. I think you're dreaming."

"I don't think so." He hooked a finger in the sheet and tugged it down. "Did you sleep okay?" His fingers brushed a strand of hair away from my face, and I felt it slide behind my shoulder.

"I did, and I dreamed a really hot guy was in my bed."

The corners of his mouth lifted in a grin so enticing, I wanted to kiss it off him. "Sounds like a great dream. This super hot guy . . . someone you know?"

I loved the playfulness in his voice, even at this godforsaken early hour. "Oh yeah, very well." I offered an impish smile, raising one exhausted eyebrow. "By the way, I never said *super* hot. Just hot. So hot that I'm sticky with sweat. What are you, a werewolf?"

He tilted his head to one side, looking confused.

"Your leg and arm were draped over me this morning." I splayed my hand on his thigh. "You're seriously hot."

He waggled his eyebrows, his irises lit with an inner glow of mischief. "You know it, baby."

"Gah!" I pawed at his hand inching up my leg. "I need coffee before I can be civil, and you'll be late for work."

"Folgers is no match for what I can do for your mood," he said seductively.

Damn him.

Warm breath caressing my ear loosened me, opening me up to the idea of his wake up call. I choked back a whimper as his inching fingers pushed past my barely objecting hand, over my hips, outlining my waist, and finally cupping a breast. I groaned, trying to feign defeat, but my body betrayed me, physically revealing my desire. Sweet, seductive kisses along my throat dissolved me. Whether it was love, lust, or a combination of both, it consumed me.

He took his time—time he didn't have—and lavished every inch of my body with soft strokes, kisses, and sweet nips. By the time he was nose to nose with me, I was so desperate for him, my body was trembling.

His lips pressed gently against mine with a control that I wanted to bust with a sledge hammer. Greedily, I reached my arm around the back of his head and pulled him to me, claiming his mouth like it was manna from heaven. I loved his lips and the way he gave me everything in a single kiss. His mouth adored me as it melded with mine, our tongues tangling together lazily, all energy melting along with my core.

His fingers hooked in the waistband of my panties and eased them down my legs, tossing them across the room to land wherever. A scorching fire raged through my body, taking over and threatening to leave a mound of ash behind. Only one person could satiate the ache inside, and he had more control than a British Royal Guard.

"Please," I groaned, stroking his rock hard length before guiding him between my legs.

He worked himself in, the final thrust sinking him to the hilt. My vocabulary disappeared; the only sounds trickling from my lips were whimpers of pleasure. Cooper on the other hand, became talkative.

"So beautiful." God, he felt so good. Not just the sex, although it was out of this world amazing, but the way he looked at me when we made love. The awe and adoration behind his eyes, the way his jaw slacked and his eyes grew heavy as he got closer. "I love to hear you moan. Fuck."

I loved the feeling of his stomach sliding against mine. But the one thing that drove me over the edge was his kiss. Deep and hungry, like there wouldn't be another chance. Mingled with the things his body was doing to mine, and I was lost. In him, with him.

He traced my lower lip with his tongue, his hot breath puffing against my throat as he spoke. "I love knowing I'm the one making you lose your mind."

I loved it, too. God, did I.

The sensations started rolling through me, a slow, tortuous voyage through my limbs, teasing my spine. I couldn't get close enough to him. I wanted our souls to intertwine and relieve the agony inside. My legs wrapped around his back involuntarily, pulling him closer, deeper.

He slipped his hands under my hips, lifting them off the bed. My breaths came in shallow pants, trying to hang onto reality. Cooper nestled his head between my neck and shoulder, whispering praises. "I love you. So damn much, Briley."

It was too much, the impending orgasm so strong I was gulping for air. My fingers dug into Cooper's back, rooting part of me in place as the rest floated into another atmosphere, reveling in the beauty of darkness freckled with sparks of light. Cooper was right behind me, riding the aftershocks with more grace than I was capable of. When I finally came back down, my senses returning, it was all I could do not to weep.

Hugging Cooper as tightly to my body as he'd allow without crushing me, I confessed, "I love you. I love you. I love you."

Falling in love with Cooper wasn't one of those knocks on the side of the head that left you dizzy and clueless as to what happened. With Cooper it was natural. Our relationship had glided from friendship to love, as sweet and easy as honey melting on your tongue.

He hadn't changed. He still offered me his coat when I was cold, opened doors, and pulled out chairs. That was Coop—big and rough on the outside, a gentleman throughout.

But I had changed.

I had grown up. Learned to let go and appreciate him more than ever. But most importantly, I trusted him now with all my heart. His love had inspired me to want to write again, pen poems on the backs of napkins and scrap pieces of paper.

Since we'd traded breakfast for sex, we shared a quick cup of coffee and inhaled granola bars.

"Want me to go with you when you talk to your mom?" Cooper asked. The compassion in his eyes pulled me in until my arms were wrapped around his waist.

I shook my head against his chest. "No, I'm good, thanks. I'm gonna go on over after I get a shower."

"Call me..." He hesitated. "If you want. You don't have to share if it's . . ." His chest expanded as he took in a deep breath. "Yes, you do. I want to know what's going on in your life, B. I always want you to feel like you can talk to me."

"I will." Pulling back, I stroked his arms. "You're my best friend, Coop. Of course I'm always going to confide in you."

He took my chin in his hand and lifted it. "Best friends that happen to be madly in love." The inflection in his voice made me wonder if he was stating a fact or asking a question.

To dispel any doubt, I reiterated, "Wildly, uncontrollably in love."

Five

Cooper

I drove home deep in thought, replaying the last ninety-six hours detail by detail. Two things were baffling me. First was how one minute our friendship had been on the line, and the next it was suddenly bonded stronger, tighter than ever before. Reinforced with rebar and concrete, nothing able to sway or crack our foundation.

The second was how I'd gotten from Briley's driveway to my own. I must've been consumed deeper in my thoughts than I'd realized.

After a shower and shave, I threw on a clean button down shirt and slacks, grabbed my coffee, keys, and phone, and made the traffic-laden trek to work. Usually by this time I'd strung out a few foul sentences about the fucking morons on the road. But today I enjoyed the slow pace. Gave me more time to think, savor the memories of our weekend together.

I'd never been the kind of guy to hold back. If I was in, I was all in, no matter what it was. A job was either done right or we'd start over. It was the same with Briley. I never once considered protecting a piece of my heart from her, in case she freaked, changed her mind, and put me back in the friend zone. There was something about our connection that had changed, had deepened to a level of no return. Like two sheets of paper glued together, if either of us separated from the other, it would destroy us both.

I parked my truck in its usual spot, grabbed my travel mug of coffee, and headed toward the front door. Sterling & Tyler was a small building with dark windows and sleek black trim. This place was my dream come true, my life. Today, however, it was the last place I wanted to be.

Even though I knew I wouldn't be able to focus on the day's tasks, I stepped through the door with a spring in my step. I was in such high spirits, not even Mr. Kinkaid's bullshit could affect me.

Colin Tyler, my partner and college buddy, was in my business before I entered the building. "How'd it go, dude?" He held the door open, the cool air conditioner issuing a blast of relief as I stepped inside.

Colin was a good friend, always had my back, but we were a rare pair, as dissimilar as two people could be. He was your typical frat boy, dressing and acting the part. We'd met in Construction Documents and Contracts class and were paired up by the professor for a project. I'd hated everything about him until I'd gotten to know him.

"Couldn't have gone any better, man." My attempt to keep a straight face failed. I couldn't stop smiling.

Colin followed me down the hall toward my office. "Details!"

"No." I shook my head. Setting my coffee down on the desk, I looked down at the stack of papers waiting for my attention. This was going to be a long day.

Colin parked his ass on the edge of mahogany—the only space not covered with documents—and folded his arms. Determined son of a bitch.

"You gotta give me something. I'm not asking for intimate details . . . unless you want to dish?" He paused, raising an amused eyebrow. When I didn't give him the satisfaction of acknowledgement, he continued. "Was she surprised? I take it she was happy to see you?"

My smile transformed into a full on grin. "Yeah, man, she was surprised. The look on her face when she heard me play our song . . ." I drifted off to that day, the expression of surprise and awe on her face forever burned into my brain.

"So, she ran away from you and then fell into your arms because you played a fucking song for her?" That amused expression turned into a frown.

"Watch it, dude." I glowered.

Colin raised his hands defensively. "No offense, brother. Just trying to catch up. You're not giving me much here."

"She didn't run from *me,* she ran from her feelings for me." I shrugged. "And apparently it was the time she needed to get her thoughts organized and realize the chance that we could work was worth the risk."

"I'm happy for you, buddy." He smiled finally and slapped me on the back. "For both of you." His last words exhaled on a sigh, "Finally."

"I know, right?" Finally, indeed.

After catching me up on what I'd missed at work, I planned my attack on the load of shit I had to get done. I'd have to work through lunch to get caught up. Starting with signing a few paychecks, I then returned two calls from Mrs. Griffin about her new addition. The woman had the biggest walk in closet in the history of the fucking universe and still wanted more. She was the most difficult client I'd ever worked with, constantly changing her mind, and I could've gotten really heated with her nagging, materialistic, old bag of wrinkles. But the money and publicity our company was getting outweighed the cons, so I sucked it up and forced as polite a tone as I could manage.

Once Mrs. Griffin was satisfied with answers, I sent Briley a text.

Hi! You OK?

She responded immediately. I hoped she wasn't driving.

Yeah. A little nervous. About to leave.

I contemplated dropping everything and driving to her mother's house. She was about to have a discussion that hopefully would give her some answers. But those answers might be hard to swallow and, although Briley was a strong woman, she was also fragile, and the thought of her falling apart made my stomach knot. I knew I needed to give her the independence she'd asked for, but just in case she changed her mind and needed my support, I offered one more time.

I can be there in 10. Wait for me?

Again, the response was immediate.

Thx, but want to talk to her alone. I need answers and will have a better chance if it's just the two of us.

OK. 143, I shot back.

But as soon as I sent the ole one-four-three, I regretted it. We were past that, onto the real thing. She beat me to it, sending the following:

I <3 U

I <3 U2

U <3 U2? I like them, but love them?

Smartass. I sent her one more.

LMAO. You'll be fine today! I <3 YOU

Just so there was no discrepancy this time…

I went back to chipping away at the stack of papers on my desk, but I was distracted. I wondered what her mother would tell her. What did it all mean? A birth certificate with the wrong name. I had told her it was probably a mix-up, but so many things didn't add up. She didn't resemble either of her parents, and where was the rest of her family? Aunts, uncles, cousins? Then there was the fact of her mother, sheltering her like a lioness protecting her young in the wild. Except we were in Tampa, and Briley was grown.

A commotion in the lobby pulled me out of my thoughts. Stalking down the hall into the lobby, I saw Madison arguing with Colin.

"There you are." She squinted her eyes at Colin and sauntered up to me. "I brought you lunch. Thought we could enjoy this beautiful day with a picnic."

"I tried, man." Colin threw up his hands and walked back into his office.

"Can't. I've gotta work through lunch." I thought I'd made it clear that I wasn't into her, but she either wasn't taking the hint, or I wasn't doing a good job of explaining myself.

She blinked, then lifted her chin, clearly determined. "You've got to eat something. Keep up that masculine physique." She gripped my bicep and gave it a squeeze. "I made the most luscious chocolate—"

Backing up, I loosened myself from her grip. "I'm with Briley."

She remained unaffected and I wondered if my words had even registered. How many ways could a man tell a woman he wasn't interested without making her feel like a fool? Not my problem. I strode back into my office, shut the door behind me, and resisted the urge to look and see if she was still standing in the lobby. I would not play this game with her anymore. Not today, not ever.

Six
Briley

Stomach twisting and churning, I pulled slowly into my mother's driveway. Normally I'd be excited to see her. I'd tell her how Cooper had surprised me on Sanibel and how our relationship had changed and morphed into something beautiful. She'd cry, wipe her tears, and then point a finger at me, saying, "I tried to tell you, Bee."

But this wouldn't be a pleasant visit. I needed to know why she had that birth certificate hidden away in her safety deposit box.

My mom always locked the front door, even during the day, so I used my key, turned the knob, and stepped through the front door. The radio was playing an old tune by Patsy Cline, and I followed the sound into the kitchen, calling out so I wouldn't scare the bejesus out of her.

"Mom?"

"I'm in here, babygirl."

I found her at the kitchen table, mending a quilt. She looked happy and content, a relaxed, easy smile on her lips as she hummed along to "Walking After Midnight." I took the seat across from her after kissing her on the cheek and watched her finish tying off the thread before cutting the end, then putting her scissors, needle, and thread back into her sewing box.

"How was your trip?" The excitement in her voice dropped my mood by at least four degrees. I desperately wanted to tell her all about my trip and time with Cooper, forgetting about the conversation I needed to have instead. But I couldn't put it off,

36

letting it fester and build until I was too chicken to talk to her about it at all.

I twisted my hands under the table, working up the nerve to start. Maybe I was wrong, questioning her about something that was none of my business, or might be too painful to talk about. It was possibly a common mistake, but I had serious doubts and I couldn't keep this inside any longer.

She scooted her chair back, ready to stand. "What's wrong? What happened?" she asked with a glimmer in her eyes.

I shook my head and waved my hand for her to sit back down. "Everything's fine . . . great, actually, and I'll . . . I'll tell you all about it soon." I paused to swallow. "Today I need . . . I have some questions."

Her eyebrows pinched together, concern aging her soft features.

Another gulp. "I—I found something that I'd like to ask you about."

At that, her face relaxed, the corners of her mouth lifting into a knowing smile. "Oh, Bee, you don't have to be embarrassed to talk to me. What did you find?" She spoke as if I had found a condom and hadn't known what it was. I had already lived with a man, for Pete's sake. Was she in for a surprise.

"The birth certificate . . . in the safety deposit box . . . it's not mine." Once the words started flowing, they came out fast and furious. Even when I noticed her expression darken, I kept going. "It belongs to an Isabella Paciello."

Her eyes widened, but she remained quiet and shrugged a shoulder as if she didn't know what I was talking about. "Must've been a mix up. Have you shared this with anyone? With Cooper?" she asked, her tone a little off. Lifting the quilt, she studied a corner piece, picking at a piece of thread. What was going on with her? Why act like it was a big secret if it was just a mix up?

"Did you steal me?" I whispered. A streak of pain rushed across my chest and my mind battled for an explanation of what I was feeling—a mixture of hurt and betrayal laced with a heavy dose of fear.

"Of course not!" She shoved her chair back and stood, wincing when the pain of her arthritis struck her knee. "You know I could never steal another woman's baby. Do you really believe that?" The tone of her voice was angry, but a thread of hurt weaved its way through.

"No," I whispered in shame, shaking my head. It was a ridiculous idea. "But how can we straighten this out? I need a copy of *my* birth certificate."

"I'll take care of it," she huffed, unable to meet my eyes. "I've got an appointment that I'm already late for."

With that, she stalked out of the kitchen and into her bedroom. When I heard the door shut, I knew two things were certain—our conversation on the matter was finished, and I was left once again to search for answers on my own.

***

For two hours I drove mindlessly down back roads, trying to figure out what to do, where to look for more clues as to what my parents had tried so hard to hide from me. Realizing I had never called Cooper, I picked up my phone and slid the bar across. Nothing. My phone was dead and my car charger had never made it back after the last business trip.

Damn. He'd be worried, but there was nothing I could do until I got home.

Twenty minutes later, I pulled into my driveway and raced inside to plug my phone in. It took forever to charge enough for use. When the screen finally lit up, I saw that I'd missed several texts wondering how things were going. A voice message waited in my inbox, I'm assuming from Cooper also. Instead of listening to it, I dialed him at work.

He answered on the first ring. "Briley, you all right?"

"I'm fine," I sighed, then went on to explain how my phone had died and I hadn't realized until I was all the way out by Apollo Beach. I rambled on breathlessly until he interrupted.

"I'm just glad you're okay. How'd it go? Did you get any answers? What did she say?"

"Can we talk about it over dinner? I just want to melt into the couch for a bit, and then I'll cook something for us—" I suddenly added, "That is, if you'd like to come over. You might have other plans." I was talking way more than I usually did, clipped words spilling out faster than normal. I was obviously rattled and needed either a hot bath or glass of wine. Probably both.

"B, calm down. Deep breath." He waited for me to follow his instructions, then said, "I'd love to come over, but no cooking. I'll order takeout. Now, pour a glass of wine and slip that fine body into a hot bubble bath. I'm cutting out early, so I won't be too long."

God, he knows me so well. "Thanks, Coop. See you soon."

One glass of wine down and another poured, I stepped into the tub. Bubbles were almost spilling over—just the way I liked it. I sank down slowly until only my head was visible, then I let out a huge sigh. Baths relaxed me more than anything. I'd never taken Valium, but I assumed a bath was the non-prescription equivalent. I even had a playlist labeled 'Bath' for such a time.

With candles lit and a full glass of Malbec in hand, I closed my eyes and let the soothing sounds of "Heaven" by Lamb fill my soul.

In the midst of my relaxation coma, I never heard Cooper come in. Somewhere in the middle of "Wicked Games" by The Weekend, I sensed a presence in the room, my heart beginning to race in panic before I opened my eyes to confirm the notion. He was leaning against the door frame, arms folded, watching me with that cocky grin he was known for.

I yelped, my wine sloshing out of the glass and spilling into the water. "Shit, Coop!" I scrambled to sit up, my hands trembling as I tried to set the wine glass on the side table. "Where did you come from?"

"Sorry." He puffed out a laugh and rushed to my side, taking the wine glass from me and setting it down. He kissed my forehead and stroked my hair. "Didn't mean to scare you."

A few deep breaths and my body was calm enough to survive the shock. "I didn't expect you for a few more hours."

"I couldn't concentrate all day, and then imagining you in the tub, naked . . ." He dipped a hand into the water and moved it across my stomach. "I was in agony sitting behind my desk."

"Well, I'm not getting out of this tub just yet. You'll have to entertain yourself for at least ten more minutes." I shot him my most seductive expression, adding a wink for good measure.

"Fuck," he muttered. "You know you can't do that and expect me to stay out here. I'm getting in."

He lowered his head, turning slightly so our lips would meet. I was completely lost, his full lips tugging against mine. Tongues intertwined in a sensuous rhythm that had my body temperature rising. My hands slid up his white button down and around to the back of his neck as we deepened the kiss. It didn't take much to pull him into the tub with me. If he'd wanted to resist, take his clothes off first perhaps, I wouldn't have had a chance; he was much too strong for me. But he slipped in easily, unresisting, and only breaking our kiss briefly to chuckle and make sure he wasn't crushing me.

Water spilling around us, he started to unbutton his shirt and undo his pants. By the time he was undressed, most of the water was out of the tub and on the tiled floor. He lifted me up, changing positions so he was beneath me, then we made out for what seemed like forever, kissing and nipping at each other's necks. Desperate and unable to wait any longer, I wiggled on his lap, swirling my hips seductively until I was sure he would take me.

Instead, he cradled my face in his hands. Hooded, lust-filled eyes stared into mine. Before I could ask him what was wrong, why he wouldn't give me what I needed, he spoke.

"I love you, Briley. So much."

"I love you, too, Cooper." More grinding, trying to relieve the pressure that was now throbbing.

"I'm serious. This is it for me." He cleared his throat and I looked into his eyes, realizing just how serious he was. "I was thinking today how it all felt too good to be true. Worried that something would happen or change and I'd lose you. But I can't live like that. I want to enjoy this, enjoy you."

The throbbing didn't ease, but this was important enough for pause. With my face still in Cooper's hands, I gazed at him, absorbing the intensity in his eyes and resting my hands on his. "Cooper Sterling, nothing will ever come between us. I belong to you. Every part of me."

Our eyes never broke contact as we made love. It was the most powerful moment I'd ever experienced, watching him and trying to keep my lids from closing as we came together. Afterward, I was so exhausted, emotionally and physically, I didn't move off of him. Instead I collapsed onto his chest, my head snuggling into his neck. When chill bumps covered my flesh and a shiver ran through me, he rubbed my arms up and down.

"Let's get you warmed up."

I nodded and stepped out of the tub. Cooper dried me off with a fluffy white towel, taking his time to make sure he didn't miss a spot. He was tender, an oxymoron for such a big, rough guy. After I was thoroughly dried, he helped me into my robe and wrapped a towel around his waist.

"I don't have anything for you to wear." I untied my robe and started to pull it off. "You can wear this, and I'll slip into some sweats."

He laughed, shaking his head. "That won't fit me, B." He pulled the belt of my robe back around my waist and tied it. "I'll stick my stuff in the dryer and hang out in this towel for a while." He looked down at himself and then back up at me with an adorable smirk. "You might have to answer the door when the food arrives, though."

"You should leave a change of clothes here." I wrapped my arms around his waist. "Seems to be a habit with you, not taking off your pants before getting wet." He chuckled like a middle school boy and I rolled my eyes. "You know what I mean."

Seven

Cooper

Chinese takeout on the living room couch and good conversation was becoming a habit of ours, and I loved every second of it. We even had entertainment—or at least I did—watching Briley try to use chopsticks. No matter how many times I positioned her fingers and showed her how to hold them, she would still pick awkwardly at her food like a toddler new to a fork. I gave her credit for trying, though.

"Want a fork?" I finally asked.

"No way, I've got this." She balanced a piece of tofu on her sticks and brought it to her mouth. I couldn't help chuckling when she dropped the saucy piece on her lap.

After, she agreed to use a fork, and we were able to talk.

"Tell me about today. What did your mom say about the birth certificate?"

"It was so weird. At first she acted like it was no big deal—a common mix up—and I was good with that. But then she freaked and shut me down."

I stopped mid bite and set my container of cashew chicken on the coffee table so I could give her my full attention.

Her eyebrows twisted, worried wrinkles forming on her forehead. "I asked her if I was stolen."

Stolen?

My eyes widened. That had never crossed my mind. "She denied it, right? I mean, no way in hell that happened." I hoped I sounded firm, although I wondered if it could be true. With the

43

birth certificate—correct date, wrong name—and the fact that she didn't resemble either of her parents, it was plausible.

"Oh, she denied it of course. Got really mad at me for even suggesting it. And I want to believe her, but she was so mad and defensive. Then she lied, saying she was late for something and shut herself in her room. It was like I'd hit the nail on the head. What the hell could she be hiding from me, Coop?"

"No, baby." I shook my head. "I'm sure there's another explanation."

"Yeah, sure. Since I'm the spitting image of my tiny, five-foot-three mother, and personality to match," she said with heavy sarcasm.

Her smartass-ness and sarcasm was shocking sometimes, coming from such a sweet girl. You never knew what you were going to get with her, and I loved that.

"Here's a theory," she continued. "There were twins. My parents figured the woman didn't need two babies, so they took one—me—" She pointed the chopsticks at herself. "—and made the birth mom think the other one died. What I don't understand is how. I mean, did she dress up like a nurse and deliver the babies, or invite her over for tea and induce labor so she'd have them at home? Hell, I can't imagine her doing any of that."

I tried not to laugh at her insane idea. "Listen," I began. I had a theory of my own, but it would mean bringing up a tender subject that I would've gladly buried. "I met someone while I was in the joint." I picked at my cashew chicken, unable to meet her eyes. I still wasn't sure how she felt about my time in prison, and I wasn't ready to find out. I needed her to see me through the eyes she had always seen me with, not tainted.

"What do you mean, you met someone?" Her nose crinkled up. Damn, she was cute.

Suddenly, I realized what she was insinuating. "Shit, B, seriously?" I narrowed my eyes in disgust. "I met a guy that was in for hacking. He's a genius. Got out a few months before I did. Anyway, he owes me a favor. I could get him to look into that certificate, see what he can find."

"I don't want to get him in trouble." Of course my girl would be worried about that.

"As long as it doesn't include stealing money from a large company, I think he'll be okay. Nothing we'd ask him to do is illegal. He'd be digging, not stealing."

"Okay," she answered, dragging out the word with caution. "If you think it would bring some answers without getting anyone in trouble, I'd be so grateful."

"Done then." I smiled. "Now that that's settled, let's see what our fortunes tell us." I handed her a cookie.

She cracked it and unrolled the tiny piece of paper, squinting to read the words. "A smooth sea never made a skillful mariner. What the heck kind of fortune is that?" She frowned, looking like she'd been gypped.

"Mine says: a faithful friend is a strong defense." I smiled. "I like it."

"Yours is good . . . and true." She paused, twisting her hands in her lap as she rested against a pillow, her legs pulled up and folded Indian style. Half-empty food containers cluttered the coffee table. "Even though our dynamics have changed, we're still friends, right? I mean, you still feel comfortable telling me things?"

I looked at her like she was crazy. "Why wouldn't I?"

"You know, now that we're intimate, you can't fart whenever you please, and you have to let me beat you every single time in basketball."

I waited for her to wink or slap my thigh playfully, but she maintained her serious expression.

"Bullshit!" I laughed. "I know you. You couldn't stand it if you thought I was letting you win. You're much too competitive. And as far as the farts . . . too bad, sucka!" I leaned in, fingering her ribs until she was breathless with laughter.

"Stop, stop! I'll pee!"

I believed her, so the tickle-fest ended.

Dinner over, we cleaned up all the empty containers, stored the rest in the fridge, then settled next to each other on her couch for *The Transporter*. We'd watched the movie at least a thousand times. I was sick of it, but Briley had a huge crush on Jason Statham, so I indulged her. Story of my life.

No one deserved the happiness I experienced when I was with her. Even while my arm tingled with the beginnings of numbness as she fell asleep on me, missing the last half of the movie. I was the luckiest SOB.

At ten past midnight, I carried her to bed. She stirred enough to help me get her robe off and get her tucked in. "G'night. I'll call you tomorrow."

Awakening then, she asked, "Where are you going?"

"Home. I've got nothing to wear, and I have to work in the morning." Might have to remedy that. Soon.

She pulled back the covers and scooted over enough for me to barely fit next to her. "Stay. You've got clothes to get you home in the morning. This weekend you can bring some things to leave here." She twisted her lips, shy Briley making an entrance. "If you'd like, I mean. I—I just don't like being apart from you. Now that you're home, and you're . . . mine. I sleep better with you here. I feel safe and . . ." She shrugged, but I understood.

She had a way of making me feel like a king, her protector, and the world's greatest lover. Of course, there was never any doubt about the latter, but it still felt good to know she felt that way.

"Same, baby." I stroked her hair, pushing it away from her face. "I'll stay." I set the alarm on my phone, making sure I'd have enough time in the morning to drive home for a shower and shave before work. I had an important meeting with some high profile clients that we desperately needed to land.

After sliding into bed, I pulled her backside into me, her body forming to mine, and I wrapped my arms around her. She fell asleep first, and I drifted off to the rhythm of her breathing.

***

The sky was still dark when my alarm blared "Happy" by Pharell Williams. It irritated the piss out of me, making the effort to get out of bed in the morning easier. I hit snooze, enjoying ten more minutes of Briley's limbs snaked around my body. It felt so good to have her in my arms. She belonged right here. If I didn't have to go into work, I'd stay in bed all day listening to her breathe.

How did I live before this?

Damn, you're turning into a pussy.

She stirred when the alarm went off for the third time, stretching her arms overhead as she yawned. "Get up, Coop." She gave me a nudge. "I'll make some coffee."

Reluctantly, I rolled out and trudged down the hall to the laundry room. I collected my clothes from the dryer and dressed, meeting her in the kitchen for a quick cup O' Joe.

"Looks like it's gonna rain." I nodded out the kitchen window at the cloudy sky. No sign of the sun.

"Good, I've got way too much to do today and I can't be tempted by that glorious ball of warmth and goodness." She sipped on her own coffee.

"When's your next trip scheduled for?" I hoped it wasn't soon.

"I don't know. I haven't heard anything." She shrugged one shoulder and paused. "Angela's got a rep for waiting until the last minute to inform me of her plans."

I kissed her goodbye, once, twice, and a final time before heading out the door. "I'll call you after lunch. I've got that meeting this morning."

"That's right. Good luck." She smiled, leaning against the frame of the front door, her robe tied around that tiny waist as she held her mug with both hands. "You're going to get it. I just know."

"I don't know." I winked. "I don't deserve this much goodness in my life. If I land this deal, I'll have to watch for planes falling out of the sky." I walked backward down the sidewalk toward my truck. Getting used to that view of her waving me off in the morning was getting addicting.

Eight
Briley

Drizzling rain and dark clouds always made for the perfect writing day. With a cup of hot tea on the desk beside me, I booted my computer and started with a poem. I had way too much joy inside of me not to express it in writing. Cooper had inspired so many new feelings, I thought I would burst if I didn't get it out.

The poem was short but gave me the release I needed to move on to my work. My article was on Truffles. It didn't take much research since I loved them and had experienced them shaved, infused in oils, and several types of truffle butters. I wouldn't write about the truffle ice cream I once was excited to sample. It was the closest I'd ever been to gagging publicly in a restaurant.

When I finished typing the rough draft, I dressed for a late morning run. The rain had stopped—hopefully long enough for me to get home from my run—and the cool breeze that came in with the storm felt wonderful.

"Move" by Thousand Foot Crutch was blasting through my ear buds as I picked up my pace, my energy level through the roof. It took all I had in me not to lift my arms in the air and cheer. Or, maybe I'd start singing the theme from *Rocky*. I hadn't felt this good in months—maybe years—and Cooper Sterling was the reason. I was crazy about him and ecstatic that the part of my brain guarding the overthinking cells had been destroyed.

Take that!

But then, my lips curved into a frown as I thought about how much time I'd wasted that could've been spent with Cooper. Why had I been so stupid to push him away? Look where it had gotten me—almost three years of my life sucked away by Blake.

I shook my head, erasing the thought of him. Nothing would ruin this euphoric feeling. No one would dampen my giddy mood.

Except her.

I never heard my neighbor, Madison Cull, coming up behind me. Now she was next to me, staring me down like a hawk. It took a good moment for me build up the nerve to look at her. We were friends, until she went after Cooper. I'd grown to hate her and was having trouble hiding that fact between furrowed brows.

She was grinning like a best girlfriend I hadn't seen in weeks, the plastered smile cartoon-like and comical. Only nasty words filled my brain so I kept my mouth shut and the music up, but after another song or two, all my energy vanished, and I slowed to a stop, bending at the waist to catch my breath.

"I'm glad I caught up with you," she squeaked. Could she be anymore fake?

My lips lifted into an acknowledging smile, and I straightened just as quickly.

"I've seen Cooper's truck in your driveway the past two mornings. Everything okay? Your ex isn't still harassing you, is he?"

"Nope," I exhaled.

"So you two just been hanging out? That's nice. I'm sure Blake won't be bothering you as long as Cooper's around." She studied my face, looking for a reaction, I'm sure. Well, she wouldn't get one. Cooper and I were together now. It was no coincidence that he'd stopped calling her and was spending more time with me. She was only trying to pull the information from me, use it somehow. I couldn't imagine how she could use anything I shared with her, but I didn't trust her.

"Well," I smacked my lips together, "I've gotta run." *Pun intended.*

"Hey, listen, Briley. You don't have to avoid me. I know you hooked up with Cooper," she finally admitted. She shrugged and forced a smile. "I can't blame you, no one would. He's the perfect distraction. I mean, you wanted a rebound, and he's a hell of a choice. An amazing lover to get your mind off things for a while . . ." She glanced at the ground, seeming deep in thought about something. It was obvious she was trying to imply that she'd slept with him, and he'd been 'the perfect distraction or rebound' for her.

Well, screw her. She hadn't slept with him. I knew that. Or did I? Now that I thought about it, I'd never asked and Cooper didn't divulge the information. What would he have said? *"By the way, I slept with Madison. Hope you're cool with that."*

Gah! I couldn't think of it without wanting to tear my hair out . . . and then pluck her eyes from her face. *And maybe punch out some teeth.*

For real, though, I needed to know or it would eat me up inside. Had she been with Cooper? Did she know what he felt like? Worse, did he know what *she* felt like?

Dammit!

I stomped out an innocent cricket on the sidewalk, feeling it crunch beneath my tennis shoe. It didn't make me feel better at all. Madison was ruining my day and working on ruining my world. Implying that Cooper and I *hooked up.*

Bitch.

I had to set her straight, even if it meant sounding like a desperate fool.

"I'd hate to think you ran all this way to catch up with me for nothing, so a few answers for you, Mads." I couldn't help the conniving smile that crept across my lips. "Cooper's not a rebound, and we didn't 'hook up.'" Holding my fingers up, I made air quotes to emphasize my point.

"Oh," She placed her hand over her heart, faking a reaction of relief. "Thank goodness. I love you both so much, I'd hate for either of you to get hurt, or for your friendship to suffer over something silly like sex."

Shit, she was evil. My relationship with Cooper wasn't her business, but I couldn't keep my mouth shut and let her walk away with the last punch.

Mimicking her with a hand across my heart, I feigned being touched by her sweet comment.

"We're so blessed to have someone care about us like you do. Just to assure you a good night's rest without worry, I'll let you in on two facts: nothing can ruin Cooper and my friendship; we've been through too much together. And . . ." I let a forced giggle slip. "There's absolutely nothing silly about the sex."

I shouldn't have gone that far. It was petty and small, but I couldn't help myself. Plus, I was madly in love and wanted the world to know it. The last thing I needed was Madison Cull tainting our relationship.

We stood there for a long beat, while I watched her fake façade crumble. The only sound was the blood pumping thick and fast in my ears.

"I'm so happy for you, Briley," she replied finally, reaching up to tuck a strand of my hair that had fallen loose from my pony tail behind my ear. It was an intimidating gesture. I knew because I had used it a couple of times myself. "You've finally found someone that won't treat you like shit."

I blinked a few times, my heart racing in my chest, but was able to regain composure before showing her any sign of weakness.

That was a low blow, bringing up my history with Blake. I was sure she'd meant to sneak it in, obviously catty. Fine. I'd take the punch, but the winning point still went to me. Cooper was mine now—that was all that mattered.

She finished with a sugary sweet, "I'm glad Cooper's not going to come between us. I cherish our friendship."

What friendship? I barely knew the girl. We'd hung out a handful of times and were neighbors. But friends? I didn't trust her. And after knowing how I felt about Cooper and going after him like she did . . . I didn't like her.

I scraped my sneaker hard against the ground, getting out some of my irritation, then replied with a smile that she could take any way she wished. *Up the ass.*

With that, I put my ear buds back in and took off back to the house, lost in thought, caught up in worry, and letting the sadness of "It's Been Awhile" by Staind permeate my soul and darken my mood like the charcoal clouds above me.

After guzzling an entire bottle of water, I picked up my phone, hoping for a text from Cooper. I knew he was in a meeting all morning, but I needed something, anything. I wasn't disappointed when I saw a single emoji waiting for me. A winky face blowing a kiss. It wasn't much, but it was enough.

***

After a quick shower, I sent Cooper a text.

Hope meeting is going well. I <3 U!

Then I shimmied into a pair of denim capris, slipped a shirt over my head, and tied my hair into a pony tail. It was time to start searching for my own answers. With the mysterious safe-deposit box key I'd found when searching for my birth certificate in hand, I was ready to tackle every bank in the area.

The first bank I tried wouldn't let me in their vault without an account. I finally persuaded the young bank manager to search their records for my father's name, but he'd never had an account there. The next two locations were ruled out immediately as they didn't have boxes matching the number on my key.

As I wandered into the fourth building, I was greeted by a sleek woman in a black pencil skirt. She was slim, her black hair twisted up meticulously at the nape of her neck. Although gorgeous, she looked like a royal bitch. I knew right away I wouldn't get far with her, and I nearly walked out.

Then I heard, "May I help you?"

"Um, hi. This is going to sound ridiculous, but I'm looking for the safe-deposit box that goes with this key."

She squinted condescendingly and acted as if helping me would exhaust her to the breaking point. "That does sound strange. Let's go to my office and see if we can figure it out."

I followed her into the back left corner of the bank, stepping into an office that looked like it had been professionally decorated. The woman sat in a leather high back chair behind a mahogany desk, and I took the seat opposite her.

"So," I began. "I found this key in my late father's safety deposit box. It doesn't belong to any of the boxes in the bank where I found it. I was wondering if he had an account here." I glanced down at the key gripped between my fingers that rested in my lap.

"Let's have a look." She smiled, still professional but warm. Once she typed in a few things, she asked me to spell the last name.

"S-h-e-f-f-i-e-l-d."

"I don't have an account for a Sheffield, sorry."

I smiled despite my growing disappointment. Today was turning out to be a bust. "Well, thank you very much for looking." I stood and shook her outstretched hand. Talk about not judging a book by its cover. She looked like the meanest woman on the planet and ended up being the nicest I'd dealt with today.

"There must be bank statements that come to the house," she stated.

"Yes, that makes sense." And it did, but was I being reduced to stealing my mother's mail now? If that's what it took, I guess. "I'll go through old statements and see what I can find. Thanks again for your help."

When I got to my car, I rested my head back and took a few cleansing breaths. I'd have to figure out a way to go through my mother's mail when she wasn't home. It felt dishonest and gritty, but she wasn't offering any answers. What choice did I have?

Nine

Cooper

Saturday night I took Briley to the fair. We used to go when we were kids and it sounded fun and different from our usual movie or picnic dates. It was a warm September evening, the thick, salty air mingling the smells of cotton candy, fried carnival food, and exhaust from the rides.

With a bag of cotton candy dangling from my hand, I pulled her toward the Ferris wheel.

"No way! You know how much I hate it." She backed up like a cat nearing water.

"Come on, B." I grinned at her. "Fulfill my fantasy of kissing you at the top."

"You want me to risk death for a kiss?" she accused dramatically. "How about you kiss me here or on that whirly ride?"

I tugged her into the line, not taking no for an answer. "One ride and the rest of the night's yours. I'll even ride the Rock-n-Roll ride with you."

On a sigh, she inched forward. But as we neared the front of the line, she gripped me tighter. I couldn't help but laugh. "Why're you so afraid of the Ferris wheel? It can't be a height thing, you do fine on the Freefall."

"I don't like getting stuck. These things *always* get stuck."

I just shook my head. "Should've known it was a control thing," I muttered, then winked. Her fingers pulsed in mine as we waited behind the gate for the next available pod. Part of me felt bad for putting her through such agony, but the other got a kick out of watching her irrational fear of a ride that kids had been riding for a hundred years.

She gripped the edge of her seat with both hands like the bottom would fall out at any moment, not even loosening her grip when I put my arm around her. At the top, it stopped for a moment to let riders exit and new ones get on at the bottom. Beside me, I felt her shiver.

"It's okay, ya big baby." I gave her knee a squeeze. "They're just letting people get off the ride. Next time I'll ask them to keep the ride going and make the people roll out while it's still moving." I laughed at that. She did not.

"Next time?" she asked, incredulous. "This is it, Coop. One ride, so get your kisses in now." She fisted my shirt and yanked me to her. Her mouth tasted like cotton candy, sticky and sweet.

We arrived at the bottom too soon, barely breaking apart long enough to step off the ride. I tried to woo her into one more trip, without success. "I could kiss that mouth all night," I said, lacing my fingers through hers.

"It was worth the risk," she admitted with a begrudging smile.

We strolled through the crowd, hand in hand as she searched for our next adventure. After the Ring of Fire, bumper cars, and Crazy Mouse coaster, she was ready for games.

"Win something for me, big guy." She ran her hands along my forearms and flashed a playful grin.

Because it's what all guys go for first, I tried my hand at throwing baseballs at the impossible-to-tip jugs. After three failed attempts, we moved on to a basketball toss. In order to win the most god-awful, humongous purple gorilla hanging from the tent, I had to win four rounds.

Briley had the audacity to laugh while she watched me lug the purple monstrosity across my shoulders as we maneuvered the crowd. "Shouldn't we take Clyde to the car?"

"Clyde?" I hiked an eyebrow at her. "From *Every Which Way but Loose?* You can't name this grape Clyde!"

She shrugged. "Okay, Kong then. Not the king but the donkey."

"Donkey Kong?" I laughed. "Perfect."

We were standing in line at one of the food trucks, trying to decide if we should go for stale nachos or the meat on a stick surprise when I heard a familiar voice.

"Cooper Sterling," a female voice purred. "Is that you?" I followed the hand on my arm—a too-friendly gesture—to her face. Amber Wilson. Hadn't seen her in at least three years. We *played* a few times. She was the girl you called when you needed to get laid without the hassle of dating. "How've you been, handsome? I haven't seen you around lately." She gave Briley a once-over and returned her attention to me, turning the drama up ten notches. "Is this the flavor of the month?"

I squeezed Briley's hand in mine while simultaneously clenching my teeth. Where did I find these women? I was surprised a piece of ass was ever worth it.

"Amber, this is my girlfriend, Briley." Even with the purple monstrosity on my back, I couldn't hide my irritation. I could only hope she got the hint and moved on.

Amber gave Briley a condescending half-smile. "She's cute, Cooper." Then she winked at me. "Give me a call sometime."

I wasn't sure how Briley would handle the situation. She had every right to be pissed, and I half expected her to walk away. Then of course I'd spend the rest of the night trying to get her out of a sulking funk.

But, no. My chest puffed with pride as my girl gave Amber a warm, but obviously fake smile, reached out a hand, and said, "It's a pleasure to meet you."

Amber's eyes went wide as she shook Briley's hand. I didn't understand why until she suddenly jumped back and shrieked. Briley had been holding a squeeze bottle of ketchup in her other hand and had emptied most of it onto Amber's legs.

I couldn't stifle the laughter when I heard Briley say, "There, that should help *you* get flavor of the month." Then Briley turned on her heels and stalked off, me right behind her.

"That was the best fucking thing I've seen all night!" I thundered, proud of her. When she didn't slow down, I caught up to her and took her hand. "Hey." I twirled her around to face me. "You mad at me?"

"No," she said, though her nostrils were flaring. "Yes . . . not really." Then she turned her fuming eyes on me. "How many flavors of the month are gonna get in my face like that?"

Shit. Ass was never worth it.

I'd tell myself to remember that little piece of wisdom, but it no longer mattered now that I was with the girl of my dreams. "I'm sorry," I stuttered, choking on laughter. I tried to pull her to me, but she stood as firm as a bull. "Look, you know everything about me, B, so you know I was a player. But those days are over. I don't care about any of those women, never did."

"I know," she huffed. "It never bothered me before. Now I'm all jealous girlfriend, and it feels bad." She hung her head briefly and then lit up. "Hell no, it doesn't. That felt freaking awesome! Served her right calling me 'flavor of the month.' Did you see what she was wearing?" Her hands were flailing with her emotion. "Really, Coop, I know you're a guy and all, but you could do better than that skank!"

"That's my girl." I chuckled and shook my head. "Come on, I've got an idea."

There wasn't a line, so we stepped right up. Briley studied me for a moment before asking, "What's the Gladiator Joust?"

I pointed to the two raised platforms. "I'll stand on one of those platforms and you'll stand on the other one. We'll both have a padded 'joust.' Whoever knocks the other one off first, wins." I pulled off my shoes and added, "Of course I'll win because I'm stronger."

She shot me a fiery smirk and slipped out of her shoes. "Never underestimate the power of anger."

Indeed.

After helping her onto her platform, I stepped over to mine and climbed up. Before I even stood up straight, I felt a whack on my ass. It wasn't hard enough to knock me over, but I took a forward roll and played the defeated roll.

"Cheater!" I shouted and pulled myself back up onto the platform. "Best out of three?"

"You're on," she answered mid-swing. I blocked her shot with my joust and swung it around to tap her on the backside. She wobbled but adjusted her stance and kept her balance. Readying her weapon, she growled and took a swing. Again, I blocked. "Go down, you brute!" She swung again so hard, she lost her footing and took a dive off the platform onto the inflated arena. "That did not count!"

"Of course it did." I laughed and pointed my joust at her "That's karma right there, babe."

"Fine. We're tied." She climbed back up and readied her feet and joust.

"How 'bout a bet?" I taunted, standing on one leg like the karate kid. "If I win this round, you have to go on the Ferris wheel with me again."

She raised a curious eyebrow. "And if I win?"

"If you win, I'll go on whichever ride you choose."

"Whichever I choose?" she repeated, dragging it out. "Even *that* one?" She nodded behind me, and I turned to see what I would be missing once I beat her. The only thing behind me was the parking lot so I had no idea what she was talking about. As I started to turn around and ask, she slammed her padded joust into the backs of my knees and took me out. I landed on my ass, still on the edge of the platform, but the balance was off. My arms flailed as I fought gravity's grip, pulling me down along with my pride.

"Dirty, B. That was downright dirty cheating!" Tossing my joust aside, I stood and held out my arms to help her off the platform, the inflatable giving into our bodies as we bounced to a halt. "What's your prize, trickster?" I asked, claiming her lips before she could answer.

"Oh, Coop," she giggled, then added softly, seriously, "You're the prize."

Call me whatever you like, but my heart fucking melted. This girl—she was the one that made a man want to settle down and change his ways. Her big brown eyes, sweet disposition, and the sound of her laughter had ruined me for every other woman out there. I'd loved Briley for as long as I could remember, but I had no idea how many different branches this love had or how powerful each one would be.

I clenched my chest, mostly for show but also because it did ache. *Briley, Briley, Briley,* I thought, shaking my head at how far she'd reeled me in. *How did we fight this for so long?*

The three of us—her, me, and purple Kong—headed leisurely back to the truck. Purple Kong took the passenger seat while Briley rode in the middle, hugged to my side. I would never be one of those country boys that drove down a dirt road, hunting dogs in the back, and a twangy country song playing on the radio. But this picture perfectly painted that scene—swap out purple gorilla for hunting dogs—and it was nice. If it meant having Briley beside me, I'd pick up a cowboy hat and boots in the morning.

Briley was half asleep when I pulled into her driveway. I tried to carry her to the house, but she stirred and slid out of my arms. "I'm awake."

"Tonight was fun," I said, walking her to the door.

"It was a lot of fun." She swapped the bag of cotton candy to her other hand while she searched for her keys.

Kong was stuffed under my arm, his cheap carnival scent wafting through the air. "Mind if I keep him at my place. I don't like sleeping alone." I tried to keep a straight face.

Briley unlocked the door, set her keys and bag of cotton candy down on the foyer table, and dragged me inside. "Cooper Sterling, now that I know what it feels like to wake up in your arms, you're never sleeping alone again."

Ten
Briley

"It's time!" I clapped my hands together, excited about my newest adventure.

"For what?" Cooper lowered his shades to glance at me. He looked divine in navy swim trunks, one arm folded behind his head on the pool float. I'd been staring at his body, day dreaming about the way he'd made love to me last night. The way he looked into my eyes, as if he knew me better than I knew myself. I rolled off my float, letting the silky water refresh my sun-warmed skin, and swam over to him. Absently I let my fingers trace the intricate tattoo on his shoulder.

"A tattoo," I mumbled, clearly distracted.

"You're telling me it's time to get another tattoo?" He chuckled. "Okay, mistress, where and what do you want inked on your boy toy?"

"What?" I looked up at my reflection in his aviators. "Not you." I splashed a handful of water across his stomach. "Me. I'm ready for my first tattoo."

His smile faded before he rolled into the water and gripped my waist. "You sure? Have you really thought about this, B?"

"I have." I tilted my head and watched him, curious about his opinion. Not that it would change my mind, but I might go smaller or let him help me decide on the location. After all, if things kept moving forward like I hoped they would, he'd be looking at this body for the rest of our lives. "Are you completely against it? Do you think it'd look trashy on me?" I grimaced. Damn double standards.

"No." He shook his head, tucking a piece of wet hair behind my ear. "You couldn't do anything to this body to make it look trashy. If you want a tattoo, get one. I just want to make sure you've thought about it. They don't wash off."

"Really? Damn. Forget it then." I let my shoulders sag and shook my head.

"Okay, smartass." He pinched my ass under the water and I jumped a little. "Tell me what you want and where."

I tested the firmness of the pool float. "This won't do. Side of the pool and you." I winked.

"You don't have to ask me twice, baby." He pulled me closer and kissed me until the water wasn't enough to cool my body off.

When the kiss broke and the world stopped spinning, I inhaled a shaky breath. "Hip. A quote. Go with me?"

"Anywhere, anytime," he breathed before lifting me out of the pool and causing my world to whirl into a wild, brilliant chaos once again.

***

Brown leather couches greeted us in the lobby of the tattoo shop, surprising me with a tasteful décor that defied the stereotype.

"Hi, can I help you?" A tall woman with thin, angular features greeted us with a smile. She had shaggy black hair and a smattering of tattoos across her chest and arms.

Cooper did the honors. "I called earlier to set up an appointment with Adam. This is Briley Sheffield, she's getting her first ink." He patted my shoulder affectionately.

"How exciting." The woman beamed. "I'll let Adam know you're here. If you'll have a seat, I've got some paperwork for you to fill out."

My hands were shaking, and my handwriting gave me away. I shook out my fingers, trying to release the jitters.

"Nervous?" Cooper flashed a grin that was clearly making fun of me.

"A little. Tell me again why I couldn't have a drink to take the edge off?" I'd wanted a shot of vodka just before getting in the car, but Coop shot that idea down.

"We want to make sure you're of sound mind when you decide to get a tat," a man answered, causing Cooper and I both to look up. "Can't have you waking up tomorrow, wondering how that bug-eyed kitten ended up inked across your face."

"Hey, man." Cooper stood and gripped his hand in a firm shake.

"How are you? It's been a while." The guy looked rough and unkempt. His shaggy beard and ponytail made me want to hightail it out of here and rethink my decision.

"Good, really good." Coop reached out his hand to help me off the sofa. "Briley, this is my buddy, Adam. He's the best and the only one I'd trust to do your tat."

"Hi, Adam." I reluctantly shook his hand, offering a timid smile. He was covered in colorful images that all worked together to form a work of art. As the guys caught up, I studied his arms, eyeing each individual piece. My favorite was the face of a little girl. It was so intricate, detailing each feature with amazing precision. If I hadn't seen it in person I would've thought it was a photograph. Beneath it was a date, and I wondered if he'd lost a daughter or sister. I wouldn't ask.

"So . . . your first time getting inked, huh?" he asked, and I nodded. "You look terrified." I shrugged at that comment. I was terrified, but I'd never let him know it. "Let me show you around, tell you how things work, and then we'll get started."

Fingers laced between Cooper's, we followed him down the hall to a larger room. Several partitions lined the walls, each hosting either a chair or table and what looked like the tattoo equipment. Adam took us to his area, showed me the machine, ink wells, and table I'd be lying on while he worked.

"What're we going for tonight, and where do you want it?" he asked as he took purchase on a round stool.

I pulled out the quote by Sylvia Plath that I wanted and showed him the placement. "I really liked this font. Can you do that or will you need to change it?"

He read my quote aloud, "I took a deep breath, and listened to the old bray of my heart: I am, I am, I am." After studying the script and holding it to my hip for a brief moment, he said, "No, this'll work. I'd like to tweak the spacing on a few of the letters, but overall the font is nice." He stood. "I'm gonna make a copy that'll transfer onto your skin. Be right back." He started to walk away but turned back. "You can give her the shot now."

My eyes widened. No one had discussed a shot, and I sure as hell wasn't letting Cooper near me with a needle. "Shot? He's joking, right?"

I backed up as Cooper reached into a sack. He pulled out two mini bottles of flavored vodka and handed them to me. "The waiver said you had to be sober when *signing*."

With an audible sigh of relief, I took one of the chilled bottles, unscrewed the cap, and drained it. "Mmm, blueberry." I took the second one and sipped on it as we talked.

66

Adam returned with the special paper that had my quote printed in mirror form. "Okay," he began, glancing down at my jeans. It dawned on me then that those had been a bad choice. How the hell was he going to get to my hip? "You'll need to pull your jeans down enough for me to get to your hip. I've got a sheet here so the only area exposed will be the canvas I'm working on."

I downed the rest of the vodka and unzipped my jeans. Cooper's jaw clenched, and I noticed his fists doing the same. For his sanity, I handed him the sheet. "Cover me?"

Cooper held the sheet up as if I were totally naked while I shimmied the jeans down my legs. Maybe it wasn't the best idea to get the tat on my hip . . . or bring Cooper along. Of course, he could've gotten a female artist. It was his fault he'd insisted on Adam.

I wondered if he was thinking that very thing right now.

As instructed, I climbed onto the table and lay on my left side. Adam told me everything he was doing as he set up his table. He handed me a large mirror so I could watch the placement of the temporary outline.

"Show me again where you'd like it."

I reached to my hip, the mirror making it difficult to coordinate the movement, and pointed to the area just above my panty line.

"I need to move those down," he mumbled to Cooper. Even with my back to the men, I could imagine Cooper's reaction. No way in hell would he let another man touch my panties. I wanted to kick myself for not planning better. I could've gone without, wore some loose-fitting sweatpants, and saved all this hassle.

"I've got it," I said, reaching for the material. *Drama, drama.* But then I gulped. "Coop, I'm nervous. Hold my hand?"

Cooper grabbed a chair, stepped around to the other side of the table, and took a seat facing me. "It's going to hurt like a motherfucker, but you've got this." He chuckled and gave my fingers a squeeze.

My heart sprinted in my chest when I heard the buzz of the machine. Adam gave me a warning before briefly touching it to my skin.

"Good, you didn't even flinch." He sounded impressed. "The next pass will have ink."

"You made a blank pass?"

"Had to make sure you weren't going to chicken out and leave here with a dot." I heard his audible smirk, then the sound of the rollers on his stool as he moved back into position. "I'll work in thirty second increments, but if you need me to stop or pause for a while, let me know."

The first pass felt like I was being cut with a scalpel, but once I got used to the feeling it was more like someone taking a safety pin to a bad sunburn. Not pleasant but tolerable.

"How you doing?" Adam asked.

"Good. Almost finished?"

"With the first part, yes."

I looked at Cooper who was trying not to laugh. "Told ya."

"I'm fine," I lied. "Which of yours hurt the worst?"

"This one." He pointed to the script along his ribs.

"Why do you keep coming back for more?" I asked through clenched teeth. The last pass seemed to last longer than the thirty seconds Adam had promised.

"They're addicting." He perused the tats on his left arm. "You see something you want and it becomes something you have to have. The pain's completely worth it."

"Okay," Adam exhaled. "I'm finished. Let me get you cleaned up, and then you can have a look."

My first glance into the standing mirror brought so many emotions, I wasn't sure whether to laugh or cry. It was perfect—better than I'd imagined—and it seemed meant to be there like it had been hidden beneath my flesh all this time, and Adam had only revealed it.

"I love it!" I finally said on a giggle. "It's perfect."

And it was.

Eleven

Cooper

Briley loved surprises, and this one was going to blow her mind. Something she'd wanted since she was a child, and hence the nickname her mother had given her. I hoped it was the distraction she needed with her being so stressed lately. It took half my day on the phone, making arrangements and paying a little extra to get everything I needed in a hurry.

Knowing I couldn't hide the excitement in my voice if I had called, I decided to just show up at her place. Hopefully she had either been successful in her hunt for information, or she had received news I could help her deal with easily. Either way, I hoped it wasn't anything bad enough to ruin the surprise I had planned.

Shifting one of the large boxes, I managed to ring her doorbell. I wished I could've seen her expression when she opened the door to find me hidden behind the stacked, unlabeled boxes.

"What on earth?" I heard the excitement behind her voice.

"Take the one on top," I suggested, bending down so she could reach it. "It's light."

After she plucked the top one from my arms, it was easier to see where I was going. I headed to the backyard and set the rest on a table.

"What is this, Coop?" she asked.

"Here, open this one first." I handed her the smallest box and waited, very impatiently, as she opened it with care.

"Should I be nervous?" She looked up at me, picking at a piece of tape with her fingernail.

"Always." I winked. Pulling out my pocket knife, I sliced through the tape, eager for her to get it open already.

Maybe the first box hadn't been the best idea. She obviously didn't get it. It was a white hat. She kept digging, pulling out the matching veil that went with it.

"Coop . . . is this a bee hat?"

"Looks like it." I shoved the next box—the tape already freed by the knife—into her arms. "Open this one."

The next box confirmed her suspicions. It contained a bee suit, smoker, and a thick book about bee keeping.

"No freaking way!" Her eyes were wide, matching a comical grin. "I don't understand. What does . . . how? When? Where?"

I was grinning like a five year old on Christmas. "The frames will be delivered tomorrow."

"Where? Here?" She glanced frantically around her backyard.

"Why not? There are honey bees all over your flowers. Who's going to say anything about a few more?"

"A few thousand!" She jumped up and down like a little kid receiving her first bike. "I'm so excited, Coop!" She sprung at me, throwing her arms around my neck, and wrapping her legs around my waist. "You know how long I've wanted bees."

I did. "As long as I've known you, you've been obsessed. If you think you'll get in trouble with the neighborhood, we can keep them at my house. I don't have an HOA."

"No, here, here!" She squealed. "No one will know with the privacy fence."

I chuckled at her exuberance. Surprising her was the best. I could get used to this. "We still need to order the bees. I didn't know which kind you'd want. They have Italian, German, Russian—"

"I'll have to do some research and see. Oh, Cooper, I'm so excited!" She picked up the beekeeping book, took it with her inside, and sat on the couch before flipping through its pages. It would take her away from me for hours, if not all night. All I had wanted was to see her light up, that smile on her face, every day.

Success.

Sitting next to her, I pulled her legs into my lap. "How did it go today? Find any answers?"

"Not really," she answered somewhat glumly, closing the book to look at me. "My best bet is to snoop through my mom's mail and find which banks she has accounts with."

I stroked her calf. "That's right up your alley, B. You've always liked those crime shows."

"It's a little different, Coop. We're talking about my mother. Or a stranger pretending to be my mother."

I tugged on her big toe. "Hey, you know that's not true, right? Nina Sheffield is your mother, and your dad . . . think about it, you really believe they stole you?" I still couldn't picture it.

"No." She shook her head, but couldn't look me in the eyes when she answered. It was obvious she was struggling with the idea.

I couldn't stand seeing her in a funk. After letting her flip through the pages of the beekeeping book for a few minutes, I scooped her into my arms.

Giggling, she asked, "What're you doing? You're such a horn dog."

True. Instead of taking her to the bedroom, though, I turned and stepped through the sliders to the backyard.

She must've caught on as she gripped me like a python and started in with a high-pitched, "No, no no no, Cooooop!" And damn, it was just too easy to peel her away and toss her into the pool, her girly screams of protest ceasing once she was in the water.

Stripping down to my boxers, I cannonballed into the water next to her, the water rippling around me and splashing out onto the concrete.

"Cooper!" She scolded, attack mode fully engaged as she splashed her way toward me. "I'm dressed!"

"I can help you with that," I teased, pulling her close and claiming her lips as I began unbuttoning her top. It might've only been a temporary fix for her mood, but it was working.

She melted into me instantly, like syrup on a hot waffle. This woman was mine, and I loved everything about her, especially the little noises she made when I hit her erogenous zones. Nothing turned me on more than making her lose her mind when I hit the spot behind her ear. Goosebumps stood at attention like soldiers, her breath stolen on a whoosh, and her back arched, pushing those glorious mounds beneath her white lacy bra into my chest.

She pulled back, cupping my jaw in one of her hands. Her dark pools of innocence fixed on me, telling me silently, everything I wanted to hear. Briley was the most stunning woman I'd ever laid eyes on, a body that drove a man insane, but she was so much more than that. I was in love with her heart and who she was on the inside. Like an M&M candy, she had a hard surface for the world to see, but on the inside she was soft and fragile. And she needed me just as much as I needed her.

Standing on tip toes, she brushed her lips against mine, whispering, "I want you, Cooper."

I don't know what it was about those few words, but it was the key to powering up a man's engine. Just when I thought I couldn't get any harder, she'd said those words, and I was revved up as far as I could possibly get.

Pool sex played out a little differently in my head than in reality. Trying to get her shorts off was impossible with the little space between us. Hoisting her up, I set her on the edge of the pool. She lifted her hips as I dragged her shorts and panties down her legs, flinging the soaked clothing aside. She started to protest about the items floating in the water, but lolled her head back when I kissed my way up her inner thigh.

I loved how responsive she was to my touch, writhing and whimpering as I took my time enjoying her sweet body. Just before I completely lost my mind, I pulled myself out of the water, grabbed a cushion off a nearby lounger, and got completely lost in Briley. Lust drove deeply into wonder and exploded into a million pieces of soul-clenching sparks. I knew I loved her, needed her, but when she looked up at me, a crooked smile skimming across her relaxed features, I knew I'd die for her.

"Move in with me," I blurted huskily, my mouth ahead of my brain.

She didn't respond, her lids blinking an SOS code in surprise. Suddenly, all my past insecurities resurfaced. Why wasn't she saying anything? What was that look in her eyes about? Did she really love me?

Stupid. Of course she loved me.

Well, then why? It was too soon—I knew that—but we'd wasted so much time already. What was wrong with moving fast? It wasn't like we had to get to know each other. We'd grown up together.

Shit. Maybe I should've made this moment more romantic, asking her over dinner with a velvet box holding a key or something.

"What?" she asked. Confusion flashed in her eyes. At least the blinking had stopped.

Okay, she hadn't heard me. A smart man would've made something up. Instead, I asked again. "Move in with me, Briley."

Her eyebrows twisted, confusion changing to disbelief like I was pulling a prank. "Are you sure?"

Damn straight, I'm sure. "I wouldn't have asked."

She was silent for a few seconds, and I could almost see the wheels turning in her head. "Why don't *you* move in with *me?*"

Ah, her stubborn streak.

"I thought about that. I know what this place means to you and if that's what you want, I'm all for it. I was just thinking with Blake—" I didn't want to bring up Blake. Not now, or ever. I hated that douche bag. But it still didn't change the fact that I felt she wasn't fully safe here, and I wanted to remedy that.

"And Madison!" she huffed. I could feel her body stiffen beneath me. Her hands came up, pushing on my chest for me to move.

Wait, what?

Madison?

We sat facing each other in some kind of standoff. Her arms were crossed over her chest like she didn't want me to see her nakedness suddenly.

"You're not serious. B, you have nothing—"

"She's vile, Cooper." I started to speak, but she put a hand up. "Let me finish. Honestly, I waver back and forth sometimes, wanting to know how far things got with you two . . ." She watched me and then flinched as if I'd raised my hand to slap her. "But I'm positive I don't want to know."

Fine. This was not going in the direction I'd hoped. I stroked the part of her leg that was closest to me and felt her relax a fraction.

"So whad'ya say then?" I cocked a half-grin and added a wink just in case. "My place or yours?" *Just please say yes.*

She looked around, seeming to weigh her options, then back at me. "Has Madison ever been to your place?"

"No."

She stared at me, cocking her head to the side.

It was obvious she didn't believe me, so I repeated, "No. She's never been inside my house."

"Then yes and yours." She flung herself into my lap then, arms hugged loosely around my neck. "Oh my God, Coop! This is a big step. You need to be absolutely sure." She brought her hand to her mouth and began chewing a fingernail. For a split second, I thought about teasing her with, *nah, just kidding.*

"I'm sure." Never been more sure in my life. "I don't ever want to wake up without you beside me."

"I'm going to have girly stuff in your bathroom." She giggled. "And I come with bees."

"I like to dabble on the guitar at odd hours." I stroked her cheek with my thumb.

"I love to hear you play," she said softly. "You can serenade me anytime, at any hour." She tucked her head into the spot between my neck and shoulder, and sighed. "A perfect fit."

Damn straight.

Twelve
Briley

Surrounded by half-filled boxes, I sat in the middle of the living room floor, sipping on a plastic cup of weak lemonade. I wondered what my father would think of me leaving this place and moving in with Cooper. I could almost hear his voice as he peered over his morning paper, a hint of parental judgment in his eyes. *"Your mother and I were married before we lived together. I know things have changed, but are you sure you've thought this through?"*

I had thought it through. Over and over and over. It was all I could think of, and now my job was suffering because of it. Cooper had become a life source of sorts. When we were apart, I counted down the hours until I could see him, touch him. I even planned out new recipes to try out on him. Not that Cooper was Prince Charming—far from it—and I was no Cinderella. I didn't need rescuing. I did need, though. I needed Cooper, and I was out of my head excited to move in with him.

Refreshed and rested, I continued the task of wrapping plates and cups in newspaper and stacking them into an empty box. We agreed to keep my dishes over Cooper's black melamine, although I was sure I saw him stash a few bowls. It was important to me not to transform his home into a floral nightmare—which would've been hard for me to do since I didn't own anything floral . . . or over-the-top girly.

"Hi baby," Cooper came up behind me and wrapped his arms around my waist. His chin, resting on my shoulder, dug in enough to massage some of the tension. "What else can I put in the truck?" I'd never seen him so giddy, over-the-moon excited these last few days over me moving into his place. He'd even helped me pack.

"All the boxes in the living room are ready to go. Except the ones against the far wall over there, those are going to the charity center." I set the last wrapped coffee cup into the box and taped it shut. "Thirsty?" I asked, filling a plastic cup with lemonade.

He drank it down in one gulp, just as I knew he would, so I filled it again. His shirt was soaked, along with his brow and a light sheen covering his arms. He was filthy with the ink of newspaper and who knew what else, and I loved it. I wasn't turned on by sweat and dirt, but watching his excitement as he packed up the last few items I had . . . *that* was a huge turn on.

"Listen, Coop." I made the mistake of running my hands along his arms and tried not to crinkle my nose as I wiped the sweat on my shorts. "These dishes don't mean a thing to me. Very few things do. I don't want you to change your entire house for me. We can keep your dishes."

"It's *our* home, B." I melted. He pulled me in, careful not to share his sweat with me, and kissed my forehead. "I kept a few of my man dishes, and it's not like you're gonna paint the place pink, right?" There was only a trace of uncertainty in his voice, but I laughed just the same.

"Never know. I do like to keep you on your toes. Better not leave me with the paint samples." I loved teasing him, it always ended well for me.

This was going to be fun.

***

Cooper loaded the last few items, while I took one more look around. I thought I would've been more sentimental about leaving my home—a place my father had helped me fix up—but I wasn't. Too many bad memories with Blake now infected the walls of this place, and I was ready to leave.

Cooper appeared in the doorway, studying me. His eyes revealed uncertainty. I assumed he was watching for signs of nostalgia or second thoughts. "Ready to go?"

I nodded, the strangest feeling coursing through me as I shut and locked the door to my house. It wouldn't be mine anymore—belonging to new owners as soon as it sold—and since it was a buyer's market, it would probably happen fast. Starting a new life with the man of my dreams was thrilling and terrifying at the same time.

A carpet cleaning truck blocked our path, so Cooper had to turn left and take the long way out of my neighborhood. Madison was standing in her front yard, watering flowers as we passed. It was evil of me, but I threw up a hand and waved sweetly, a prissy Scarlett O'Hara smile spread across my face.

Pulling into his driveway ten minutes later brought a fresh string of emotions. I'd always known this place to be Cooper's, but now it was mine, too. Would I always feel like a roommate, or would it eventually sink in that it was my place, too? Cooper scooped me into his slippery-with-sweat arms and carried me over the threshold. I giggled and kissed his salty cheek before he set me down in the living room. I loved hanging out at his house—typical bachelor pad with brown leather couches and blank walls—but now that I was living here, we'd have to dress the place up a bit. Curtains and a few framed prints would ease him in. Thankfully I wasn't a fan of the floral print, as giving as Cooper was, I was sure he wouldn't go for that.

After a quick rinse in the shower, Cooper joined me in the living room, unpacking a stack of books and settling them into the bookshelf. "Whoa there." I removed the stack. "They have to go in order. Grouped by author and then tallest to shortest."

He chuckled and rolled his eyes. "I forgot about your weird quirks. I'll leave the books to you."

I expected him to attend to another box or task, but his hands were all over me. *Books can wait.* I tossed a few paperbacks back in the box and turned to face him as we sat on the living room floor. The pads of his fingers made feather-light strokes across my shoulders, down my arms, scripting something along my lower back. When he moved up, skimming the outer edge of my breast, my muscles failed me, and I relaxed back into his arms.

With my head in his lap, he bent down and kissed me. My lips were upside down for him, so he kissed my lower lip, so tenderly I felt myself dissolve into him. I don't know what it was about Cooper Sterling, but he did crazy things to my insides. It always felt like there was a battle inside of me between raging fire and calming pools. It was an effort to participate, give back, when he elicited such an all-consuming control over my body.

It took every bit of energy I had left in me to sit up and straddle him. I wanted to be closer to him, wanted to feel the fullness of his mouth on mine, and needed to get lost in his addictive green eyes.

Foreplay wasn't in the cards this time. I was desperate and needy, a starved animal. I pulled away just long enough to pull my shirt over my head and toss it aside. Thank God I'd chosen to forfeit underclothes today.

His hands were on me immediately, kneading and sucking my aching breasts.

"Cooper," I moaned. "I need you . . . now." I considered finding the opening in his boxers and taking him right then and there, but he lifted me up and slid them off in a flash.

We made love sitting on the floor of the living room. It was fast—not as romantic as I would've planned for consummating our new living arrangement—but powerful and perfect. As the last of the shockwaves rippled through me, we both laughed, and I buried my head in the crook of his neck, holding on to him tightly.

My phone came to life next to us, but I ignored it. It was probably my mom. Seconds later, it went off again, the braying of a donkey alerting that Blake was calling. Cooper grabbed the phone and pulled it apart, glass and wires scattering across the tiled living room floor, effectively pulling me out of the wonderful buzz of after-sex.

"What the hell?" I could feel the heat rising in my cheeks. "I needed that." My body jolted upright into a sitting position. Aware of my nakedness, I felt vulnerable and exposed so I crossed my arms over my chest.

He was completely at ease, his expression relaxed and sure as he lay there with his arms behind his head. "Get a new one. If you're not going to block his number, *you're* getting a new number."

"I can't afford a new phone right now," I lied. It wasn't out of my budget, but it *was* a pain in the ass to redo everything.

"I'll get you a phone, B. If it means that fucking maggot leaving you alone, hell, I'll buy you a dozen phones."

He wasn't wrong. Cooper had done the one thing I should've done months ago, yet it still pissed me off. Why, I wasn't sure. But all of the new feelings and emotions were making me feel like a hormonal teenager. I wasn't about to apologize. He should've asked before he busted my phone, even though it would prove to be a good thing. I did, however, let the anger float away.

"He's never going to leave me alone, is he?" I sighed, not daring to look at Cooper. It came out before I could stop it and wished it hadn't. I had to be careful not to rile him as I knew how badly he wanted to send a message to my ex.

"He'll leave you alone. I'll make sure of it."

"No." *Keep your mouth shut, B. You want him locked up for good?* "I'm sorry I let that slip out. Please leave it alone. I can't lose you again, especially not now."

He sat up and looked me in the eyes, his expression serious. "I'm not going to do anything stupid, B. Now that I've got you, I'm not letting you go—"

Cooper's phone began to ring.

You've got to be kidding me! I was tempted to throw *it* against the wall and let him buy two new phones.

He growled. "Jeez, can't everyone leave us alone for one fucking minute so I can enjoy my girl?" He ignored his phone and pulled me down to lay on the rug with him. As soon as the ringing stopped, it began again. "What the hell?" He scooped up his cell and checked caller ID. "It's my dad."

I nodded for him to answer and sat up.

"Hey, Dad, what's up?" Cooper's expression transformed into something I recognized as worry. His brows cinched together as he looked at me, transferring that worry to me. Whatever his father was telling him . . . involved me.

"We'll be right there." He ended the call. "Baby, your mom's been in an accident."

I shot up, too fast, then sat back down until my tingly legs received the message that I wanted to stand. "What happened? Is she okay? We have to go. Oh God!" I was a frantic ball of nerves, zooming around the living room looking for my bra. I hadn't worn one, but I needed one now. *Where did I pack my underwear?*

"Briley, she'll be okay," he insisted. "What do you need?"

"Bra. Where the hell did I—?"

"I'll get you one." He went straight to my suitcase and fished out a purple bra. I dressed haphazardly and ran to the truck, Cooper right behind me.

"The other car?" I asked on a sob, my emotions beginning to take over. "Are they okay?"

Cooper glanced at me and then back to the road as we drove toward the hospital. "It was a hit and run," he began, his voice low and thick. "She was on foot, crossing the street in Bellaire Plaza."

Thirteen

Cooper

The next two weeks didn't allow us to get cozy and play house like I'd planned. Briley spent most of her time at the hospital with her mom. Nina would be fine, but the healing process would take some time. Two broken ribs were the worst of it, which caused her a lot of pain when she tried to move, eat, or even breathe deeply. She'd received a hip replacement since the ball that fit into the socket of her hip was shattered so badly they couldn't fix it, but she was lucky her injuries weren't worse. Police never did find the bastards that had run her down. Assumed it was a car full of reckless teens.

I thought last Monday would be the last time I'd have to lie to Briley. I'd been telling her for over a week now that I couldn't stop by the hospital because I had to work through lunch. When instead I'd been going to her mother's house to sift through the shoebox of mail the neighbor had been collecting. Briley needed answers. We both did. Two bank statements had arrived. I took them both and, without opening them, shoved them in the glove box of my truck.

When the time was right, I'd give the statements to Briley so she could find that damn safe-deposit box and hopefully unlock the mysteries of her family's past. I felt like an asshole at times, keeping the envelopes from her. But she was under a lot of stress, and I wouldn't let anything take her over the edge. What if she was right? What if the Sheffields had taken her and passed her off as their own?

Briley looked like she'd been hit by a car herself when she walked through the door late Thursday night. Dark circles marred her usually flawless complexion, and her shoulders slumped with fatigue.

"Hi, baby." I took her purse and keys and guided her to the couch. "How is she?"

"Fine. Still in a lot of pain. She's not sleeping, which makes it worse, and she won't take pain meds until the last minute when it's so far out of control, it's hard to get relief. The doctor said she needed to take her meds *before* the pain really kicked in, so she could stay ahead of it." She slapped her hands on her thighs. "But why would she listen to a doctor? I mean, she's Nina Sheffield for chrissakes. She knows all." Her words were bitter, and her face pinched. My girl was exhausted, and I was just the person to rescue her.

I poured a glass of Malbec, handed it to her, and sat down, tugging her legs into my lap. "I'm sorry, B. At least now I know where you got your stubborn streak from." I chuckled, but she was too tired to return a smile. The most I got out of her was a slight lip curl. I rubbed her legs, urging her to finish the glass. "Drink up, you need it."

She obeyed, holding the empty glass against her chest. "They're releasing her next week. She'll have to go to rehab, but she's walking around the hospital like nothing ever happened . . . when her pain is under control."

"That's good news. Listen." I kneaded her calf muscles. "I'd like to take you out of town for an overnighter." I'd been forming a plan in my head for a few days, but hadn't actually put it into play. It wouldn't be anything fancy, but hell, even a hotel in the next town would be good for us. "Two nights max.

Let's go before Nina's released. I know you won't want to be out of town when she comes home, so let's go this weekend."

"That sounds wonderful." She stroked the length of my arm, and I reveled in the feeling of her soft, loving touch. "But I can't."

I frowned at her. "Why not?"

"I have the best news," she suddenly sang with renewed energy. Her eyebrows pulled up and a wide smile spread across her flawless face. "Angela wants me to do an article on tapas. I have to travel, but I'll only be gone a few days."

I lifted her hand to my mouth and kissed her knuckles. "That's great, B. When do we leave?" I was only teasing, but if her boss let me tag along, I was all in. Hell, I'd pay for my airfare. There was no reason I couldn't go.

"You can't go, Coop," she said, disappointed. "Your parole."

"Where's she sending you? Africa?" I asked, knitting my brows together.

She scrunched her nose, and her excitement about the trip seemed to fade. "Barcelona."

"As in Spain?" My eyes widened.

"Uh-huh."

Shit, really? "Can you put her off a few months?" I asked, knowing I couldn't leave the country. I still had a few months meeting with my parole officer.

But Spain . . . *Spain with Briley* . . . sounded fucking heavenly.

"I can't, Coop. I leave Thursday."

"Thursday? *This* Thursday?" I realized I was being too aggressive with her calf muscles when she winced in pain, so I stopped rubbing altogether. "I'm not gonna lie, B. I'm not thrilled with the idea. Besides, you don't have a birth certificate or a passport."

"First of all, I worked that all out—my mom had it in her purse. Said she cleared the mix-up and they sent her a new one immediately. And the passport is on rush. Should be here tomorrow or the next day. Second, why not? You're worried?" She folded her arms across her chest, a defensive move I'd seen too many times. "This isn't my first rodeo, and I'll have the photographer with me."

"I'd worry less if it was a rodeo." I paused, thinking that through. "No, a rodeo filled with cowboys—scratch that." All I could imagine was Spaniards flirting with my girl. I'd seen the movies. Those dudes meant business.

"Cooper Sterling! Do I sense a little jealousy?" A puckish grin stretched across her face. "I like it."

"I'm serious, B. You have no business traipsing through that country without me."

She started laughing, the kind of laughter that took over her entire being, causing tears to spill from her eyes. "Stop. Oh my God, Coop!" She held my stomach as the cackling continued.

What the hell was so funny?

"Traipsing? Am I wearing a white sundress with a daisy chain around my head?" When she noticed my narrowed eyes, she sobered up a bit. "Okay, I won't traipse, and I'll have the photographer with me," she reminded me again.

I sullenly crossed my arms over my chest. "Like some little nerdy girl with a camera will protect you."

Her laughter cut off then, and she sat up to face me. "You've got to be kidding me!" she huffed, palming her forehead. "First of all, I'm not a weak little girl who needs protecting all the time. Second, the photographer is not a nerdy little girl, it's a guy, and third—"

Hold the fucking phone. "A guy?" I interrupted, eyeing her suspiciously. She didn't deserve it, but I couldn't hold my tongue. I was worried, maybe a little pissed I couldn't go with her. "No way in hell you're going on this trip. I'll call your boss myself."

"Cooper!" She poked her index finger into my chest with each disjointed word. "I swear . . . if you . . . I'm going. I'm a grown ass woman with a career. I've worked really hard to get to this place, and you will not ruin it for me because you're afraid some chubby man in his forties with three kids and a wife, that drives a minivan to work, is going to pick me up." She sucked in a deep breath. "And yes, I'm aware that was the longest run-on sentence in the history of the world."

"Fine," I barked, feeling maybe a hair better after knowing he was a chubby forty-something. "But if anything happened to you," I started, my voice calmer. I gulped, not even able to finish that thought. Her mom's accident had been reality enough.

She placed a finger over my lips. "Shh. Nothing will happen to me. Fate has worked too hard to get us together, Coop. She wouldn't risk tearing us apart after all this time."

"So fate's a girl?" I smirked. "Figures."

***

Deception never felt good, but sometimes a man had to take care of things the only way he knew how. That's how I justified lying to her one more time. This would definitely be the last as I watched her sleep, her chest rising and falling in a rhythmic pattern. The moonlight was touching her face, highlighting her beautiful features. Long lashes rested on her cheeks, her relaxed lips plump and soft. She was so exhausted; I couldn't wake her if I tried, so I pressed my lips to hers for a moment. Her keys were next to mine on a hook by the door. After sliding the one to her mother's house off the ring, I replaced them and snuck off to do what I thought was best.

It took a good two hours to thoroughly search through files and try to find hiding places for special documents in Briley's father's home office. Not wanting to alert the neighbors of my presence, I used a flashlight to guide me through the dark room. I wasn't sure how, but it still smelled like a man in here, leather, the faded scent of strong cologne, and something that made the hairs on my neck stand at attention. I knew I shouldn't be in her father's office. Even though he'd been gone for years, I felt like he was scolding me from beyond the grave.

I studied a safe I'd found tucked in the wall behind a painting—why did people hide things in the most obvious places? It took a few tries, but I finally opened it with the same code they used on the security system.

Two things caught my attention: a loaded Smith & Wesson .38 Special and a young picture of Briley's father with a group of men. All were dressed in suit and tie, hands clasped in front. Four of the men had numbers handwritten above their heads. Mr. Sheffield's was a four.

After taking a picture of the photo with my phone, I replaced everything carefully, walked into Briley's childhood room, and lifted the one thing that would help carry out a plan, tucking it under my arm.

***

I was burning up with Briley's leg draped over my thigh and her arm across my chest. But it was totally worth the sweat trickling down my side to have her beside me, my arm resting on her back so I could feel her body move each time she inhaled and exhaled. She was out. My left arm had already gone numb, a tingling sensation traveling to my fingertips, so there was no point in trying to move her head. Instead, I brushed her hair away from her face so I could watch her sleep.

All hell was going to break loose when I shared the information I found in her parents' house. I knew she'd want to leave immediately and find the bank that possibly held some answers. It made sense to wait to tell her about it. But, damn, I hated keeping secrets from her. Who was I to hide this from her?

Briley didn't even stir when I pulled my phone from the nightstand and emailed my buddy, Rowland. He was a guy I'd met early on in prison—in for computer hacking—a genius from what I'd heard. And he owed me a favor for saving him from a massive dude wanting a new bitch. He'd gotten out seven months before me and on his way past my cell, he'd said, "If you ever need anything, man, find me."

Well, I needed his expertise now, and it gave me an excuse for not telling Briley right away. I had her best interest in mind as I dug deeper, giving her more than the insignificant clues I found.

Rowland,

I need a favor. Can you find out who's in this picture? Any information will help.

Thanks.

p.s. Please keep this on the DL.

*attachment

C

After a few games of life-sucking Candy Crush, I heard back from Rowland.

C,

I'll just use my face recognition software and get back with you. Kidding. Will have to do some searching. Might take some time. Do you have anything else? A name? Reason for the numbers?

Row

I held my phone down low, trying to type with one finger. Rowland would have to deal with my shorthand.

#4 - Gerald Sheffield. All I have.

The last message came through, and I read it quickly as Briley started to stir.

Cool. I'll see what I can find.

Fourteen

Cooper

Just after midnight, Briley shut off her computer. I'd been missing her laughter, her touch, her happiness. I loved the way she would dance through the house, walking on her tiptoes while humming a tune. She hadn't done that since she'd moved in with me. We hadn't made any good memories since my home became hers. Tonight I planned to change that.

As I watched in the doorway of the home office we shared, she stood and stretched, waiting for her computer to shut down. I wasn't quiet when I approached, wrapping my arms around her waist from behind, but she jumped.

"Sorry. Didn't mean to startle you. All finished?"

She tried to catch her breath, her hand on her chest as she gripped the back of the chair. "Yeah. I thought you were asleep?"

"No. Wanted to wait for you. I flipped through the channels and watched the end of a movie." I leaned in, careful not to let any other part of our bodies touch as I licked the seam of her lips and let my breath hover over her jaw until I reached her ear. A little nibble caused her breath to hitch. Sucking part of her lobe into my mouth elicited a long moan.

Her arms flew up to wrap around the back of my head, trying to pull me in. I was much stronger than her so I held firm, shaking my head. "Patience, baby."

I stepped back, gazing at her beauty. She was wearing one of my T-shirts that swallowed her frame but didn't minimize her sex appeal in the least. I lifted the hem of the shirt and trailed a finger along the edge of her lace panties. Her stomach tightened in response. Keeping my eyes locked on hers, I lifted the shirt over her head.

She was beautiful, a body so perfect I felt like a teenage boy every time I was near her. The way she looked at me, like I was the king of her castle, the only one thing she'd ever need, had me desperate to be buried deep inside of her.

This had not been my plan for tonight, but with her standing here in nothing but a pair of white lace panties, her tits heaving as she breathed, I was coming undone. Keeping our bodies from touching, I hooked my fingers in the lace and slid them down her long legs. She reached for me, but I stepped back and shrugged my boxers off.

With a devilish grin, I scooped her into my arms, slung her over my shoulder, and carried her toward the pool outside.

"Cooper! Put me down. Where are we—the pool?" She tried to wiggle out of my arms, her hands smacking my ass as we got closer to the door.

I gripped her firmly, not letting her loose. Walking to the deep end where the hot tub connected, I set her down. Offering her a hand, I eased into the water, helping her join me. She looked around, her eyes darting from left to right to see if any of the neighboring houses could be seen through the thick landscaping.

"No one can see past the bushes. Trust me. Besides, this is our place. We'll do whatever the hell we want."

I hoped she could let lose, enjoy the moment with me. She seemed to relax once submerged to her shoulders, the hot water hopefully releasing her inhibitions.

"How do you feel?" I pulled her into my lap, nibbling on her earlobe.

"Like I'm the only woman in the world." She sighed.

I'd done my job well if she truly felt that way. I wanted her to feel as beautiful and sexy as I knew she was.

"Good." My palm rested on her thigh, stroking up and down her smooth leg. "I know it's a rough season for you right now. But I'm here."

She cocked her head to the side, a smirk pulling at the corner of her mouth. "You're still worried about my trip aren't you?"

"That's not what this is about." Although she was right, I hated the idea of her traveling out of the country the day after tomorrow. "Since you moved in, you haven't experienced much happiness. I want to change that."

Briley's smirk softened into the sweetest smile. "You're wrong." She adjusted herself on my lap and reached up, cupping my face. "I'd be a disaster without you. You're the one happiness in this jacked up world of mine."

"It's not jacked. It's . . ." I didn't know what it was. Upside down, full of pot holes, and shooting flaming balls of shit at her. But I wouldn't say that out loud.

"Jacked. It's okay. Life can't always be rainbows and butterflies."

It wasn't the best time to laugh, but I couldn't help it. Briley Sheffield baffled me. Most women did, but she was so fickle. One minute she was freaking out because of the chaos in her life, the next she's telling me it's not all rainbows and shit. If we got married—when we got married—I felt sure I'd still be in the dark after sixty years together.

"What's so funn—?" Before she could finish her question, I claimed her mouth. Memory number one in the Sterling-Sheffield home was christening the hot tub.

Fifteen
Briley

Barcelona was wonderful. I'd soaked in the culture and feasted on Spanish flavors, while taking in the sights. When given the opportunity, my photographer, Stuart Morrow, and I sat outside. We talked about random things—a little of my relationship with Cooper, a lot about his family and how his career path had shifted from sales to creative—but there was an obvious disconnect.

Not a moment passed when I didn't wish Cooper was with me. I imagined the excitement in his eyes as he studied the stunning architecture of Barcelona. I wondered what he would've thought about the tiled inlays, wrought iron railings, and decorative moldings around various shaped windows. I wondered what he'd think about the history, the culture, the food. I wanted the warmth of his hand in mine when I strolled along Port Vell at sunset. And I craved his laughter when Stuart and I were served small portions, displayed beautifully on square plates.

Though I was sure Cooper would've been looking for a burger joint as soon as we left.

By the time we landed in Florida, I had the article finished. I was ready to be home again and couldn't wait to wrap myself up in the arms of my guy.

***

It felt like someone had punched me in the gut when I realized what had been done. Holding the two bank statements addressed to my parents, and a manila envelope Cooper admitted to taking from the safe in my father's office—a safe I'd never been privy to—I couldn't breathe. Hugging my arms around my stomach seemed to hold me together, but I couldn't get enough oxygen to satisfy my burning lungs.

"You broke in?" I gasped. "I would've let you in." Planting myself on the arm of the cloth sofa, I sucked in a deep breath off too-thick air. "Why, Cooper? Why did you go behind my back?"

"I don't know." He raised a hand up behind his head, rubbing a spot on the back of his neck. "I wanted you to forget this whole thing, leave the secrets buried where they belong. I mean, what if you *were* stolen? What then?" He crouched down in front of me, resting his hands on my knees. "But I couldn't go through with it. I know you're not going to stop until you figure this out."

"So you agree with me?" My voice was barely audible as I added, "You think they took me?" Instinctively, I shivered at the thought. How could my parents not be who they said they were? Dropping my shoulders, I sighed. "If that's true, I'm not Briley Sheffield."

"We don't know that for sure, B. In fact, I don't believe that at all. I think there's an explanation out there, something your mom doesn't want you to know, but I feel certain it's not a stolen baby story."

"How can you be sure, Coop?" My body drooped against the couch. "All the evidence suggests so."

"Look at the picture, B. There's a lot more going on."

I reached into the large manila envelope slowly, as if a mousetrap was engaged and ready to snap my fingers. Inside was a bank statement from L & M Bank & Trust and a photograph of my father amongst a group of men.

"What're the numbers for?" I asked. I didn't expect Cooper to have an answer, but maybe he'd found more than what was in the envelope.

"I don't know. I sent the picture to the buddy I told you about. Maybe he'll have an idea. It could be a code . . . or it could mean nothing." He exhaled a deep, steady breath. "Look, B, I'm sorry I went behind your back—"

"Don't do it again," I snapped. My tone was harsher than I'd planned. Trying to soften it, I added, "Let's figure this out together."

Cooper took the contents from my hands and set them on the coffee table. "Sounds good to me." He stood, helped me up, and guided a hand under my chin. "We'll figure it out together. But know this . . ." His thumb brushed against my cheek. "No matter what we find, I love you, and I'm not letting you go."

"Even if my name is Olga?" I wanted to laugh but the moment was too serious, stifling the emotion.

His eyes sparked with amusement. "Hey, now, that might be pushing—"

I gave his arm a firm pinch, eliciting a laugh.

"We should go." I checked the time on the microwave clock. "It's too late to make it to the bank, but I'd like to see my mom."

***

Getting my mother settled at home was a feat. Something had changed after the accident, breeding a stubborn crankiness in her that was grating on my nerves. But I needed to get her

98

home and comfortable before I could ask her about the contents of the envelope Cooper handed me three days ago.

"But the doctor said—"

She cut her eyes up at me, lowering herself into the chair opposite the television. "I'm a grown woman, and I know my body better than some kid straight out of med school."

The doctor was at least late forties, but I wasn't about to argue with her. I'd made sure her fridge was stocked, which, according to her, was all wrong.

"How about a cup of hot tea? You find us something to watch."

"It's way too hot for tea," she groaned. This woman was *not* my mother. Before my feelings were fully hurt, she took my hand in hers. "I'm sorry, Bee. It's the pain. It makes me grumpy."

"Let me get your pain meds, Mom," I pleaded. It was a waste of time. I knew she'd refuse them, but I had to try.

Flipping through the channels, she landed on a gardening show. We sat in silence, watching an older lady with auburn hair teach us how to grow a potted pineapple plant. Lacking the courage to look my mother in the eyes as I asked her about the contents of the envelope, I twisted the fringe of a throw pillow, braiding the short strands and pulling them loose to start again. Although I'd rehearsed what I was going to say and how I'd word each question, in the moment, I was nervous. I wouldn't tell her that Cooper had broken in and found the information himself. She wouldn't know what to think about that, and I couldn't risk her having a faulty opinion of him.

"Mom," My body stiffened as I tried to make the words flow. "I found something a few days ago that I'd like to ask you about. It was in with Daddy's things. An old picture of him with some buddies, I guess. He had a number above his head, and I wonder if you know what it means?" I waited for her answer, but she didn't respond. Not a sound or a single movement to cue me in on her mood. "Mom, please. I know you're keeping something from me. I need some answers."

Braving her stern gaze, I peered over at her. Eyes closed, breathing rhythmic, she was sound asleep. *Damn!*

While she was asleep, I searched my father's office for something, anything. I thumbed through drawers, ransacked cabinets, and even his shoeboxes lining the back of his closet. Mom had kept most of his things, except for a few suits that she'd donated to a young pastor. Nothing caught my attention, so I put everything back, laid a blanket over mom's lap, and locked the door behind me when I left.

Greeted by air that felt like a blast from a hair dryer, I sucked in a deep breath and exhaled some of my frustrations. Nothing was going as planned, and I wanted to shake it all off before I got home. I had been so excited to move in with Cooper so we could spend more time together, but now that we were there, it didn't seem to be going at all how I had pictured—us sitting on the couch while he played guitar, going skinny dipping in the pool late at night, sharing fancy candlelight dinners that I'd cooked. None of that.

Instead I spent my days looking for answers to who I really was and my evenings by my mother's side in a hospital that smelled like death and antiseptic. I wasn't good at hiding my emotions. Cooper could always see right through me. This was not how I had wanted to start our relationship—me moping around while he walked on egg shells, trying not to set me off.

We were supposed to be having fun, and that's exactly what we were going to do.

I didn't have time to create a gourmet meal, so I called Gianni's Italian restaurant and ordered dinner to go. But because I'd had such a shitty start to the day, karma apparently decided to go the extra mile and make it a doozy. Before I could get to the door, Blake stepped in front of me.

Groaning like a child with too much homework, I threw up my hand. "Don't even!"

"Don't even what?" he asked, looking the part of a charming gentleman as he held the door and smiled. He was different somehow. Same preppy attire and hairstyle, but the boyish charm that lured me in was gone. Either I'd finally seen him for who he really was or someone had finally shaken him out of his bullshit.

Using too much force, I pushed it shut. "Are you ever going to get it, Blake? Won't you ever leave me alone?" I pulled my purse strap onto my shoulder. "I know you don't want me. You only want to win."

"You're wrong, Briley. I was—"

I put a hand up. "Stop. Just stop. I know your game. You're going to keep harassing until Cooper does something stupid and ends up back in prison. You'll do anything to see him locked away for good. Well, listen up." I stepped into his personal space so he'd know I was serious. "You might get your wish, but hear me when I say, if Cooper goes back to prison, it'll be for your murder, not something small like smashing your face."

"Shit, B. I'm done." He raised his arms in surrender, backing up like I had a gun to him, a flash of fear in his eyes. "You're not . . . it's not worth the trouble. Obviously he's got someone on the inside and . . . well, that's beside the point. I get it. You're *with* him."

He made it sound dirty, giving me another reason to hate him. At least he was giving up. I'd take it any way he offered it.

I narrowed my eyes at him. "Yes, we're in love and very happy." Though I don't know why I felt the need to explain anything to him.

He shoved his left hand into his jeans pocket and leaned against the building. "You're selling our house I see." He lowered his head and glanced up at me. It was the first time I'd seen a look of regret from him. He reminded me of the Blake I'd first met and fallen for. I had thought I loved him, but now that I knew what love was, it was clear that what Blake and I had was excitement and lust. Puppy love maybe, but not love. Not the real thing.

"It's *my* house," I retorted. "And yes."

"Where're you going?" he asked with a bitter edge. I searched his eyes for sincerity.

Surely he knew Cooper and I were living together. How could he not? I debated on how to answer him. If he really didn't know, I wasn't sure I wanted him to. He said he was done harassing me, but I'd have to be stupid to trust him.

"I found a place not far from here. Better neighborhood." Hopefully he'd buy that and not ask any more questions. Before he had the chance, I quipped, "Well, my order is waiting. I need to go."

We walked in together, the busyness of the restaurant not offering an opportunity to talk further. I settled with the hostess, took my bag of food, and nodded a polite goodbye to Blake. Sitting in my car, I exhaled a sigh of relief. Maybe it really was over, and I could finally move on with that part of my life.

The house was mostly dark except for a glow coming from the dining room. Jazz was playing softly through the wall speakers.

"Cooper?" I called.

"In here."

I followed his voice to the dining room and found him pouring wine. The table was set, candles lit, and the smell of basil and melted cheese floated through the air.

"What's this?" I asked, glancing around at the scene, looking for the cause of that glorious smell.

"I know it's been a rough few weeks for you." He walked toward me and pulled me into his arms. The bag of food, still in my grasp, dangled at my side. "I thought we'd have a nice dinner and then you can soak in the tub, or we can watch a movie."

Relaxing into his arms, I let the bag drop the few inches to the floor, then I laughed into his chest as I wrapped my arms around his waist.

"What's so funny? Too much?" he asked, looking back at the table, overdone with new taper candles resting in my crystal holders and two full place settings atop a white tablecloth. Sweet that he had tried so hard. If he cooked, too, I'd bow down at his feet and admit my unworthiness.

"No. It's perfect. You're perfect." Pulling away, I gripped the handle of the food bag and lifted it up. "I had the same idea. I hoped to beat you home and put this food into containers so you'd think I cooked it all."

"No way." He peered into the bag. "Giovanni's?"

"Yep." I sucked on my bottom lip. "I'll stick it in the fridge for tomorrow."

"No, let's eat it tonight while it's fresh and hot."

"That's okay, it'll reheat. You've already gone to all this trouble, and I'm starved." I started toward the kitchen, but he tugged on my arm.

"Seriously, B. You're going to be disappointed. You know I can't cook so I picked up dinner, too." He gave me a sheepish smile.

I chuckled at the irony. "What did you get?"

The look on his face made me want to giggle. "Pizza."

"That sounds wonderful, Coop." I kissed him lightly and put the food in the fridge. When I returned, we enjoyed easy conversation and pizza loaded with so much cheese you could've stretched a bite into the next room without breaking the strand.

"I'm sorry I've been in a funk. Everything got so stressful all at once." My life had gone from complicated to utter chaos in a couple of months.

"It couldn't be helped." He shrugged one shoulder. "Your mom needed you."

"I know, but she's home now, and I want to focus on us. What do you say to a game of basketball or . . . skinny dipping?" I waggled my eyebrows.

"It's a tossup." He held out both hands, as if weighing something in them. "Have my girl dressed and trash-talking, thinking she can beat me in a game of basketball, or have her smokin' hot body, naked, in my pool."

"I'll clean up and meet you in the pool, then." I flashed him a smile and wink as I stood to clear the table.

"Oh no you don't." He stopped me with a tug of my arm. "You've got me fired up. Start stripping before I throw you over my shoulder and toss you into the pool myself."

"What about the dishes?" I asked, feigning coyness.

"A pizza box and two wine glasses?" He stood, blew out the candles, and held out his hand. "It'll wait."

I took his hand and let him lead me out of the dining room. We left a trail of clothes from the living room, through the sliders, and outside beside the pool. The water felt like silk as it enveloped my skin.

Cooper slid his hand under my chin and turned my face toward him. "It's just you and me." Leaning his head to the side, he bent down and claimed my lips with his own. Then the world melted away, and his words became truth.

Sixteen

Cooper

The buzz of my phone startled me out of a deep sleep. Slapping the nightstand until I found the object vibrating across the wood, I picked it up and barely opened one eye to see it was only six forty-five in the morning. It was Roland, my tech buddy from prison.

Before answering, I cleared my throat, trying to rid the sleepiness from my voice. "Hello?"

"You're asleep."

"No, no, I'm up. What've ya got?" I tried to keep my voice low as I stepped out of the room so Briley could sleep. As I was shutting the bedroom door, I watched her stir, flop onto her side, and then still as she settled back into sleep.

"Can we meet up?" He wasn't a man of many words, his tone short and clipped. I never pegged him for an early bird. Always thought of him staying up late, his eyes bloodshot from looking at a computer screen. If you met him out you'd think he was one of those geeky perverts that watched porn all night. And maybe he did, but he was a good guy. Harmless. Wouldn't hurt an animal, let alone a person. He had served his time and deserved it for hacking into those accounts, but I understood his desperation. Needed the money and that was an easy way to get it.

"Yeah. I need to get ready for work, but I can meet you in—" I looked at my watch. I had a couple hours before I needed to show up at the office. "Give me thirty minutes."

"Dane's coffee shop on thirteenth?"

106

"See you in a few."

Briley was up and had coffee ready as I stepped out of the bathroom.

"Morning, beautiful." I kissed her forehead and took the cup from her outstretched hand. "Sleep okay?"

"Mmm." She nodded. "Why were you up so early?"

"I got a call from Roland. He might have some answers. I'll call you as soon as I know."

"You're meeting him?" Her body straightened. "I'm coming with you."

"No." I set my cup down and held her in place by the shoulders. "I'll tell you everything later."

"It's *my* family secret," she argued. "*I* should be the one meeting him." Her fists rested on her hips, one leg jutted out in front. She was ready for battle.

"I agree with you completely, but it's not happening. This guy has been in the joint. I don't want him anywhere near you." *No fucking way.*

"Cooper Sterling! *You* were in that very same joint. If he's that dangerous, maybe you shouldn't meet him either."

I rolled my eyes. Stubborn ass woman. "He's not dangerous, baby. I just don't want his eyes on you. He's a little . . . off. Just let me be the overprotective boyfriend, okay? I promise I'll call you and tell you every detail. In fact, come by the office, and I'll reenact the entire conversation."

She scrunched her eyebrows and grunted before turning away from me. "Fine. I'll indulge your stupid caveman ways, but you'd better not leave out a single detail, or you'll face my cavewoman wrath." She turned and smirked before shutting the bathroom door. "I'll meet you at the office."

Before I could turn around, she opened the door and came to me. With arms draped around my shoulders and eyes pleading, she asked, "Did he sound like he had good answers or bad?"

"He didn't say. He may not have anything. Maybe he needs more information?" I stroked her hair and lifted her chin. "We'll figure this out, I promise."

"I know," she answered, though her voice was laced with uncertainty. "I trust you." She pulled away and went back into the bathroom, peeking around the door frame. "Cooper?"

"Yeah, baby?"

"I love you."

I'd never get used to hearing her say those words, never take them for granted. Her love meant everything to me.

"I love you too, B."

***

The coffee shop was packed at seven-thirty in the morning, everyone sucking down their morning charge before working themselves to empty. I envisioned them all as robots, hooked up to battery cables.

Roland wasn't there yet, so I waited for a couple to finish up and then slid into their dirty booth. A waitress appeared, clearing the mugs, and asked for my order.

"Coffee, black, please."

Roland sat down as she was stepping away, and he ordered a coffee with cream.

"Hey, buddy, how've you been?" I asked. He looked good. Better than he had in the joint.

"Good." He nodded. "Real good."

He laid a folder on the table, but pulled it back as the waitress poured our coffee. When she was gone, he leaned forward. "It's not good, man. This is serious shit. I suggest you walk."

I shook my head. "I need answers."

He slid the envelope toward me, glanced over his shoulder, and then back at me. "You familiar with the Zeretti's?"

I frowned. "No."

"They go way back. Generations. This guy here," he pointed to a man in a fedora, one person over from Mr. Sheffield, "This is Nico Cavezza. See how there's no number over his head?"

I looked up at him, wishing he'd get on with it.

"These numbers are a warning. A death order. Cavezza doesn't have a number and he's the only one still alive. Must've been the only one that didn't piss off the Zerettis. I did some searching and each of these guys died in the order of their number."

A chill lit up my spine at the thought of Briley's father being murdered. He didn't have enemies, couldn't have. I knew the guy and he was as decent a guy as I'd ever known. It didn't make sense. Rowland let me down.

"You've got it wrong, Row. Gerald Sheffield didn't have enemies. Everyone loved him."

"Maybe Gerald Sheffield didn't, but this guy," Roland tapped the photo again. "Giovanni Scoza did. He pissed off the wrong people.

Impossible. I knew him. Or so I thought. "You're saying number four is Gerald Sheffield?"

"No, I'm saying number four is Giovanni Scoza." He looked at me as if I was too dumb to understand. "You're girlfriend's father must've led a separate life."

"And Sheffield died last?" It can't be right. That's not how he died.

"Yep." Rowland tipped his head then took a sip of his brew. "It has to be a mistake, dude. He died of a heart attack."

"I don't know what to tell you. My information's confirmed. I don't know the details of his or this guy's death," he tapped the head of the chubby, balding man next to him, "but names are confirmed and they were definitely picked off by the Zerettis . . . or someone who worked for them." He pointed at each man, left to right as he named them. "Marcus 'Marky' Licata, Giovanni 'Little John' Scoza, Vincent 'The Vet' Forgione, Nico 'The Old Man' Cavezza, and Anthony 'Tony the Nighthawk' Destefano."

I blinked at the photo a few more times. "This just can't be right, man. This guy is my girl's father." I gritted my teeth. As if my anger would snap him into telling me the truth. Change the story he was trying to make me believe. "I'm telling you, I grew up next door to him. He was in pharmaceutical sales and liked to work on model trains."

Roland took in a nervous breath. "I'm telling you what I've got, and you know my information is tight. Maybe your girl isn't shooting straight with you?"

I gave him a warning look that had him sitting back in his seat. "There has to be another explanation. Everyone has a twin, right? It's a coincidence."

He nodded his head sarcastically. "Yep, and how many have a picture of their 'twin' framed and mailed with a death order? There wasn't much information on Scoza, but it looks like he was a rat. When there's a death order listed, they save the best for last. Gets him good and scared, wondering when and where."

"Rat?" I shook my head. "No way he was affiliated with the mob. Besides, if any of this were true, wouldn't there be police reports, news stories, court documents?" Roland had let me down with bogus information and I was pissed. None of this made sense. Gerald Sheffield was no mobster, and definitely not a rat. Although he didn't care much for my presence around his daughter, he was the last person on earth I could imagine holding a gun to someone's head . . . but he *did* have a gun hidden in the safe. *Gun. Safe. Faulty birth certificate. What the fuck?* I cracked my neck from left to right, trying to relieve some of the tension. *Nah. Roland's reaching. He's been in the cage too long.*

"Normally, yeah. That's what makes this strange. I dug deep and couldn't find much on the guy."

"Fuck!" I growled in a low voice, gripping the edge of the table. "What am I supposed to do with this shit?"

"You want my advice? Drop it. You're in over your head and these guys are dangerous."

Whatever. I slid out of the booth—skidded was more like it—the faux red leather sticking to my jeans in spots that I assumed was dried syrup. "Appreciate it." I nodded, not able to look Rowland in the eyes. My girlfriend's father is a mobster rat. No fucking way.

***

Fuck, I thought again as I drove back to the office. I'd have to tell Briley something, but what? I thought about making up a lengthy story that would explain the picture. But when I saw her standing outside of her car, biting her nails as she waited for me to tell her what I'd learned, I couldn't do it. I tried to tug her inside, sealed up in my office with total privacy, but she wanted the information now. So I spilled everything. Except the part about the mob. And Mr. Sheffield being a rat.

Briley's breaths became shallow as she processed the overload of information. "You're telling me this guy is not my father? I know it's him, Cooper. You think I wouldn't know my own father?" She backed up and leaned against her car, palming the door with one hand to steady herself.

"I don't know what to tell you, B." I wanted to pull her into my arms, throw out some empty promises to take that pained look off her face. Instead, I stood close, ready to give her whatever she needed, whether it be my arms or space. "This guy's name is Giovanni Scoza." The name felt so foreign on my tongue. I'd grown up with this man. It was so hard to believe.

She bit down on her pinky fingernail as she studied the photo. "Oh," she whispered. She pushed off the car and started pacing. "Oh," she repeated. Watching her pace back and forth along with the crazy information still swirling in my brain had my head spinning. "Oh my God, Coop."

"What?" She stopped and looked at me like I'd missed the billboard announcement.

"Don't you see? Giovanni Scoza . . . Gerald Sheffield. Both initials are G S. They're the same person. My father, Gerald Sheffield, is Giovanni Scoza." Tiny goose bumps sprang up on her arms. "I've heard of this before. People use aliases with the same initials. Remember the serial rapist, Adam Anderson? His real name was Alex Avancho. He also used the alias Axel Aimes."

Where did she get this information and why was I more freaked out than she was? I didn't know whether to be creeped out by her facts or concerned about her current state. She had to be in shock. The Briley I knew wouldn't be this calm learning her father was in the mob. I played along, not wanting to upset her. "I think I remember hearing you talk about that story."

"Question is . . . which one is real?" She glanced up at the sky as if she'd find the answer in a wispy cirrus cloud. "Is my father Gerald or Giovanni?"

"I'm sorry, baby." I checked my phone for the time. "I've gotta get inside. I have a meeting with a client in thirty minutes. Let me cancel before they—"

A black car pulled in at a diagonal, much too close to Briley and me. The dark tinted window rolled down halfway, giving me a glimpse of the man inside. He looked to be in his fifties, salt and pepper hair, and an intimidating smile.

"We're trying to find the aquarium," he insisted.

He seemed friendly enough, so I pointed toward the road. "You're close. Take this road two blocks to Meridian. You should see signs, but—"

He interrupted, holding a police badge where I could see it. "If you want to keep Briley safe, don't make a scene." He held his hand out through the window as if he wanted to shake. "Take the envelope, point toward the road again, and read the instructions once you're inside your office."

Briley was frozen next to me. Panic rendered me motionless for a few beats, but I shook his hand, discreetly accepting the small envelope, and pointed aimlessly at the road until he rolled his window up and the car sped off.

"What the hell was that?" Briley whispered as I stood there in shock, gripping an envelope the size of a gift card.

"Uh," I glanced around wildly for anything out of the norm, then ushered her toward the front entrance of my office building. "Come inside."

The place was empty, thankfully, but in a matter of minutes, my partner and our employees would be coming through. I hauled Briley into my office, shut the door, and urged her to sit.

"Open it, Coop!"

The print was small and neat with these instructions:

126 Piedmont Avenue

7:00 p.m.

Park in back lot, parking space #54

*both parties must be present

Briley and I shared a look, both of us silent. *Damn it, damn it!* This was all my fault, getting Roland involved. I'd most likely gotten him in trouble, too, and now the two of us would be questioned.

"I'll go alone," I insisted. My jaw ached as my teeth ground together, angry over my stupidity. I shouldn't have dragged Briley into any of this. Not yet. I should've made some shit up and saved her. A few speeding tickets was the extent of her dealings with the police. This was way out of her league, and I'd make sure it ended here.

"Oh no you don't!" She snatched the card from my hand and shoved it in her pocket. "This is my mess, and if anyone is going, it'll be me." Turning on her heels, she stalked off toward her car. I was right behind her, ready to set her straight on the matter, but she held up her index finger as she started the car and rolled down the window.

"Briley, I'm telling you—"

"I know, Coop," she interrupted with a soft smile. "You've always been my protector, and you won't let me go alone." She raised her hands in defense. "I give. We'll go together. Want to meet at the house, or should I pick you up here?"

We both knew what she was doing, turning it around and making it seem like she was *letting* me go with her. I let out a long, frustrated sigh. It was no use arguing with her. When her eyes darkened and her lips curled up into that fake smile, it meant she was all in. Nuclear bombs couldn't shake *Stubborn Briley.*

"I'll see you at home," I conceded.

Seventeen

Briley

Fear tried to settle in my bones, raising the hair on the back of my neck in warning. I couldn't let Cooper see it, or he'd turn the car around and drop me off. Knowing him, he'd take something out of my engine so I couldn't drive. Slow, steady breaths and imagining the way the ocean rolled in and out seemed to work the best at relaxing me.

Cooper pulled around back into parking space fifty-four as instructed. The lot was used for the three surrounding buildings, and we had no clue which one to enter. I pulled out the card and read over it again.

"The address is one-twenty-six, so I assume it's this one." I pointed to the red brick building in front of us. The only door on the back side was a grey metal with a card reader slot for entry. Cooper tried the handle with no luck so we stood there, wondering what to do next.

At exactly seven o'clock, the door opened. A pudgy man with a blue ball cap and a blank expression ushered us inside and led us to a room with a few folding chairs. Cooper never loosened his grip on my hand as we chose the two seats farthest from the door. While we waited, I peered around the room, taking in the frightening environment. It wasn't anything like I'd seen on television. Cops usually questioned you in a back room of the police station, one of those reverse mirrors lining a wall so other officers could see.

This room was windowless, the white walls unadorned and giving off a musty smell like a neglected basement. There were no noises besides the blood beating behind my ears, until Cooper's voice echoed through the room.

"What the hell's going on?" He exuded a relaxed confidence which eased my mind a fraction. "Why have you called us here? This isn't police procedure."

Men's dress shoes clanked against the concrete floor, the sound competing with the beat of my racing heart. The man from the car earlier entered the room. He was dressed in slacks and a light blue button down shirt, making him seem even more intimidating than before. I wondered if he'd changed for that very reason. His black hair was slicked against his head, one tendril out of place and falling across his forehead. I sucked in a breath of courage, refusing to let any fear show. Cooper and I hadn't done anything wrong, had we?

"You're probably wondering why you're here," he began, taking a seat and crossing his legs. His right ankle bobbed up and down as it rested on his restless left knee. "I—"

"Why we're here," Cooper interrupted. "And who the hell you are."

"I'm U.S Marshal, Billings." He nodded toward the man in the ball cap. "And this is Kroegen."

"Marshal?" Cooper was on his feet, jaw clenched and eyes blazing. The hand that had held mine gently was now balled at his side. "What—?"

"Please, sit." Billings waited for Cooper to calm down and take his seat. Cooper's reaction had my sweat glands in overdrive. I glanced up at him, gauging his reaction which seemed to be calmer now, and I blew out an unsteady breath. I was nervous enough. I didn't need him losing it.

Looking at the man claiming to be someone important, I asked with a shaky voice, "What's a U.S. Marshal and what do you want with us?"

Cooper answered before the man could get a word out. "Federal Law Enforcement."

My eyes bobbed from Cooper to Billings as each took their turn interrupting the other.

"You've been snooping around, digging for information that you've no business with." He gave Cooper and I equal time with a stern glare.

Cooper's voice startled me when he spoke. "Last I heard, the internet was free game."

The Marshal uncrossed his leg and straightened. "I'm not asking, I'm informing. Stop digging, son." He tossed a fatherly glare at me and then back at Cooper. "If you care about this girl, drop it. You're young . . . in love—am I right?" His lips curled slightly as he looked from me to Cooper again. "You've got enough to focus on. No more digging."

"But I have questions," I said, my heart slamming against my chest as I spoke. "I need to know who I am. And you have answers, don't you?" I leaned forward in my seat. "Who are you, and why do you care if we find those answers? Who is it going to hurt? Right now the only person the secrets are hurting is me." Tears trickled down my cheeks unexpectedly, and I swiped them with the backs of my hands. "Why is everyone trying to hide things from me? I have the right to know!" I was shouting now, my voice echoing off the walls and making me sound a lot stronger than I felt.

Just as I thought my heart would explode and my body would go into shock from shaking so violently, Cooper's arms were around me, pulling me into his lap. He cradled me like a child, and I clung to him as if he were the life force I needed to survive.

Over and over, he whispered, "It's okay, baby."

The officer waited a few moments for me to collect myself. Once I was able to look at him, he explained the situation. It wasn't what I had expected, but at least I had something.

"Miss Sheffield," he cleared his throat, leaned forward, and rested his forearms on his knees. "I hope the information I'm about to give you will help you understand. What I'm about to tell you may put you in further danger, depending on how you choose to deal with this information." He gave me a pointed look, making sure I absorbed the warning.

I nodded my head, urging him to continue.

"Your parents were put in the WPP."

I drew my eyebrows together, trying to figure out what that stood for.

He answered my question before I could ask. "Witness Protection Program. Your names were changed." He gave me a few seconds to process the information before continuing. "Your father was involved with some very dangerous men. He was working with us to obtain necessary information to put these men away." He took a deep breath, leaned back in his chair, and glanced at the man in the ball cap who narrowed his eyes. "That's all I can tell you, and I hope to God I've made the right decision telling you as much as I have."

With that, he stood and left the room, the other man following behind. Cooper and I sat there in silence for what seemed an eternity.

Cooper was the first to break the silence. "It's probably safer to talk here before we go home. How are you feeling? What are you thinking, B? What do you need right now?"

Hell if I knew. I was numb. "I don't know." I shrugged. "I'm dumbfounded. What just happened, Coop?" Once the dam broke and my mind came back to life, I was full of questions. "Witness protection? Why? What did they do or who was after them? Don't they put people under protection for testifying against a big time criminal?" My eyebrows twisted with each question. "You know my parents, Coop. My mom bakes, my dad was simple and kind. This has to be a mistake, right?"

Cooper nodded, and then shook his head. "Doesn't make sense."

"It doesn't. You know what I think? I think that creepy dude made this all up so I would stop digging for the real truth. He thinks I'm naïve enough to believe his B.S. and back off. Well, not Briley Sheffield. Nope. I'll find the truth—"

"Okay, stop right there." Cooper bounced his knee, shaking me out of my rant. "Whether he made it up or not, this has all gotten out of hand. He said you were putting yourself in danger, and I'm not taking a chance on your life. I love you too much."

"I'm not in danger, Coop, he—"

"No." His jaw tightened and his lips formed a straight line. "It's over."

"The hell it is!" My arms flew up in the air trying to make myself seem bigger and more determined. This was my life, not a game. No one, not even Cooper, would tell me when it was over. "I need to know who I am." My voice echoed off the concrete walls, a higher pitch than I'd intended. Clearing my throat, I asked, "What if you found out you weren't really Cooper Sterling?" I spat out his name like a rotten piece of cheese. I couldn't help it, I was mad. "Wouldn't you want to know what was going on?"

"I know who you are. Whether you're Briley Sheffield or Olga Wollowkowski—" He paused briefly at my narrowed eyes. Now was not the time to attempt humor. "You're beautiful, sweet, smart, stubborn as shit, a brilliant poet and writer. You suck at making pancakes, but you're a fantastic cook, you can whip anyone's ass in basketball aside from mine, and the most important thing . . . you're mine." His face was fierce and soft at the same time. "I'll do whatever it takes to protect you and keep you safe. If that means pissing you off and not having you talk to me for a week, I'll take the chance. You're dropping this shit. Understood?"

My body stiffened, and I slid off his lap, standing before him with hands on my hips. "What-ever," I answered with the snappiest voice I could muster. I was still fuming, adrenaline making my face hot, but Cooper wasn't to blame. If the table was turned, I'd feel the same. Truthfully, I'd all but asked him to let Blake piss all over us as we stood there and took it because I didn't want him back in prison. I hated being told what to do, though, so I wouldn't let him know at that moment that I wasn't mad at him.

Stalking off toward the car, I heard him right behind me and smiled secretly. By the time we got to the car, I'd lost the anger I'd been trying to hang on to. Lifting my arms, I wrapped them around his waist and rested my head on his chest. This was where I felt safest. I shook my head a fraction, thinking about how over the top Cooper could be.

This man. I loved everything about him. The way he exhaled a shaky breath after every kiss, the random, stupid jokes he told to make me laugh, and the depth of his love for me. If I believed in fate or the idea that everyone had a mate specifically matched for their soul, I knew without a doubt

Cooper was that match for me. I couldn't live without his friendship growing up, and now I couldn't live without his love.

"If this is angry Briley, I can deal," he chuckled a little, enveloping me in his strong arms.

"I can't be angry with you for wanting to keep me safe, Coop." My stomach growled loudly and it dawned on me that all I'd consumed was a cup of coffee and cereal bar this morning. "Guess I should eat something." I rubbed my stomach. "You hungry?"

"Starved." He opened the passenger door for me, waited until I slid in, and shut the door. I watched him walk around the front of the car and hoped for both our sakes we'd be able to forget this day.

Sitting in a booth at the back of Café Nonna, we picked at our meals, Cooper pushing a piece of lasagna around his plate while I swirled pasta onto my fork, making spaghetti towers.

"I thought you were hungry." He frowned at me, disapproving of my food architecture.

"Sorry, the stress has taken my appetite."

"Same. I'll have them box it up."

I nodded and drank the last bit of wine in my glass. Cooper's phone buzzed with an incoming text. He glanced down, but slipped it back in his pocket.

"Ryan," he said, knowing I'd be curious. Ryan, his bandmate. "We've been offered a gig this weekend at Octane."

"That's great, Coop."

He shook his head. "I'm not feeling it. Meeks can take my spot." He laid his credit card on the table so the server would know we were ready to go.

"What? Why not? Because of all that's happened?" I rubbed my hand over his on the table. "Coop, you've gotta do it. It'll be the perfect distraction." His expression was unchanged. "Please, Coop, for me? I haven't gotten to see you since . . . last time." And I hadn't been invited last time. We hadn't been speaking, and he had invited Madison. It was a sore spot I had no desire to revisit, but I wanted to remind him. Maybe this would clear out a lot of things, our overloaded brains and some bad memories.

"Okay." He offered a soft smile. "For you." Pulling out his phone, he texted his reply.

It was already working, my mind releasing the stress of our meeting and focusing on what I would wear, wondering which songs they would play, and what Octane looked like from the inside. It was a bigger club, and I'd heard rumors about half-naked women dancing in cages set up on platforms above the crowd.

"I'm so excited for you!" I rubbed my hands together. "This is huge, Coop. What do I wear as one of the cage dancers?"

His eyes shot up at me and widened, making me laugh.

Eighteen
Briley

Three days passed at the speed of a prisoner walking to his death. Each minute of the day was filled with unanswered questions, my mind debating whether or not I should talk to my mother about the supposed witness protection program. My only distraction was helping Cooper get ready for his gig. He had practiced with the guys two nights in a row at our place, and I busied myself making way too much food—enough to feed all twelve bands at the Big Guava Fest—let alone my man's small group.

By Friday night, my nerves were frazzled. Our bed was completely covered in skirts and blouses, shoes scattered all over the floor. I still hadn't picked an outfit.

"What happened in here?" Cooper asked as he stepped out of the bathroom. His wet hair appeared darker, making his green eyes more prominent than usual. He was stunning in nothing but a pair of distressed jeans.

I scrunched my nose. "I don't know what to wear."

"Seriously? Slip on a pair of jean shorts and that black top that goes around your neck." He swirled his finger around his neck, in case I didn't understand his description of my silk halter top. "The one with the silver beads."

I giggled at his attempt to help me dress. *Jean shorts? Men.* "I'll find something." I let my eyes roam over him from head to toe. Lucky bastard. All he had to do was step out of the shower to look hot as hell.

He gripped my waist, pulling me in against his bare chest. My hands impulsively slid up over his shoulders.

"I see you checking me out." His voice was cocky and playful, turning the knob on my temperature gauge up a notch.

"Stop, Coop." I lowered my eyes from his gaze and chuckled. "You've got to go."

"They can set up without me. I'll be there in plenty of time to go over the music." He dipped down, letting his hot breath linger on my ear. Damn him for knowing that was my undoing every time, and I was sure he could feel my body give in. "Besides," he said, his voice low and husky. "You don't want to watch me play an entire show with a raging hard on, do you?"

"Of course not. Anything I can do to help you have a good show. I *am* your number one fan." I gasped when he reached into my robe and went straight for the prize. The shock of his sudden touch was replaced with a craving that only he could satisfy.

"I need you now, baby." His voice, low and sexy, vibrated against my ear.

I reached between us and fumbled with the button of his jeans, giving up after only a few seconds. "Get these off," I demanded.

As soon as he pulled the last leg of his pants off, I untied my robe and let it fall to the floor. Backing up, I found the edge of the bed. Cooper closed the space between us, pulling me to him. With his hands on my waist, he looked into my eyes and then at my mouth, watching as my tongue darted out to wet my lips, then he leaned in and kissed me.

His mouth moved to my neck, effectively sending a thrilling sensation up my spine. I groaned, his name spilling from my lips. Flipping over, I bent at the waist and gripped the comforter with one hand while reaching behind to stroke him with the other, urging him to take me.

An animalistic sound vibrated from deep within his throat as he pressed against me. His fingers traced along my spine, down the side of my waist, and over my ass. Gripping my hips, he took me hard and fast. It was uncomfortable at first, the sting of my body trying to accommodate him from that angle. But the ecstasy far outweighed the discomfort, and I was teetering on the brink of orgasm.

"Fuuuuck," he growled, low and guttural as he thrust into me, his hands digging into my hips. He kept moving, his fingers reaching around to stroke me until I was white knuckling the comforter. When he bit down on the tendon between my shoulder and neck—just hard enough to release the most erotic sensation—and the sound of my name, dripping from his lips like warm honey, I came. He was close behind me thankfully, my legs unwilling to support me any longer.

My chest and arms collapsed onto the bed, Cooper coming with me but keeping his weight from crushing me somehow. He kissed my shoulder, neck, and nipped at my earlobe. "I'm going to play so good for you tonight, baby."

"Well, Coop." I giggled which got me a firm smack on the ass when he stood up. "Okay, okay. Play well, play good." The way he smirked when I corrected his grammar had a part of me wishing he made more mistakes.

"I love you." He stroked a thumb along my cheek. "Now get that fine ass dressed. I'll see you in a few."

***

I couldn't have felt sexier when I'd finally picked an outfit and straightened my hair. I wore a black mini dress with a deeply cut, gold sequined bodice. A thin strip of black tulle layered over the gold bodice, serving as straps and came up around the neck in a halter fashion. It was just enough to cover but still leave an ample amount of cleavage. At the last minute, Cooper's partner Colin and his fiancée Claire decided to join us. They offered to drive, picking me up first and then Ryan's newest girlfriend, Joselyn.

"God, Briley. You look amazing," Claire beamed as I got into the car. "Cooper's gonna freak."

"Thanks, I hope so." I giggled. "Your hair looks great up like that."

As instructed, we approached the large, bald man at the door and handed him the purple pass Cooper had given me.

"Good evening." He smiled. "Go on in. Ethan will show you to your table."

I stepped through the doors and found Ethan waiting with arms folded across his chest. He matched the doorman in size and build but had a full head of bristly blond hair.

"Hi," I offered, handing him the pass.

"Right this way." We followed him to a round high top table close to the stage. It was on the left side of the room so I would be looking right at Cooper. "Drinks are on the house for you tonight. What can I start you off with?"

Colin ordered a round of Patron for each of us while we perused the specialty drinks. Ethan turned toward the bar, and my eyes took in the room. It was a beautiful club, from what I could see. The space was dark, the only illumination from sapphire blue accent lights. There were no cages for dancers, as rumor had it, but the cocktail servers were wearing bikini tops and barely-there black miniskirts.

I was happy to see the place filling up, a line of people outside, waiting to get in. Cooper could easily quit his day job and make a living out of playing if that's what he wanted to do. It wasn't the life I wanted for us—always worrying about the women throwing themselves at him after a show—but I'd support him if he wanted to take that road. He was a great musician, and I was glad he was getting to use his talents.

A petite redhead brought our shots to the table. "I'm Gia, I'll be taking care of you tonight."

"Ladies, have you decided?" Colin asked.

"I'll have this." Joselyn pointed to a picture on the menu. "The Rock Star."

"Sounds good to me, too." Claire added.

"What's your favorite?" I asked Gia, our server. I usually knew what I liked, but there were so many good choices. She'd surely know what was best.

"This one." She pointed to The Rock 'N' Roll. "If you like rum."

"Yes, perfect. Thanks."

"I'll try The Golden God," Colin quipped, flashing a wink at Claire, who in turn rolled her eyes and slapped his thigh.

When Gia left the table, Colin held up his shot glass. We all joined him and waited for his cue. "To Ryan." He looked at Joselyn, who grinned with pride. "And Cooper. Here's to rockin' this club tonight!"

I swallowed the glass of smooth liquid, feeling its warmth travel down deep before sucking on a lime to finish the experience. We all slammed our glasses upside down onto the table and laughed.

"Smooth," I said, appreciating the slight buzz a single shot could bring.

Gia returned to the table, setting down another round of shots and the drinks we'd ordered. I'd never been treated like a VIP before. Intentionally trying to calm my inner geek, I lifted the shot glass and stifled the desire to wiggle with excitement.

Joselyn offered the next toast. Something about us all getting laid after the show. She seemed like a fun girl, full of life and empty of fear. Her honey-streaked curls bounced as she tossed back her Patron and then rested perfectly around her face as if someone had personally placed each one. Ryan was a handful, and I wondered if she was the one that would finally rein him in. Most girls grew tired of his immaturity, but she was just quirky enough that they might be the perfect match.

"Did you meet Ryan at one of the gigs?" I asked.

"No." She shook her head. "He came into my shop one day and we started talking."

"Your shop?" I asked, my curiosity piqued.

"Yeah, I own Music & Arts on Henderson."

"I've been in there." I leaned in so I could hear her better over the crowd. "Do you play?"

"Piano." She beamed. "You?"

"No." I shook my head. "I'm not musically inclined. I love it, though. I'd give anything for an ounce of talent."

She gave my hand a gracious pat. "Sometimes you just need a good lesson. Come on by and let's see what you've got hiding away."

"I'll do that, if you don't mind wasting an afternoon laughing." I gave a cheesy grin. Ryan had better hang on to this one. She was different, and I liked her.

The lights dimmed, causing the crowd to cheer and whistle and me to panic. I felt it every time Cooper played in front of strangers. My pulse rate would increase, rising even higher when he stepped onto the stage. Then, with the first strum of his fingers against the strings, my pulse would decrease to a normal but excited level.

The music began before we saw the band, an electric guitar bringing the first notes as the stage lights slowly illuminated each member. My eyes focused on Cooper as he watched his fingers to make sure he hit each note. He had the courage of a lion, standing before a packed club and opening with a guitar solo. I knew every song they were going to play, but not in which order.

"Are they singing *In The Air Tonight?*" Claire asked, leaning in so I could hear her.

"Yeah, but they've given it a rock n roll edge. It's amazing."

The crowd went wild during the drum solo, everyone beating the air in unison with faux drumsticks. The next song had everyone on their feet, bouncing to the beat and singing along.

When Ryan began the next song, he pointed to Joselyn, gripping the mic stand with his other hand. She swooned, leaning on me for support. It was an intimate song, making me feel uncomfortable, like I had a front row seat in their bedroom.

She was a mess the entire song, grabbing my arm, singing along, screaming when he sang, "All the sounds you make."

I was sure I didn't want to know . . .

After covering songs by Pearl Jam, Kings of Leon, and Seether, the band took a short break and we ordered another round of drinks. Surrounded by cool people, listening to great music that just happened to be played by the man I was crazy about, the night couldn't have gotten any better. With a tap on the shoulder, I turned around and realized however . . . it could get worse.

"Hi, everyone." Madison addressed the group with a counterfeit smile. She was dressed in a black mini dress that hugged her curves perfectly but looked like something a stripper would wear—barely covering the necessities.

I flashed a puckered brow and excused myself. "I need the restroom. Be right back."

Standing in front of the mirror, I looked myself over and straightened my dress. Madison was suddenly next to me, determined to ruin my evening. Whether it was the alcohol taking over, or my fuse had been shortened by too many jerks burning it, I wasn't sure, but I lashed out before she could say a word.

"The fuck do you want?" Admittedly I hated that word, but I felt like a badass saying to her.

She straightened and stepped back, her eyes wide with shock.

My shoulders automatically pushed back in a defensive stance.. "Cut the bullshit, Madison. Why are you so hell bent on messing with me?" I waited for her to lay a hand over her chest and act offended.

She didn't disappoint. "I'm not messing with you. I wanted to say hello." She pulled out a tube of red lipstick, leaned in toward the mirror, and coated her lips.

"Well, then *hello.*" I couldn't keep the snappiness out of my voice.

"I saw your house was for sale. Are you staying in town or relocating for your job?"

Oh, this is too perfect. I couldn't wait to tell her. "Actually, Cooper asked me to move in with him." The most divine feeling came over me as I watched her squirm.

Her slate eyes darkened with a flash of anger, but she recovered quickly, smiling as if she was happy for me. "How nice. I'm truly happy for you, Briley." She said it with such conviction, I almost believed her. Maybe she had moved on and was mature enough to accept her loss with dignity? "Listen, I'm so happy I ran into you. I'll just give this to you, since you're living with Cooper now." She reached into her purse, pulled out Cooper's black Pearl Jam T-shirt, placed it in my hands, and walked out.

A deep rage came over me, causing me to do something I'd never done before. Still holding Cooper's shirt, I caught up with her and took a chunk of her long blond hair in my fist, effectively twirling her around to face me.

"What the—?"

"Listen to me carefully, you lousy bitch!" Someone gripped my arm, pulling me back. I whipped my head around to see Colin.

Madison laughed, a high pitched, unnatural sound. "I wonder," she began, stepping out of my reach, "how long until he's bored with you, sweet girl."

I lunged forward then, eager to slap the smile off her face. Everything in sight disappeared, a film of red rage blurring my vision. The only sound was the blood beating against my ears. My nails grazed her arm as she jerked back and Colin tugged on my arm.

"C'mon, B. Don't let her get to you." His voice was steady and calm. He led me away, back to our table, but my eyes followed her all the way into the arms of a tall, blond man. They must've been there together. I hoped and prayed he would sweep her off her feet and move her out of the country so she'd finally leave us alone.

"Are you okay?" Colin quirked an uncertain eyebrow at me.

"Yeah." I handed him Cooper's T-shirt. "Can you take this from me, please? It smells like her, and it's all I can do not to go over there and choke her with it." Tears welled up in my eyes, partly from the altercation that almost took place between us, but mostly because she had confirmed my fear that Cooper had slept with her. It was my fault for pushing him away, but all the hate was easily directed at her. *Stupid, stupid move.*

I waved down Gia, asking for two more shots of Patron.

"Whoa, B," Colin warned. "Cooper only has eyes for you. You're all he talks about." He reached across the table and squeezed my hand. "He's crazy about you. Don't waste another thought on Madison. I can assure you, Cooper doesn't." He was right, of course. But I was still wrecked and it would take more than a few words from his best friend to take that pain away.

"Yeah, but he screwed her, and I have to deal with her rubbing it in every chance she gets." I felt sick as the words left my mouth, images forming in my mind like a horror movie.

"You don't know that. She could've borrowed the shirt."

Joselyn and Claire remained silent, their eyes going back and forth between me and Colin as we volleyed comments.

"Have you seen her? Tell me you wouldn't sleep with her if given the chance." My eyes bounced to Claire when I realized what I'd said. "I mean, if you weren't with Claire."

"Honestly, Briley . . ." He reached his hand behind his head and massaged his neck. "I don't know. Cooper was pretty distraught over you. If I know him like I think I do, he wouldn't have touched her. However, get a man drunk enough—" Claire must've kicked him under the table as his body jerked, and he changed his tune. "No, he would've told me. I'd bet all my money he didn't sleep with her."

I slid one of the shots across the table to Colin. "Thanks. Here's to believing you're right."

After the show, I'd ask him. It might kill me knowing the truth—if he was with her—but my sanity was at risk. I had to know.

The band was back on stage and the crowd went wild as they covered "I Want You" by Kings of Leon. The tequila, along with Colin's convincing nod, calmed me enough to enjoy the rest of the evening. I glanced back at Madison once to see her making out with her date.

Colin is right, I told myself. *Cooper is mine.*

It was Cooper's turn at the mic, and he had my full attention. He strummed his guitar a few times, stepped up to the mic, and looked at me when he spoke, his voice throaty and low. "This one's for my girl."

A hush fell over the crowd as they watched him. His fingers manipulated the guitar pick over the strings, eliciting a euphonious sound. He began to sing the words to our song, "Everlong" by Foo Fighters, and the crowd cheered and sang along. My heart melted watching him sing to me, only taking his eyes off of me occasionally to look down at the strings.

He came to my favorite verse in the song—asking me to promise not to stop—and I held my breath so I could focus on his lips, his voice, the words.

Everyone sang along, and Cooper flashed an appreciative smile that made me weak in the knees. I was sure every girl in the room fell in love with him at that moment. The way his jeans sat loosely on his hips, his muscles flexing as he handled the guitar, and the glisten of sweat highlighting his scattering of tats. One more shot of tequila to loosen my inhibitions, and I would've thrown my panties at him. It was hard to believe this was *my* Cooper as he jammed out on a guitar solo.

They played a few more songs and ended with Creed's "My Sacrifice." Cooper sang lead, and his voice surprised me. It was deeper, but I picked up small resemblances to Scott Stapp's voice. God, Cooper was sexy as hell, and I couldn't wait to get him home.

Nineteen

Cooper

The show had gone smashingly well, despite all the distractions. I'd wanted to get Briley's attention during the break, blow her a kiss or something, but she wasn't at the table. Just as I spotted her, with a handful of Madison's hair in her grip, Colin showed up, saving my girl from a fight she would've lost. Briley was tough as nails, but she didn't have the street smarts to fight. Her little punches to my arms wouldn't hurt a kitten.

I don't know, though, she looked pretty pissed. Maybe she would've knocked her out?

The other distraction was Briley's dress. Where the hell did she get that come-fuck-me dress? It took all the concentration I had to hit the right notes. I was first to pack up my shit, wanting to get out of the club so I could get Briley home and peel that dress off her body. I stepped out of the bathroom and changed my shirt before she'd made her way through the crowd and found our dressing room.

Before I could say a word, she ran up and flung her arms around my neck. "Holy shit, Coop, you were amazing!" Her mouth crashed into mine, eager and unrelenting.

I heard Colin say something in the background, so I held out my fist and waited for him to bump it with his own. My hands gripped Briley's waist, guiding her against the wall. I pulled away, not taking my eyes off her. "Some privacy," I demanded.

A few crass remarks and chuckles preceded the sound of the backstage dressing room door shutting. Finally, we were alone.

"This fucking dress," I breathed. My palms glided over her hips, skimmed over the dip of her waist, and cupped her half-masked breasts. "You drove me insane tonight."

"Good," she panted. "We're even then. I can't wait to get you home."

"I'm not waiting that long. I want you . . . right here, right now."

Her chest heaved with each chaotic breath. "Do it," she challenged, her eyes lit up with excitement.

Palming the wall, I found the switch and turned off the overhead light. Pale streaks of light from the bathroom illuminated her face as I watched her tongue dart out and lick her bottom lip, urging me to devour her. Brushing my lips against hers, I pulled her lower lip between my teeth and groaned in appreciation.

I lifted the hem of her skirt, letting it gather around her waist. Feeling for her panties, I realized they weren't there. "You didn't wear panties?" I pulled back to look at her, my eyes wide. That was a stupid move in a club like this.

"I did." She held them up and laughed. "I planned on giving them to you so you'd get the hint and take me home, but . . ."

I exhaled and flashed her a grin. "You're killing me, baby."

Dipping two fingers into her, she moaned and tightened her grip on my shoulders. She was as turned on as I was, and I couldn't wait another moment. I lowered my jeans just enough to free myself and lifted her up so she could wrap her legs around my waist. We both gasped at the sudden feeling, and I almost lost my footing. She felt so good, I knew I wouldn't last.

The way she clung to me with her head resting in the crook of my neck made me feel powerful and wanted. She was louder than usual, and I knew anyone outside the door could hear.

"Shh," I whispered in her ear. Either she didn't hear me or didn't care and the sounds she made brought me closer and closer to releasing the sexual tension that had built over the last two hours. Finally, she cried out my name as I gripped her ass and titled her just enough to hit the sweet spot. It was all I could do to hold the two of us up as my body was overtaken by a surge of pleasure. My knees weakened, but I remained steady, gripping the mortar line of the concrete wall as we rode the last of the waves.

"Fuck," I groaned. My forehead pressed against hers, both slippery with sweat. We shared an I-can't-believe-we-just-did-that-here look as I eased her down to the ground and zipped my pants. "I couldn't wait."

She shook her head, a shy smile on her flawless face. "Me either. Watching you on stage . . . your voice, the way you looked at me when you sang "Everlong." I almost jumped you right then and there."

I helped Briley step into her panties and straighten her dress. Hugging her from behind, I whispered in her ear, "Thanks, baby. It was good to have you in the front row. I know we're just a group of guys playing around, but you make me feel like a rock star."

She turned to face me, her expression serious. "You are, Coop. You could easily quit your day job." She put her hands on her hips, when I smirked.

"You've known me all my life, yes?"

I nodded, swallowing back laughter at her tone.

"You know when I'm lying. Look at my face." She swirled her finger in a circle around her sweet face. "Am I lying now?"

"It's hard to tell. You're flushed from the sex." The laughter escaped, and I received a much deserved smack on the arm. "No, your ears aren't that red. I believe you."

She finger-combed her hair and waved her hands next to her face. "I am flushed," she said, suddenly sheepish. "Everyone will know what we were up to."

I'm sure everyone heard what we were up to. "I don't give a damn." I took her in my arms and stroked her cheek with my thumb. "Let them all know how much I crave you and can't keep my hands off you. Jealous fucks."

"Such a guy thing to say, Coop." She rolled her eyes and punched my arm softly.

I twisted my lips into a half smile. "I'm a guy."

Stepping through the door into the hallway, we were greeted by Ryan and his girl, Joselyn. "If you ever do that to me again, motherfucker . . ." He shook his head. "I shouldn't have to babysit your ass while you fuck—"

I stepped closer to him and gripped a fistful of his shirt. "Watch it," I warned.

He looked from me to Briley, and then raised his hands. "Whatever. I should've left the door unguarded." He took Joselyn by the hand and stalked off down the hall.

Briley looked mortified, standing there like she'd been slapped. "Oh, God," she said, her voice barely a whisper. "He knew. They heard us." She began pacing the short length of the hallway. "Were we loud? Was I loud? I think I screamed your name." Her hands reached up to cover her eyes like she was hiding.

"Hey." I cupped her chin and lifted it. "Look at me." She took her time removing her hands, finally looking into my eyes. "You were so quiet. Not a sound. In fact, I wondered if you'd forgotten my name or that you weren't into it. That's how quiet you were. He was just being an ass."

"You're so full of shit," she muttered, a smile creeping across her face. "Funny, but full of shit."

"There's the smile I love. C'mon, let's go home," I urged, holding out my arm.

There was something about stepping through the front door of your home that made your body realize it could shut down. I was completely exhausted from the night and couldn't wait to crash. I only had enough energy to pull off my clothes and fall into bed. Briley went through her ritual of brushing her teeth and washing her face before joining me, then she tucked herself into my side, resting her head on my chest. It would've been so easy to slip into a deep sleep but curiosity wouldn't let me be.

"What happened between you and Madison?"

I felt her body stiffen, and her toes began to trace a pattern on my leg. "You saw us? Where?"

"I was backstage, looking for you."

"We had a disagreement." Her tone was flat and I could tell her teeth were clenched.

"It looked heated," I said carefully.

"Yep." Her tone was clipped.

"Hey." I lifted her chin to look at her. She was visibly upset. "What happened?"

She gulped. Not a good sign. "I need to ask you something, Coop." She pulled away from me and sat up, her fingers fumbling around in her lap. "I know we weren't together and you're a man with needs, and you had every right to . . . just tell me the truth. Did you sleep with her?" Now she was picking at the hem of the sheet.

All exhaustion left my body, her question acting like a jolt of caffeine. Pushing off the bed, I sat up and leaned against the headboard. I had no idea she was going to ask me something like that, and I paused too long before answering.

"I'm no saint, B," I told her. She cut her eyes at me and then looked back down. "But, no. I did not sleep with her."

The look of disbelief she gave hurt. "Then why did she hand me your shirt tonight and imply that you did?"

I shrugged. "Hell if I know why your crazy friend does the shit she does. I loaned her the shirt. I did not sleep with her."

"She's not my friend." She twisted the sheet around her finger and unwound it. "Did you screw her?"

I blinked. "I just told you I didn't."

"You said you didn't *sleep* with her. You could've screwed and left." She crossed her arms over her chest and squinted her eyes.

"You're pissing me off, B." My shoulders straightened, making the position I was in uncomfortable. I jerked back the covers and climbed out of bed. "My word should be good enough." Stalking around to her side, I pulled her around to face me and lowered to her level, resting on one knee. "I know Blake took your trust away, but this is me, B. Look at me." I waited for her to lift her gaze to meet mine. "I have never and will never hurt you. I have no problem admitting my faults—I can be a real piece of shit—but if I tell you something, believe it."

She nodded and blew out a noisy breath. "Okay. I believe you. How did she get your shirt then?"

"She spilled her ice cream. The shirt was in my truck. I loaned it to her."

She nodded, clearly still pissed, and I sighed. "I took her out. A movie and ice cream. Like you said, we weren't together."

"So why didn't you sleep with her? Too full from the ice cream?" she snapped.

My jaw clenched. "Fine. You want the truth?" I gripped the back of my neck and rubbed it as I stood up to pace the floor. "I tried. Believe me, I tried everything to get you out of my head. It didn't work." I knelt down in front of her, pulling her to the edge of the bed. "You wrecked my world, B. I loved you too much to push you, but I also loved you too much to let you go."

Everything about her softened then, and she gripped my head, pulling it to her chest. I inhaled the scent of her silk slip before moving out of her embrace and climbing back into bed. Without another word, I wrapped an arm around her waist and tugged her into my side.

"I love you, Coop, and I do trust you," she said in the moonlit dark.

"I love you, too, baby."

"If we have a chance to see Pearl Jam in concert again, I'll buy you another T-shirt. The other one's in the trash."

I fell asleep smiling, with my girl in my arms.

Twenty
Briley

Sunday was perfect—a lazy day by the pool with my guy. If I were a superstitious person, I'd assume the sun-filled day of bliss was prepping me for the cloudy, shit-storm that would consume my Monday.

The first thing that happened Monday was a phone call from my editor. She wanted me in her office "as soon as physically possible."

With my hair in a messy bun and a pair of wrinkled shorts, I looked far from a professional, but this was what *"as soon as physically possible"* got you. I stepped into Angela's office and took a seat, waiting for her to finish yelling at whoever was on the other line.

Thanks a lot for getting her riled before she lets loose on me!

She slammed the phone down, looked up at me, and sighed. "Can no one do anything right this week?"

I didn't answer.

"So," she began. "This article sucks." She pulled out a folder holding my piece on Tapas. "There's nothing in here that half the world doesn't already know and . . ." She searched the paper with her eyes and tapped a spot with one finger. "This paragraph about Croquetas is awful. You make them sound like a Spanish version of mozzarella sticks with ham inside. Even I can do better than that. Nothing you've written here makes me want to try those. What the hell's going on, Briley? I've never seen you write so poorly. Look," she sighed and turned the paper around so I could see her marks, "you misspelled five words and left out a comma." Her glare turned soft as she studied me.

"I'm sorry, Angela. I've had a lot on my mind, and I see it's affected my work. I'll rewrite it."

"I thought things were fairytale happy in your world right now?" she asked.

"For the most part, yes." I liked Angela most of the time. She was easy to work for and usually praised my work. We never lunched together or shared too much personally, but I could tell she was probably good to her friends, and outside of the workplace we'd get along.

Known for opening my mouth and spilling whatever chose to come flooding out, I paused and chose my words carefully. "My mother's been in the hospital. She's home and settled now, but the whole thing has left me exhausted. It won't hap—"

"I'm sorry to hear that." She seemed sincere. "Now, take your intern-worthy article and fix it so it's Briley-worthy." Her expression was flat, except for a flash of a twinkle in her eye, letting me know we were cool but she still meant business.

I left the building in a rush, thankful that Sophie wasn't there for the usual chat session. I liked her a lot, but this meeting was upsetting, and all I wanted to do was get to my car.

My focus should've been on the article and how I'd make it *"Briley-worthy"*—a compliment hidden amongst an insult— instead, my mind was back on that stupid key that sat waiting in the bottom of my purse, wondering what answers it would unlock. I'd had more time to think about it this weekend—and Coop's and my strange encounter with the Marshals. Now that I had the name of the bank, all I had to do was walk in and open the box.

Instead of my original plan to get groceries and head home, I found myself parked at the bank. As I rolled the key in my palm, I tossed around the idea of going inside. The parking lot was practically empty, so it would be easy to slip in and out without too many eyes on me. Fear gripped me, reminding me of the warning the Marshal gave. Was I in over my head? Probably. But I couldn't let it go. No one was offering answers and I wouldn't settle for leaving my life a mystery. After a deep breath of uncertainty, I exhaled and got out of the car.

Inside the vault, I found the safe-deposit box and slid the key in, turning it to the left until it clicked. *It worked!* My heart skipped. I pulled the box out carefully, as if an alarm might sound, alerting the police of my disobedience and further digging.

After setting it on the table, I stared at the long metal container, a medley of emotions bounding inside me. The contents would most likely reveal truths that would either set me free or destroy me. I shifted my weight from one foot to the other as I teetered on what to do. In the end, nails jagged and sufficiently trimmed from chewing, I started to lift the top. I had to know what was inside.

No bright light emitted from the box, revealing a golden prize. Only a single legal-sized envelope rested inside. I slid my finger beneath the glued edge, opening the flap and removed a hand written letter.

My darling neonata, it began.

Italian?

One day, when ~~Mr. and Mrs.~~ your parents feel it is safe to say the truth to you, you will read this and I hope understand. I read the words, imagining a woman with dark, flowing hair in a white gown with a thick Italian accent.

I love you and wanted you the moment I knew you were growing inside me. I used to talk to you and sing fa la ninna, fa la nanna each night before bed.

Fa la ninna, fa la nanna,
nella braccia della mamma
fa la ninna bel bambin
fa la nanna bambin bel,
fa la ninna, fa la nanna
nella braccia della mamma

I couldn't wait to hold you in my arms and tell you about the world. Explore dreams and a future with you. Teach you how to cook, paint, and grow a garden.

But my life became dangerous, and I had to give you up to protect you.

I wish you happiness, my beloved daughter. Enjoy life to the fullest, love deeply, and marry someone worthy of you. Someone who makes you laugh. Someone who will lay down his life for you, if he has to.

Your father was that man for us. He loved you so much. If it is ever safe enough for me to find you, I will. If not, know how much I love you, and I will meet you on the other side one day to hold you in my arms.

I cannot say goodbye, so I will say to you once again, I love you more than words can express, my beautiful, perfect baby girl.

Love,

Your mother

I stood there, stunned. I knew without a doubt she was talking about me. The birth certificate I'd found for Isabella, it wasn't a mistake or a misprint. It had been mine all along. They must've gone to great lengths to change my name, have another certificate drawn up, and pass me off as Briley from Tampa. What I didn't understand was why it wasn't hidden in this box? Instead it was out in the open for me to find. Had my father set that up, knowing it was his last shot at leading me to the truth?

A feeling of relief washed over me knowing that I hadn't been stolen. At the same time I was sad, knowing my birth mother had to give her child to strangers in order to keep her safe. I didn't know for certain this letter was meant for me, but it made sense. The only way to know for sure was to ask my mother for the truth.

I wasn't sure how I made it from the bank parking lot to my mother's driveway, the short trip a blur as questions swam through my head.

"Hi, Bee," my mother greeted from her recliner in the living room.

"Mom," I answered, not sure how one was supposed to broach the subject of an under the table adoption.

"Everything okay?" She sat upright, lowering the leg rest on the chair.

"No." I shook my head, my brows cemented in a pulled together position. "I—I have some questions, and I need you to shoot straight with me."

"I always have." Concern invaded her features as she watched me.

"No, you haven't." I gazed at her affectionately. Even if I did have another mother, this woman before me was still my 'mom'. "I love you, Mom, and I know you're trying to protect me, but I need answers. May I speak freely or do we need to turn on music or something?"

She must've understood my meaning as she shifted in her chair, her expression changing from concern to frustration. "Not today, Bee."

"I'll take my chances, then." I paused to see if any panic reflected in her eyes. She remained stern, so I continued. "I found this letter in a safe-deposit box that Dad held secretly." I walked to her chair and handed her the note, waiting until she finished reading it.

It was a long moment before she looked up and met my eyes. "You found this?"

I nodded.

"It has nothing to do with you, Bee." She kept a straight, stern face but I saw something in her eyes. Panic? Frustration?

"Stop! Just stop!" I held my hands up. "This letter was meant for me one day. That day is now. Start talking, Mom, or I'm going to the cops." Fear flashed in her eyes, but I continued. "I know we're all in the witness protection program."

She lowered her eyebrows and blinked a few times. The look on her face made me feel sorry for spilling so much, so fast. "How . . .?" she began.

"A cop found Cooper and me. He took us to a building and tried to scare the crap out of us. I'm sorry, Mom, but I need to know what's going on. You can't expect me to live like this forever. Don't keep me in the dark." I plopped down in the chair next to her so she'd stay put. Getting up was still difficult with a healing hip replacement.

"You what?" She flinched. "Bee, are you all right? Who was this man? What did he look like?"

"I don't know, he was your age, maybe a little older. Salt and pepper hair."

"Did he have an accent?" Her voice was shaking. "Any noticeable tattoos or markings?"

I shook my head, getting more frustrated by the minute. It was my turn to ask the questions. "No, he didn't have an accent or any marks. He had a badge. Said he was on our side. Please, Mom. You have to tell me the truth. If I keep digging, he said I'll put us in danger. Just tell me what I need to know."

"Okay." She lowered her head a moment. "Damn your father. I love him, but he shouldn't have left those clues for you. This is not the right time." Looking back up, she repositioned herself, grimacing as she moved. Inhaling a deep breath, she began, "This letter was written by your mother. Like it says, her life was in danger. Her husband—your biological father—was murdered by some really powerful, bad men. We adopted you secretly and gave her enough money to flee."

My next question had me knotting my hands. *Stop digging. Let it go.* But I had to know. Curiosity far outweighed the danger. "Was Daddy murdered? Was his name really Giovanni Scoza?"

"Who told you that, Bee?" Her eyebrows knit together before she leaned back and swallowed hard. "Where did you get this information?"

"I followed the trail." A deep breath did little to calm my nerves. "There's a picture of Dad with some men. He has a number four over his head." I watched my mother's face twist into different expressions. I'd always been able to read her. Not this time. "Who are those men, what does the number mean?"

"He was—" She sucked in a sob and let it settle before continuing on an exhale. "It was a warning from the Zeretti's. They're cruel and sadistic. The name of their game was 'guess when, where, and how'. The only thing they told you was who would be taken out before and after you. Your father was last in line to be . . ." She couldn't finish, couldn't say the word. Her breaths became shaky as she inhaled and exhaled, but she kept going. "We landed in the witness protection program because your father helped your biological parents hide you. The Zeretti's wanted your entire line wiped out, and they won't stop until they find you."

Wiped out? Someone's trying to wipe me out? My bones rattled with terror but I pressed on. "So he didn't die of a heart attack? They . . . killed him?"

"I choose to believe both. The official cause of death was a heart attack, but I believe it was due to the stress they'd put on your father. You can't imagine how hard it is to live in fear for your life and that of your family." On the verge of tears, she rung out her hands. "We were always looking over our shoulder, making sure you were safe."

I thought I had wanted the truth, but it was a lot to process. I slumped back in my seat, trying to absorb all my mother had told me. We sat there in silence for a long moment. I could only imagine what was going through her mind as I hardly kept up with the sprint going on in my own. She'd given up so much— her family and friends—to protect me, and she'd loved me as deeply as if I were her own. I wondered if her parents—my grandparents—were still living, and what they were told when she'd left and changed her name.

"I love you, Mom." I watched tears spill over her lashes, feeling my own gather in my eyes. "I'm grateful they picked you."

"I've always loved you, Bee. The moment they put you in my arms, I knew that whether or not you were my own flesh and blood didn't matter. You were mine. I think I went overboard sometimes, making sure you knew how much you were wanted, cherished."

"Is she still alive?" I asked. My mother shook her head. After another beat, I asked, "Do I have any other family?"

"You had a brother. Matteo. They called him Matt, I believe." She paused, clearly shaken.

"Had?" I asked, wishing I hadn't as soon as the words left my mouth.

The nod of my mother's head was slight, but not missed.

"How old was he?" I asked thickly, mourning the loss of a brother I never knew. Somehow it still hurt.

"Sixteen."

"Good God! How could they hurt a kid?" I felt my heart squeezing tight.

"They're cruel people, Bee. They have black souls. That's why we've gone to such lengths to protect you. That's why I begged you to stop digging for answers. If they find you . . ." She lowered her head, unable to finish the sentence. I knew the end; she didn't have to voice it.

If they found me, they would kill me.

Twenty-One
Cooper

I didn't want to greet Briley with stress written all over my face. A wise man once told me to never bring work home. It would be there waiting for me tomorrow. Briley had enough to worry about without me bringing the pollution of a douche bag builder into our lives.

After taking a deep breath, letting the disastrous day melt off my shoulders, I stepped inside to see Briley waiting in the living room.

"Hi, baby, how was your day?" I asked, trying my best to leave the day behind.

"Hmm, okay. Yours?" Her legs were pulled up beside her on the couch, and she seemed to be deep in thought.

"I'm gonna grab a beer. Can I get you anything?" I called over my shoulder. I'd been craving a cold one since ten this morning, so I was in dire need.

"I've got a glass of wine already, thanks." She sounded off, a little dazed.

After popping the top off a Rolling Rock and sucking back half the bottle, I joined her on the couch. "Tell me about your day."

Hopefully she wouldn't ask about mine. Although I could sum it up in a single sentence: jackass builder rants at poor, unsuspecting contractor.

"I don't even know where to begin." She pulled her knees to her chest.

"What happened, B?" I set my beer on the end table, hooked my arms under her legs and pulled her toward me.

"Well," she began on a huff. "First, my boss chewed my ass. Said my article seemed a little 'amateur' in quality." She made air quotes over her head, and I had to hold back a smile at how cute she looked. "Then, I found something." She seemed to be lost in thought, so I waited her out a few moments before nudging her.

"What'd you find?" I rubbed a knuckle over her arm.

She peered up at me, looking as if she was surprised I was there. "You're not going to believe what I'm about to tell you, Coop." I saw uncertainty in her eyes, like a child that didn't trust the stranger offering candy.

"Briley," I took her hand in mine, caressing the soft skin with my thumb, "you can trust me. Tell me what you found."

She watched her hand, focusing on the movement as I drew a pattern across her flesh. Finally, she looked up and declared, "I found a letter from my real mother."

My body remained still, trying not to react until she was finished. With a flat expression, I urged her to continue.

"It was in a safe-deposit box. I used the key and the bank statement you found, and . . . there was a letter inside. She—my mother—wrote it so one day I'd understand why she gave me up."

I nodded slowly, not taking my eyes off hers. "And you're sure it was your mother who wrote the letter?"

"Yes." She nodded absently. "Mom . . . my mom—the one who raised me—confirmed it. She and my dad adopted me under the table. My biological father was murdered by those Z people."

Holy shit. "The Zeretti's?"

"Yes." She busied herself with my hands, trying to distract her emotions as she talked. After tracing my veins with a finger, she began pushing on my thumbnail, watching the blood fill up when she let go. "My . . . real mother—God, that's weird to say—felt our lives were in danger. She gave me up to protect me."

"Is she still alive?" I asked.

She shook her head. "They killed her . . . and my brother."

"Brother? Your twin?" Tiny hairs on the back of my neck pricked my skin. The information was too much. Sensory overload.

"No, he was older. Sixteen."

"Those fuckers killed a kid?" This information confirmed my fear about the level of danger Briley was in. She nodded her head and lowered it, but not before I saw the tears.

"I'm sorry, baby. So sorry." I pulled her into my lap and held her quaking body until she settled and the tears stopped.

"So . . ." She drug out the word. "I'm not who you thought I was."

I choked out a nervous laugh, trying to lighten her mood. "Should I call you Olga now?" She didn't respond to my humor like I thought she would.

"I would've been an Isabella." A small smile started to form in the corner of her mouth, but she dropped it.

"That works out perfectly then."

"How so?" she asked, one eyebrow lifted.

"I never would've called you Isabella, it's too long. I would've shortened it and called you Izzy B and, because I'm lazy, would've eventually shortened it even more and called you B. So see, you've always been and always will be my B." There it was . . . a smile that crept up the side of her mouth into

154

a crooked grin. I couldn't stop, though. I needed a full smile out of her, maybe a giggle if I was lucky. I could always get a laugh with a stupid joke.

"Have you heard the one about the peaches?" I asked. She shook her head. "A farmer is selling peaches on the side of the road. He's got any flavor peach you want. First man thinks he's gonna be a smart ass and asks for a peanut butter and jelly peach. 'Here you go.' The farmer hands him the fruit.

"The man takes a bite and is surprised by the taste. 'Peanut butter!' he says. 'But where's the jelly?' The farmer smirks and says, 'Try the other side.' Sure enough, tastes like jelly on the other side.

"Next man walks up, amazed, and asks for caramel popcorn. He takes a bite, and it really tastes like caramel. He tells the farmer, 'That's nice, but there's only caramel, no popcorn.' Farmer smirks and says, 'Turn it around.' Sure enough, tastes like popcorn on the other side.

"Finally, this punk walks up, thinking he'll pull a fast one on the farmer. 'How about one that tastes like pus—'" I stopped short, knowing she hated the word.

"Lady parts." Briley finished.

"Yes, lady parts." I couldn't say that phrase without sounding like a fairy. I shook my head and smirked. "Anyway, the farmer hands him a peach and the guy takes a bite, then spits it out. 'This tastes like shit!' he says. The farmer smirks and tells him, 'Turn it around.'"

Briley was doubled over in laughter, holding her stomach as the giggles flowed.

Mission accomplished.

"Did you . . . make that . . . up?" she asked between cackles.

"No." I pulled her into my lap. "Heard it a long time ago." Lifting her chin, I kissed her. Really kissed her. She needed to know that no matter who she was, I loved her.

"You're free this weekend." It wasn't a question. I had checked her calendar. "I've made plans for us to take that trip." I hadn't organized anything, but it wouldn't be hard to do. I had four days to pull everything together, and I didn't plan on anything exotic, just a short weekend trip.

"I don't know, Coop," she sighed. "So much has happened, and I have so many things to process. I don't think I'd be any fun."

She needed this trip. I needed it. I missed her and I wanted some time alone with her. "I've already booked the room, and there's no refund." Another fabrication, but she seemed to be softening to the idea. "You need this time to rest and refresh, B. I need it, too. Say yes."

She nodded a sluggish but agreeable confirmation. "Okay. Where're we going?" Her eyes lit with a hint of excitement.

"Trust me."

"With all my heart." She nuzzled her head in the pocket between my shoulder and neck, closed her eyes, and after a few minutes, was out for the count.

After tucking her into our bed, I went out to the back porch with another beer and my acoustic. Three bottles later, I was fully relaxed and had a plan.

***

During my lunch hour the next day, I drove down fifty-third avenue and pulled into the cemetery where Briley's dad was buried . . . or where his tombstone was rather. He'd chosen cremation, and his ashes had been taken to sea via sailboat and scattered.

If I believed in that stuff, it would've made more sense to talk to the water, but this would have to do. If he could hear me at all, it wouldn't matter where I spoke to him. This just seemed more legit than taking a boat out.

I'd been with Briley so many times to talk to her father's headstone, it should've been easy to find, but I had to walk up and down several rows before I found it.

Gerald Sheffield

Loving husband and father

Feeling like a fool, I glanced around cautiously to make sure no one was watching. A big guy like me, holding interlocking teddy bears and talking to an engraved concrete block, would've made a kid famous via Vine or Youtube.

"Listen," I began, clearing my throat. "Mr. Sheffield, you know I've loved your daughter since I could walk." I pulled the bears apart several times, letting their magnetic bodies pull them together again. This meeting was a lot harder than I'd thought it would be. Even though he couldn't tell me to get lost or kick me off his porch—asking for something I didn't deserve—it was insane talking to the air. "Remember these bears?" I stopped to remember myself. "I knew I wanted to marry her in fifth grade." I chuckled and shook my head at the memory. "I know I don't deserve her, she's way out of my league, but I promise you this . . . no one'll ever love her more than I do, and I'll do everything in my power to protect her and make her happy. I want your blessing to marry her." A salt water film blurred my vision, betraying my manhood as I poured my heart out. Thumbing the corners of my eyes, I blinked a few times and shook my head. *Pansy.*

I waited for a crack of thunder or a bird to shit on my head—a sure sign he was laughing at my dumbass idea—but nothing happened.

"Well," I placed my hands on my knees and started to stand, "I'll take your silence as a yes and let her know we have your blessing."

Something happened then that most would call coincidence. A quail called out in the distance, "Bob White." No one would ever hear this story, but I took it as a definite sign.

Briley's favorite bird—thanks to a game she and her dad had played when she was growing up—was a quail. Her father would whistle, and the bird would answer. Briley swore the bird was saying, "Bob White."

All I could do was nod my head and grin.

Thank you.

Twenty-Two
Briley

Bags packed and by the door—check.

Updated article turned in to editor—check.

On time getting home—nope.

Cooper took off work early so we could get a head start on traffic and have most of Friday night to relax. I had a meeting and was running late.

Rushing through the door, I greeted an awaiting Cooper. "Hi, love. Are we ready to go?" I huffed out a breath of air, blowing a stray hair off my forehead, then charged him and pecked him on the lips. "Everything packed? Lights off?" I pulled away, now distracted by everything that needed to be done before we could take off. He took me by the wrist, twirling me back into his strong arms.

He chuckled. "Everything's packed, lights are off, dog's fed, and the world hunger issue is solved. You're free to relax and enjoy this trip."

"We don't have dogs, smartass." I rolled my eyes, trying to hide how much I loved his ability to make me laugh.

"You, me, and an entire weekend with no interruptions," he sighed, brushing a thumb across my cheek. "Whatever will we do, Miss Sheffield?"

"I don't know, Mr. Sterling. Should I pack a deck of cards, or would you rather read?" I smirked, receiving a much deserved smack on the ass.

"Let's go. I can't wait to get you alone, strip off your clothes, and . . . kick your ass in a game of gin rummy!"

***

Since Cooper wouldn't tell me where we were going, I sang every lyric of "Burning Ring Of Fire" by Johnny Cash and bobbed my head as he drove. He stopped me on the third go-round.

"Baby, as much as I love your sweet, very much in tune," he coughed, "voice, and your weird obsession with Johnny Cash, it's really not a big secret where I'm taking you."

"Sanibel?" I asked, hopeful. I liked to discover new places, but we were looking for time alone, hopefully locked up together with just enough food to survive.

"Yeah," he exhaled. He sounded disappointed, like he wished he'd chosen another place.

"Perfect!" I squealed. "Why do you sound disappointed? Don't you like it, too?"

"I do. I want to try new places with you, make new memories some day, but familiarity was important for this trip—no distractions—just you and me." He reached for my hand, gave my fingers a squeeze, and flashed a wink that made me want to pull over and take him right there in the car.

"I can't wait." I hoped the double meaning wasn't lost on him. A smile, stuck on my face, wouldn't fade until well after we crossed the Causeway, passed the lighthouse, and pulled into our parking spot at the condo. Even then, it would probably remain. More often than not, because of Cooper, I was even falling asleep smiling.

At the start of our drive, my mind had been lost in all the things I'd discovered. I had another mother, father, and a brother. I wondered what my life would've been like being raised in their home. Would I have gotten up early, forcing

Matteo to watch cartoons with me while our parents slept in on Saturday?

No. If my parents hadn't rescued me, I'd be dead. They were all dead. My heart ached for the loss of a family I never knew and would never know.

Once I shook off the sadness, my thoughts were consumed with the idea of Cooper unlocking the door to the condo, carrying me to the master bedroom, and making love to me. I was fully charged and ready to start this trip off right.

But he did none of that. Instead, he took his time unpacking and placing his toiletries in the mirrored medicine cabinet above the sink. Had he already grown tired of me? Were we in that rut that long time couples experienced sooner or later? Although I'd known Cooper my entire life, we'd only just begun romantically. This was not how I'd seen things playing out, and not what I wanted in life. What happened to the uncontrollable hunger we had for each other? I liked the playful Cooper that couldn't keep his hands off me.

I tried not to mope as I unpacked. I also tried not to notice how Cooper avoided being in the same room with me. When I walked into the bathroom to put my toothbrush away, he went to the kitchen. And when I stepped into the kitchen to tell him something, he rushed back to the bedroom.

All luggage in its place, the only thing left to do was sit on the screened lanai and watch the waves roll in. Confused and on the verge of tears, I pushed everything to the back of my mind. Why had he invited me for a weekend only to avoid being in the same room with me? Maybe Madison had been right—Cooper was finally bored with me.

After a few minutes, he stepped out and handed me a glass of wine.

"Everything okay?" I asked, begging my tear ducts not to betray me.

Cooper took a seat next to me, rubbing a firm palm up and down my thigh. "Yeah, I've just got a lot on my mind." He cocked a crooked smile my way. "But from this point forward, I'm shutting it all off, okay?"

I nodded instead of saying anything, uncertain of my tear ducts' loyalties. Speaking with a lump in your throat almost always guaranteed a flood.

"I'm starving. Dinner and sunset sound good?"

"Mmhmm," I answered. The lump was dissolving, so I risked words. "I'd like to change first."

We dined at my favorite restaurant, sipping on flavored martinis while we waited for our food.

"How's your drink?" Cooper asked, fidgeting with the white table cloth.

"Divine. It's like a dessert. Here, have a taste." I watched as he carefully sipped the caramel laced glass.

"Holy hell, that's rich." He made a face. "What's in it?"

I giggled and swiped a strand of hair away from my face. "Kahlua, caramel vodka, and Bailey's Irish cream. Let me taste yours." I tried not to make a face after I sipped his extra dirty martini. "Talk about hell, that doesn't have an ounce of holy."

He laughed, a little too loud for our surroundings, and pulled his glass back to sit in front of him. "Lightweight."

My competitive side trumped my sanity, and I decided I'd prove him wrong. I could hold my liquor better than most women. He knew that. "Hardly. I can hold my own—"

He held up a hand. "I know you can and, as much as I love provoking you, I need you conscious tonight." The predatory

162

look in his eyes had me squirming in my seat, wishing dinner was over.

"Oh, don't you worry about me. I can play gin rummy drunk or sober." My insides lit up when I saw the flash of concern cross his features before he remembered our joke earlier.

He reached across the table and took my fingers in his. "I love you, B. Everything about you." He was serious, bringing my insecurities back like a dark plague. His moods were all over the place. Happy and fun one minute, serious and brooding the next. To say I was freaked was an understatement.

"What's going on, Coop? You've been strange all day. Was this weekend a mistake? Do you have something at work that's keeping you from relaxing, or is it me?" *Please don't say me. Please.*

"No, baby." He let go of my hand as the server approached our table and set down our plates. After she was satisfied we had everything we needed and left us alone, Cooper continued, "Don't ever think it's you. When're you going to get it through that thick skull that I love you?"

My lips twisted, contemplating what he was saying. All I'd heard was *thick skull.*

"We're having dinner in your favorite restaurant," he reminded me, "about to watch an amazing sunset . . . Why can't I tell the woman I love that I'm crazy about her? Do I sound like a pussy?"

I cringed at his choice of word.

"Sorry." He relaxed back in his chair and rubbed his hand against the back of his neck. "I don't care! Shoot me. I'm happy and I want to make sure you're happy. I know you've had a lot on your mind, it's a lot for anyone to digest. I hoped this weekend would allow you relax and forget all that for a little while. You with me?"

"Mmhmm." I nodded, regretting being so cynical.

"Just let me love you this weekend, B. No more dissecting my every word and action. Trust me."

"I do trust you, Coop." I hoped he could see the sincerity in my eyes. It was Blake who had hurt me, and I had to find a way of separating the two. They were nothing alike. "And I love you. You've always been so giving, taking care of my needs before I even knew I had them. Why are you so good to me?" With every fiber of my being I was in love, but there was still that trickle of fear that it wouldn't last.

He rolled his eyes playfully. "Hell if I know."

"I mean it. I'm happier than I've ever been in my entire life, yet I'm still terrified of the fall. I can't help worrying about it. It's built into me somehow."

"Not this time, B." He shook his head, eyes soft, almost glowing in the dim lighting. "We've both waded through enough shit to last two lifetimes. Please, for both our sakes, get that doomsday crap out of your head. Pluck those weeds at the root before they finger beneath the soil and take over."

"Oh my God, Cooper!" I held my hand over my mouth so I wouldn't laugh too loud. "Where did you come up with that poetic analogy?"

He jerked his head back and grinned. "Is it so hard to believe I came up with it on the spot?"

"Yes," I laughed.

"Well, I did. Damn good line." He drove his fork through garlic mashed potatoes and took a bite. "And it made you smile."

"You always do." I winked and stabbed a scallop, placing the perfectly bronzed bite into my mouth.

After dinner, we crossed the street and cut through a row of cottages to the sandy beach. He seemed to be in a rush, which was foreign to me on the island. Beaches were meant to be strolled on while enjoying the sights, sounds, and smells. Although the sun had just begun its descent, the wispy clouds were saturated with bold colors that resembled flames. Wanting to take time walking hand in hand down the sand, occasionally stopping to watch the colors change as the sun dipped lower, I slowed and looked at the water. Cooper tugged me along impatiently as if he couldn't wait to check the beach stroll of his list and get back to the condo.

"What's the rush, speedy?"

"Sorry." He let out a breath and slowed down. His hand was slippery with sweat and he looked strange.

"You feeling okay? Want to head back?" I hoped it wasn't food poisoning.

"Yeah, fine. You know it's hard for me to slow down." He released my hand and wiped his on his pants.

In the distance I could see candles lighting a path for a wedding or maybe a romantic dinner for two. I'd have to remember that for a future trip. When we were close enough to see that the candles were scattered across the sand, encircling something, I stopped and tugged on Cooper's arm.

"We should turn back. I don't want to interrupt."

"We'll walk closer to the sea oats." He took my hand, leading me away from the water's edge toward the tall grassy plants. "See, we're not the only curious ones." He lifted his chin toward a couple that was also approaching the scene.

"So rude," I exclaimed quietly. "Not that I'm not super curious myself, but someone worked hard to put that together. They need to walk away." The couple circled the scene and took a few pictures before continuing on down the beach.

"They're not hurting anything. No one is even down there yet. Let's have a look."

"No! Cooper Sterling," I scolded. "Control your nosy ass." I had to admit, as we got closer my curiosity grew. There was something in the middle of the heart-shaped outline of candles that I couldn't quite make out at this distance.

"C'mon, B. If we see the couple coming, we'll split. Just a peek."

"A quick pass by." I huffed and then smiled when he picked up the pace.

At closer look, I saw two massive hearts dug out of the sand and filled with sun-bleached white scallop shells. In the center, where the two hearts joined, sat two stuffed bears hugged tightly together. They looked just like the bears Cooper had given me when we were kids.

Weird.

"Look at that," I half-chuckled and squeezed Cooper's fingers. "Looks just like . . ." When I glanced up at Cooper and saw the smile on his face, I realized they *were* my bears. "Are those—?"

He gulped once. Without answering me, he pulled me to the center of the heart and picked up the bears. It felt like I'd swallowed a golf ball, my throat constricted and unwilling to let me breathe without difficulty. Tears pooled. Had Cooper placed all of these shells? When?

"Do you remember the day I gave you these bears?" Cooper asked, handing them to me. I hugged them to my chest and nodded, the first tear finding purchase on the furry head of the other. "Take the note out," he encouraged. "I know you kept it."

This was no time to deny it, even if I was embarrassed that I'd kept his note all these years. Fishing for the note that I'd kept tucked inside the shirt pocket of bear number one, I pulled it out and unfolded it. In a child's handwriting, only slightly resembling Cooper's now neat, architecture penmanship, was the following:

Will you marry me?

Circle one: Y/N

When I looked up from the notepaper, its folds fragile from time and having been read a thousand and one times, Cooper was on one knee. Something rested in his hand, but all I could focus on were his amazing green eyes. As fierce as the raging sea and as gentle and loving as I'd ever seen, I let myself get lost in them.

"Briley Sheffield, I've loved you my entire life," he began, getting somewhat choked up himself.

My heart melted, then oozed through my chest cavity. Blood pounded behind my ears, making his voice sound distant. I shook my head in disbelief. This wasn't happening, it couldn't be. "Coop—"

"God, Briley, please let me finish before I screw this up." He wiped his hand across his forehead, then rubbed it on his thigh. "I have a lot I'd like to say and I don't want to forget anything."

I nodded, hugging the bears so tight I'd have an indent on my chest.

"I love you, baby, and even though I've done some things— screwed up more than a few times—you're the one thing I've done right. Could you spend your life with someone like me?"

I dropped to my knees, feeling very aware that I was towering over him as he knelt. "You know I love you, Cooper, and any woman would be lucky to spend their life with you. Don't ever question that fact." My knees sunk deeper into the sand as I squirmed under his intense gaze. He was nervous, more than I'd ever seen.

Yes, I loved Cooper with all my heart, but I was about cause him a great deal of pain. Because of who I was, always making things way more difficult than they had to be, I was going to screw this up.

I had to say no.

It was the wise thing to do. I'd just come out of a failed engagement—a blessing, yes—but failure all the same. And did he really know what he was getting into? I was a product of the mob after all. Born and bred from a family of evil practices. Maybe that's where I'd gotten my selfish streak. The mafia didn't care who they hurt as long as they got what they wanted. I couldn't let Cooper throw his future away on someone like me.

Me . . . who the hell was that anyway?

I'd need to choose my words carefully, and make him realize we were moving too fast. I did want to marry him one day. It was all I wanted and everything I needed. But I couldn't offer him anything right now except a burden.

Filling my lungs with air, my lips quivered as they spilled my answer to his unasked question, "No, Coop. I can't marry you."

Twenty-Three

Cooper

She said no. She said no? I hadn't even asked yet. Not really.

What started as an ache in my chest was now growing into a sharp pain. It felt like someone was carving out the words '*I don't want you*' on my heart muscle with a dull blade.

"What are you saying, B?"

"Coop, think." I waited for her to laugh and tell me she was joking, but she was serious. Her eyebrows creased, trying to hold the emotion back. "We're moving too fast. How can we trust these feelings? You don't know who I am." She shook her head back and forth as if she were trying to convince me of a simple truth I'd overlooked. "I don't know who I am. My parents were Italian mobsters. It's in my blood, part of me."

"That's ridiculous!" *Comical. Insane.*

"Look at us," she yelled. "Me, straight out of a failed engagement. You, straight out of prison, and lonely. What if—?"

"Stop." I gripped her around the waist, making her focus. Her eyes locked on mine and remained there as I spoke. "All that bullshit sounds like something you've heard on a soap opera." My voice cracked. I was angry and hurt, my words clipped and harsh. "I loved you *before* prison. You think something changed while I was away? Sure, it did. I realized how close I came to losing you. Realized how short life is and how easily mistakes can ruin your fucking life.

"I loved you before I knew anything about your parents. Seriously, B?" I speared my hands through my hair and let out a heavy breath. "First of all, they couldn't have been that bad. They loved you enough to give you to a good family and try to save your life. Second, their past has nothing to do with who you are today. You're Briley fucking Sheffield. Have been since I've known you . . . and I've known you your entire life."

"And Blake," I went on, though I couldn't say his name without spitting it out through gritted teeth. "Blake was a mistake, not a failure. Are you going to let that mistake ruin your life, suck every ounce of happiness from you before you even taste it? That's not the Briley I know."

Damn, she was a mystery that frustrated the hell out of me. I had to make her see the truth before she ruined both our lives.

"You're a fighter like me. Maybe not physically," I squeezed her tiny biceps, offering a smile to calm the rage inside both of us, "but you're a fighter. You've never taken shit from anyone until now. Don't let him break you, B. He's nothing. Don't give him undeserved power." I searched her eyes for something—anything—as she remained silent, gaze fixed on me like she was watching her reflection in my pupils. Was any of it sinking in?

"I know you love me, B, I can see it in your eyes, feel it in your touch." She dropped her gaze. I gave her a few beats to let my words settle in before lifting her chin and making her look me in the eyes again. "Can you live without me? Were you happier before I came home?"

She blinked away the flow of tears and shook her head.

"Because I don't want to be without you. When I'm at work, I can't wait to get home and feel you in my arms."

She held up her index finger, asking for a moment. I knew she was swallowing the lump in her throat so she could talk. When she did speak, her voice was small. "I don't like being without you, either. I feel best when I'm in your arms. Safe, warm, and loved. I just want to be sure. I can't stand the thought of hurting you, and I don't think I'd survive you hurting me."

Damn all this doubt. "The last thing I want to do is hurt you."

"I know, I know." She shook her head. "And I'd never hurt you. I've never loved anyone this much. I wonder now if I've ever loved anyone at all, really. I'm terrified of messing it up. You're the most important person in my life, Coop."

Finally we were getting somewhere. I rested my forehead against hers. "I've loved you for twenty-six years, B."

She rolled her eyes playfully. "I'm only twenty-five."

"Fine," I chuckled. "I've loved you . . ." I had to think back to the first time I knew. "Fourteen years. That's still a long-ass time."

"It is." With the back of her hand, she swiped a few strands of tear soaked hair from her face.

I didn't know where we were at the moment, but I wasn't giving up on her. Most of the candles had burned out and the only light was a half-moon reflecting off the water. On a boombox hidden in a patch of sea oats, our song played on repeat, but I hadn't noticed it until now. I wondered if anyone was watching us in the darkness. Curiosity tugged, but I resisted the urge to take my focus off Briley. Pulling the bears from her arms, I tucked the note back into the designated pocket, set them down next to the ring box on the sand, and took her hands in mine.

"I love you, Briley, and I know I don't deserve you, but I also know neither of us deserves to be without the other." I looked away from her, my head down when I spoke the following, "I asked your father for your hand, and I believe we have his blessing, too."

"You what?" Her voice squeaked, and I knew the crying would erupt again.

"I went to the cemetery and properly asked for your hand. I know it sounds ridiculous, but I'm sure he gave me an answer."

"What do you mean? You asked my dad?" She shuffled her knees in the sand to move closer to me. "How?" Eagerness clipped her voice. She loved the paranormal. I thought it was stupid, but I couldn't deny what happened.

"I talked to his headstone," I began, feeling stupid as shit as I retold the event. "Afterward, a quail flew close by and kept repeating your 'Bob White' song." I shook my head. It sounded even more asinine out loud.

"Oh my God." She released a hand from mine and covered her mouth. New tears pooled and spilled down her cheeks.

"I've made you cry . . . again." I let out a loud whoosh of a breath and cursed.

"No, Cooper. Thank you for telling me that." She flung her arms around my neck and hugged me in a death grip. I couldn't feel her breathing.

"Breathe, baby."

She released me and sucked in a breath. "My dad never liked you." She giggled. Her laugh was intoxicating, filling my miserable bones with a hopeful happiness.

"He does now." I lifted a brow and smirked.

"So do I." A shy smile played on her lips. "But you're a moron for pursuing me."

"Marry me, Briley," I said softly.

"Wait. I wasn't ready." She wiped her face dry with the back of her hands, then raised her chin and took in a sniffly inhale through her nose. "Okay, say it again."

I couldn't help but grin. The Briley I knew was back. She pushed her hair back behind her shoulders and looked into my eyes.

Shit, this had all gone so differently in my head. My nerves were back, taunting me to screw up. Finding my place on one knee again, I picked up the box, dusted the granules off, and took her hand in mine.

Twice, I cleared my throat, then began, "Briley Beatrice Sheffield, I love you more than I've ever loved anything. Will you stand beside me as we go through the rest of this crazy journey and let me love you, protect you, and make you laugh? Will you marry me?"

She cupped my face in her hands, her lips inches from mine as she answered, "Yes, Cooper Sterling, I'll marry you."

I don't know who moved first, but our mouths crashed together in a desperate kiss, sealing the deal. I could've stayed there all night, enjoying that sweet mouth, but there was one more thing I had planned, and I didn't want to miss our opportunity.

I stood, offering her a hand and helping her out of the sand. "You know I don't dance, but they're playing our song. Actually, it's been playing on repeat for the last hour." I stepped out of the shell circle, onto fresh sand, and twirled her once before pulling her body tightly to mine.

"Everlong" played in the distance while I trampled her feet, trying not to ruin the moment. She laughed, her head cocked to the side as the moonlight lit her beautiful features.

"Here, let's try this." She put one sandy bare foot on top of mine, then the other, and we danced like that until the song ended—a torturous four minutes for me, but she seemed to love it.

I had forgotten about the ring box clenched in my grip, until the song ended. "Shit! The ring." Popping open the velvet box, I pulled it out and slipped it onto her finger. It fit perfectly and she couldn't stop staring at it—and gushing. I guess that's what women did. I hoped she liked it as much as she went on about it.

"The jeweler said emerald cuts were in now, but I went with the round. I liked that there were no corners. I want you to always be open with me and never feel like you need to hide. You know I like to go to my own corner sometimes, but I want you to hold me accountable and don't let me do that to you."

"It's perfect, Cooper. I love it and I love you, so much."

"I love you too, baby. But I'm getting eaten up out here." I smacked at my calf, itched the side of my arm. Damn bugs.

"You must be a lot sweeter than I am. They're not touching me." She laughed and gathered the bears into her arms, looking at the ring on her finger once more.

"No one's sweeter than you, B. Sweet like honey—"

"Gah! Stop that. You're going to spoil me." She flicked her hand in the air, then bent down and started picking up the candles.

"Leave them. It's taken care of." I scooped her up and tossed her over my shoulder. "No more cheese ball. Caveman take woman now."

"Put me down!" She laughed, beating her fists onto my ass as I marched down the beach. I couldn't wait to get my fiancée back to the condo and show her what true happiness felt like.

Fiancée. This was new for me, the feeling that my heart was so full it spilled over into every part of me. If I died on the spot, I wouldn't be able to tell the difference between heaven and earth.

Twenty-Four
Briley

Cooper set me down on the sand near the jutting rocks where we'd left our shoes. I couldn't stop looking at the ring on my finger. A brilliant stone set in platinum. It was perfect for my small fingers, but probably much more than he needed to spend.

We made it back to the condo in record time, the drive mostly silent and the air filled with a crisp energy that I'd never experienced before. Watching Cooper unlock the door, I suddenly saw him in a new light. He was mine, fully and completely. Our love story wasn't conventional or perfect by any means, but it was spectacular. A conscious-altering kind of love. I'd fought hard to take things slow—making sure we were doing the right thing—but his words rang true.

Life was too short not to go after what you wanted.

I couldn't wait to tell my mom the good news and see Mr. and Mrs. Sterling's reaction. They would've been happy with a straight-out-of-high school wedding.

"What're you thinking right now?" Cooper asked as he pinned me to the wall, his hands on either side of my head.

"I was thinking about your parents' reaction. They're going to be thrilled."

"Seriously? That's what you're thinking?" He stroked his thumb across my cheek and chuckled. "I'm thinking of how difficult it'll be not to tear this dress when I peel it off of you."

"Sorry." I shook my head for show. "Okay, back in the game now." I brushed my lips along his bottom lip and whispered, "This old thing is begging for the trash anyway, and if you don't rip it off soon, I'll be doing some begging myself."

All it took was my nod of approval to put Cooper's plan in place. He gripped the seam on the side of the dress, one hand on each side, and yanked. The fabric separated easily in his grasp, as if it knew it didn't stand a chance against his burly strength. I wasn't sure why or which emotion had grown stronger since I had agreed to be Cooper's wife, but the level of lust, carnal need, and love that soared through my body was almost more than I could process.

Cooper led me to the back bedroom step by step, his lips never once leaving mine. It was a wonder we weren't bruised and banged up by the time I felt the edge of the mattress hit the backs of my legs. He'd been an amazing kisser before, but tonight he took my breath and made my limbs feel boneless. I inched back onto the bed, Cooper crawling with me as if one break in our kiss would separate us forever.

After stripping me of my bra, he finally broke the kiss long enough to pull his shirt over his head and toss it aside.

I made a tsk tsk sound when he came toward me. "Everything off." It was only fair as I lay there in a white thong. It was as close as going commando.

He swallowed a grin and stripped, then he broke the strings of my thong and slid the material from underneath me. *I actually liked that thong.* My thoughts wandered, trying to recall if I had packed another. Panty lines were a serious pet peeve.

My thoughts vanished suddenly, all senses focused on Cooper's hot breath between my thighs.

"Cooper, not tonight. I need you, all of you—"

"No fucking way. I'm savoring you, baby. We've got all night."

"I need—" I lay back and whimpered as he ignored my pleas and worked his magic.

He always did miraculous things to me, and I was wound up and so tense already, I had to grip the sheets at first touch. In a matter of moments, I lost all sense of reality, passion efflorescing throughout every fiber of my being.

As I caught my breath, he kissed a path along my waist, across my arm, and finally working his way to my throat, jawline, and lips. Although my body was still reeling, I needed to have him. I couldn't seem to get close enough to satiate the deep ache inside.

"You're so beautiful." He raked his hand up my side, sending chills all over as he grazed the outside of my breast. "Your body . . . so fucking amazing." He growled the last part and had me on the edge again already.

"Cooper," I pleaded, lifting my hips to grind into his arousal. The throbbing was so intense it was almost painful. His fingers dipped down between my legs, but instead of easing my need it only intensified. "Please, Coop."

He propped himself up on elbows, hovering over me. "Is this what you want?" He grinned. Cocky son of a bitch, but I loved it.

"Yes," I breathed.

When our bodies came together, it was beautiful and breathtaking. I was completely focused on the power behind our connection. It was as if my life had been created just for him and his for me. Falling over the edge was intense, as I knew it would be. My focus now taken over by this rapturously beautiful moment. When my clarity returned, my limbs resting like noodles beside me, I basked in the feeling of being engaged to Cooper.

This man, the one that I loved more than myself, felt the same about me. Besides my father, no one had ever loved me enough to die for me, but I knew Cooper would lay down his life to protect mine.

"I love you," I mumbled, unable to move my head to look at him as he lay beside me.

He must've found his strength as he scooted onto his side. "I love you, too, B. What's on your mind?"

"Bliss. Pure, unadulterated bliss," I answered, still unable to control my spent body.

"You don't know how happy it makes me to hear you say that." He plopped back onto his pillow. "Want a snack?"

I looked at him then. "Seriously? It's the middle of the night."

"It's only ten o'clock. We can sleep when we're dead."

He was such a kid sometimes. I could see our future now. I would probably spend the rest of my life trying to get him to grow up, and he'd probably spend the rest of his reminding me to be young and live life. I hoped he'd win.

With a sheet wrapped around my body, I joined Cooper on the screened-in lanai. Two forks and a half-eaten Key lime pie sat between us as we watched the waves roll in. The moon's light caressed the water, the massive dark pool both beautiful and terrifying all at once. Just like our relationship. I knew everything there was to know about Cooper, yet I felt there was so much I didn't know.

"How do you feel about kids?" I asked, spooning a bite of the tart dessert into my mouth.

"I want them. You?"

I had wanted a baby all my life. Having never been around them, I didn't know where that desire had come from. A psychologist would probably say I needed to fill a hole in my heart. But now that my heart was full, maybe I didn't need a child.

"I've never really been around them." I watched his expression, fearing disappointment. He was patient, listening to me ramble. "But they seem cute. Of course, they grow up, and bite, and—"

"Don't overthink it, babe," he said easily. "If you don't want kids, we won't have them. But I know you, you'll want them someday. You'll be an amazing mother."

"How do you know? What if I'm mean," I growled, making clawing motions. "What if I leave it in the basket at the grocery store? That happens, you know. Women grab a gallon of milk and, since it's around the same weight as the baby, they think they've got everything."

"You love making shit up, don't you?" He laughed, giving my ribs a poke.

I chuckled and shrugged. "We have plenty of time to think about it. You don't want them soon, do you?"

"Nope." He gave me a mischievous grin. "I don't want to share you with anyone. Let me get good and sick of you before we add a baby to the mix."

"Hey, now!" I protested. In the darkness, I could see his shoulders shake with laughter. "I'm gonna get on your nerves, though." I pulled the sheet tighter around my body. The night air had changed and it was starting to get chilly. "I have weird quirks."

"I know all about your weird quirks, B, and I still want you."

"Do you know about my toothbrush fetish?" I cocked an eyebrow.

"What, that you have a bigger stash than a dentist's office, and after you brush it has to be put away in a drawer so no dust or germs settle on the bristles? No, didn't know that."

"Hmph." *Okay, he wins that round.* "How about the fact that I dig out extra marshmallows from the cereal box so the proportion of marshmallows is greater than cereal?" *Take that!*

"You got me." He sighed dramatically. "I did not know that about you. I guess we aren't compatible after all. I mean, it wouldn't make sense to get two boxes of cereal, would it?" The sarcasm oozed.

"What don't I already know about you?" I asked, hopeful it wasn't anything terrible.

"I fart the National Anthem every single morning before I get out of bed."

"You're an ass, Cooper!" I elbowed his side. "Be serious."

"Okay, let me think . . . I hide candy bars in the freezer. Even though I live alone—or used to—I'm like a squirrel, only I prefer chocolate."

I rolled my eyes. "Because your sister ate all your Easter candy two years in a row. Tell me something I *don't* know."

"I'm an open book, B." He scratched the back of his neck as he thought. "Okay, here's one. If I get up to go to the bathroom in the middle of the night, I go outside."

"Why? You like to draw pictures in the grass?"

"On the fence actually," he deadpanned.

"Gross!"

"I'm kidding." He shook his head at me. "I don't know why, but once I'm up, I like to look at the stars, enjoy the silence for a while. Makes sense to pee outside if I'm heading in that direction anyway."

"So far I'm not freaked out by any of your quirks or weird habits." I smiled, hugging my knees to my chest and rubbing my hands up and down my legs for warmth.

"Cold? Let's go inside."

I climbed into bed and Cooper spooned me, his body warming me instantly, and I drifted off into a peaceful sleep. I didn't have any dreams that night, probably because nothing could top the dream I was living.

Twenty-Five
Cooper

My sister, Carleigh, insisted on an engagement party. Her words exactly: "We're celebrating. Don't even try to stop me. If I have to strap these baby girls to my back and throw the whole thing together myself, I'll do it. We've all been waiting for this day to come, and it's a very big deal."

Of course she wouldn't do it herself. My mother would either help, or hold her new grandbabies while Carliegh worked her magic. As much as I tried to tell everyone that Briley wouldn't care for all of the fluff, my mother and sister were now out of control.

Briley stepped out of the bedroom in a silk dress with a navy and green pattern—paisley? Her hair was pinned up with a few loose curls spilling over. Trying not to mess her up too much, I reached a hand out to her waist and pulled her in. I loved the way the fabric felt as it slid under my palm.

"Beautiful as always."

She twirled around. "Is it country club worthy? Are the earrings too much?"

"You look perfect," I said, lifting her hand and kissing two of her knuckles. "I have a feeling my sister went overboard. She usually does. Just be prepared." The last thing I wanted was her getting overwhelmed. "Country club," I blew out a puff of breath and tugged on the tie choking my throat. "I don't know why we couldn't have had it at the house.

"It'll be great, Coop. Your sister's so sweet for putting this together. I don't know how she does it, being a new mom." She squeezed my arm. It was a loving gesture, one I could get used to. "You know—" She paused by the door. "Once we enter the doors of the club, it's official. You'll have a fiancé, and your buddies will start calling me the old ball and chain. Last chance to run." She flashed a sassy grin, and I couldn't stop myself from kissing it.

I wiped any remnants of lipstick off my lips and lifted her into the truck. "It's already official, baby, and I'll appreciate having you chained to me every damn day." With a wink, I shut her door and jogged around to the driver's side.

***

Just as I imagined, the room was overdone. I couldn't help feeling embarrassed for Briley as we entered a room. It looked like something Willy Wonka would appreciate—flowers, candles, framed pictures, and every kind of hors d'oeuvres imaginable.

I sighed at the same time Briley squealed. "Oh my God, Coop! Isn't it amazing?"

Nodding in disbelief, I watched Briley take in the room. Her eyes sparkled as if she'd entered a fantasy world. I would've sworn she'd hate it, but I'd been wrong.

Carleigh was the first to bound over and wrap her arms around my girl. They embraced in a hug that lasted a few beats longer than I expected, but I appreciated my sister's affection for Briley. Two years older than me, she graduated before Briley entered high school so they didn't run in the same circles. But anytime they were in the same room, they acted like they'd been friends for years.

"Finally!" my sister drawled. "I don't know what I'm more excited about—seeing you two together where you've belonged all along," she flashed me an irritated look, as if blaming me for our not being together all these years, "or gaining a sister!"

"I thought having babies made people grow up, sis? Briley won't want to play Barbie's with you, ya know."

She put both hands on my chest and pushed me with all her might. She was petite, but actually managed to move me a little. Becoming a mother must've given her some strength. "Shut up, Coop!" We shared a laugh before she turned her attention back to Briley.

"This is too much, Carleigh." The smile that lit up Briley's face contradicted her words.

"Do you like it?" My sister looked way too pleased with herself.

"It's perfect. I can't believe you pulled this off, and with two babies! Where are the girls? I can't believe I haven't met them yet." Briley glanced around for my twin nieces, Eden and Emma.

"Mom has them." She nodded toward a back corner. "I need to feed and change them, so look around, grab a drink, and then come see them. Can you believe they're already four months old?"

"No. God, I wish you lived closer."

Carleigh smirked at me as Briley danced away. "Told you."

I shook my head and smiled. She was right. I was wrong. *I get it.*

She spun on her heels and headed toward her babies, and I just chuckled. Did all siblings act like they were still in kindergarten? I'd never tell her, but I was proud of her and thankful she'd made Briley so happy. After the party was over I'd tell her thank you in my own way. Maybe a spa day for her and Briley. I'd offer to watch the girls, although I knew she'd never go for that.

My father appeared out of nowhere and gave me a firm slap on the back before pulling me in for a man hug. "Your mother and I are thrilled, Son. You know we've always felt like Briley was family, but now it's official. Have you set a date?"

"Hello to you, too." I smirked and looked at the beer in his hand. I could use a drink.

***

Once Briley and I had a glass of wine in hand, we browsed the room. There were framed pictures on each dining and hors d'oeuvres table, representing the two of us through the years.

"Look at this one, Coop." Briley held a picture of us that I'd never seen. My wide grin showed a mouth full of metal. Briley was riding piggyback, her arms wrapped around my shoulders. "My hair!" she shrieked. "Why didn't anyone stop me from that catastrophe?"

It was the year she'd cut her hair short—really short—and got a perm. I'd thought she was beautiful no matter what, but I had to admit, this hadn't been her most flattering year.

Flipping the picture upside down, I set a platter of bacon-wrapped dates over it. "That wasn't my best year either. I thought it was cool to choose the school colors for bands on my braces. Note to future brace faces: green is never a good idea when dealing with teeth." We shared a laugh and found our seats as the toasts began.

By the end of the evening, I'd actually had a good time. My buddies were cool, offering advice that ranged from hilarious to good-to-know. I hadn't seen Briley in a while, so I glanced around the room as Ryan made another crack about married life.

When I found her, I couldn't take my eyes off her. She was holding one of the twins. It looked as if she was in her own world as she rocked Emma or Eden—I still couldn't tell them apart—and told her some kind of intricate tale. If I hadn't loved her with every ounce of my soul before, I did now. There was something primal about watching your girl with a baby. I wanted that for us. Not now, not anytime soon, but one day.

"Excuse me, Ryan." I nodded and made my way to Briley. Standing there quietly, I watched her. When she looked up, she grinned bashfully.

"What? She needed to know where to get the best truffles." She looked back down at the baby and the pitch of her voice rose. "The difference between Swedish and American chocolate is colossal."

"Necessary information, I agree. Which one have you got?"

"Eden. Want to hold her?" She stood and placed her in my arms. I'd held her before—in the hospital when she was brand new—but she wasn't as wiggly. It was obvious she wanted to be back in Briley's arms. "She likes to sit up a bit." Briley helped me get her into a better position, and my niece seemed to be satisfied.

I was looking down at Eden, noticing her tiny features when Briley said, "Okay."

"Hmm?" I glanced up.

"Okay. I'm in. I want this." She flicked her eyes from the baby to me. "Seeing you with her, it's—I live for the day I can watch you hold *our* daughter."

"Or son," I quipped with a smirk.

"Or both." She was quick to come back at me when I thought I'd flustered her. Last week she hadn't been sure she wanted to be a mother. Now all of a sudden she wanted one of each?

"One day." I leaned in, careful not to squish Eden between us, and kissed Briley's forehead. "I'm not ready to share your attention just yet."

My mom took Eden from my arms as Carleigh called Briley and me up to the front of the room for a game of Trivia, each guest reading from a card.

Colin, my business partner, went first. "Where was your first kiss?"

I glanced at Briley, wondering which answer to give. Did he want to know about the first kiss ever or the first kiss after she accepted the fact that we belonged together?

Briley, apparently with the same thought, answered, "The first kiss we shared was beneath the Birch tree in his back yard, if a peck counts." She chuckled and shook her head, seeming to be back in the moment, under that tree. "He was ten, I was eight."

A lady that worked with Briley's editor—a receptionist, I think she said—read the next question. "What does he do that annoys you and vice versa?"

"Hmm . . . absolutely nothing about this man annoys me," she said sweetly. "But to appease the crowd, I'll give you something." She tapped her chin, as if she were struggling to find an answer. "Okay, the way he flips through the channels like he's in a race. I don't know how he even knows what's on, he never lands on anything until he's made the entire loop." She cocked one eyebrow at me. "Your turn."

Shit, how was I supposed to announce to the room something that annoyed me about the woman I was crazy about? If she had a weird tick of picking gunk out of her toes, I would probably think it was cute. The only think I could think of that annoyed me in the least was her lack of self confidence in her work sometimes. Hands in the air, I surrendered. "Not a damn thing." The crowd gave a boo and I heard a few of my buddies make disappointing sounds. I'd pay for that pussy response.

Carleigh chimed in, "Speaking from experience, now that you're engaged, everyone will ask you 'when are you getting married?' Next will be 'when are you having kids?' And then, 'when are you having another?' So, I get to go first with the unnerving question." She looked down at her card briefly, then set her focus on me. "This question is for both of you. "Cooper, how many kids does your future bride want. And, Briley, how many does your groom want?"

Leave it to my sister to bring an uncomfortable silence to the room. We were barely engaged and already talking kids. Thankfully Briley was on board, and she didn't look flustered.

I spoke up first. "She wants one of each, a boy and girl."

Briley nodded, smiled, and then answered, "Cooper would like three sons, but that's not happening!"

"Not true," I yelped. "Three boys? If they've got my genes, we'd be in trouble."

That got a laugh out of the room, and my father clapped.

My Aunt Debbie was next. "If money wasn't an issue and you could go anywhere for your honeymoon, where would you go?"

Briley and I answered in unison, "Thailand."

We continued to answer questions about favorite foods, songs, and movies. During the last toast of the evening, I thought I caught a glimpse of Blake in the doorway. But when I stood to move toward him, he disappeared. *How the fuck did he find out? Stupid small town.*

Briley's gentle hand to my arm distracted me from my vision of throwing him over a balcony when I got a hold of him. "Are you having a good time? I know it's a bit girly, but—"

"It *is* girly, but I wouldn't miss celebrating us for anything." I pulled her into my arms and kissed the top of her head. "I might need to spit a few times and scratch my balls when we get home. You know, make sure my man card is still in my wallet."

She giggled, placed her hand on my cheek, and looked at me so intently with those brown eyes of hers, the rest of the room melted away. "I don't ever want this dream to end, Coop."

Twenty-Six

Briley

Dreams don't seem to last as long as nightmares do.

Monday afternoon, I moseyed to the mailbox and noticed a long black car parked across the street. Something didn't feel right. The tiny hairs at the back of my neck were standing at attention. My hands trembled at the thought of someone watching me and a few pieces of mail slipped away, falling to the ground.

I heard the car pull away. With a sigh of relief, I gathered the few pieces of junk mail that had gotten away, then each of my senses was suddenly assaulted as the car pulled up. I heard the sound of heavy rubber tires crunching against the gravel bits in the pavement. A door creaked open and the smell of cheap aftershave, applied in excess, wafted out into the air. Everything happened so swiftly, there wasn't time to look up before I felt strong hands grip me around the waist, jerking me backward. The only sound I made was a grunt as the wind was knocked out of me by their forceful grip.

I always thought I'd be a fighter, someone who couldn't be taken. Since the night Matt Lasko had tried to rape me, I'd planned for a moment like this. I'd bite and claw, kick and punch. But as the heels of my bare feet dragged helplessly across the pavement, I was frozen with fear and my brain was failing me.

It happened so fast, yet seemed like it was all in slow motion. I had time to wonder if I had dropped the mail again, if I had left my straightener plugged in, or the front door wide open. My captors were oddly gentle in their movements, tucking my head as they pulled me into the backseat. Maybe they didn't want to leave traces of hair or blood? I wondered—hoped—one of the neighbors had peeled back a curtain to witness my abduction. Of all the times to snoop, this would be it. Please get a license plate number. *Find me. Help me.*

Tears stung my eyes, which had an odd effect on my state of mind. Instead of crying out for help or begging for my life, I was pissed. The fight that had abandoned me moments ago, I now felt building inside of me. If my life was going to end—my family name finally wiped out for good—I was going to leave a mark.

Looking down, I noticed the arms of the two men touching me. A firm grip pinned my arms behind my back while his hairy, tattooed arm snaked around one of my legs. The other arm had hairless older flesh, and was locked around my chest like a pageant sash. That was the one I went for. I bit into his flesh, my teeth scraping against his arm as he jerked it away. "Dammit!" he barked. "Have you got her?" I assumed he was talking to the man slamming me down onto the leather of the back seat.

"Who the hell—" I started to say to the first set of eyes I could focus on. A familiar face gazed back at me from the seat across from mine. He was gripping his arm where I'd sunk my teeth in.

"Settle down. I'm sorry we had to do things this way, but time isn't on our side." He spoke through gritted teeth, clearly upset that I'd bitten him. Served him right taking me like that. Just because he showed a badge last time we'd met didn't mean he could be trusted. If what he'd said was true, and my life was in danger, I couldn't trust anyone.

The car moved, picking up speed as we left the neighborhood. Tinted windows darker than I thought was legal veiled the view, and I felt disoriented as the car traveled. I took a moment to realize the backseat was larger than most. Two black leather bench seats faced each other. The man across from me was the U.S. Marshal from the warehouse and the one next to him was his partner, minus the ball cap this time.

"I warned you to back off," he snapped. "But you just had to keep digging."

"So what, going to the bank is a crime now?" I snapped. "All I did was open a safe-deposit box. It's not like I Googled the Zerretti name or something." I wondered how much they knew and . . . how? I had searched the internet for anything and everything I could find on the Zeretti's. But I'd also covered myself by using the computer at the library.

"Just like a Sicilian," I heard him mumble under his breath. "Do you know why we've protected your family all this time? Why I've gone above and beyond my duty?" His tone was harsh.

Staring at my reflection in his unnecessary sunglasses on a cloudy, sunless day, I tried to sum up his character. I imagined he was a divorced father of three, heating a microwavable dinner each night before watching a repeat episode of CSI Miami. He'd light a cigarette but never remember to puff it. He'd light another one, take a drag, and stamp it out into a nearby ashtray.

"No," I answered, feeling the weight of his scrutinizing glare.

"Your dad was key in solving a case we'd been working on for years. He and I became friends through that process. He was a good man."

I knew my father was good. I didn't need some schmuck telling me that.

"He loved you and I promised him I wouldn't let them get to you." He removed his glasses, revealing the eyes of an overworked and overstressed cop. "Everything was fine until you opened Pandora's Box."

Something wasn't right, I could feel it. "So they've found me?" I tried to keep the confidence in my voice, playing the role of a sarcastic fugitive. But I was shaking on the inside. Death was the least of my fears, although I wasn't ready to die. Torture, on the other hand, terrified me.

He didn't move, but I thought I saw a slight nod. "Not yet, but they're getting closer." He paused, wiping his brow with a palm and replacing his shades. *Tinted windows. Overcast. You don't need them.* I closed my eyes, letting them rest a few seconds longer than a blink.

He lifted a notebook from the seat next to him and handed it to me. Flipping through the pages, I noticed times and locations jotted down in a handwriting that had to belong to a guy—young, most likely left handed.

"What's this?" I shrugged.

"A log of every move this person has made in the last two months." He handed over a photo of a woman I didn't recognize.

"Okay. Are you seeking my detective skills on this case, Marshal?" I smirked.

"Take a closer look, Miss Sheffield." As he talked, I studied the picture more closely. "Dark hair, dark eyes. She's the same age as you. In fact—and you might find this interesting—you both share the same birth date."

I felt the warning in my chest before it registered in my brain. "They . . . think this is me?" I watched the slow nod of the Marshal's head. "Did they hurt her?" I felt the need to bolt out of the rushing car and try to save her myself. "Is she okay? You didn't let them take her, did you?"

The Marshal waved his hand and shook his head. "No, no, she's safe. We've got her in a safe house until—"

"Then why are you coming to me? If they think she's me, and she's safe . . ." A small part of me was glad this whole thing was over and I could move on, knowing they would never come after me again. A bigger part felt guilty that someone was holed up away from their friends and family, probably scared to death. "Of course she can't stay locked away. What's the plan?"

"They'll figure out it's not you very soon—if they haven't already—and resume their search." He let out a heavy breath and relaxed back into the seat. "Problem is, they're close and it won't be long before they're on your trail."

"How close?" I asked, needing to know but scared to death.

"Georgia."

"So we all have to move again? Change names?" *My mom, Cooper, Cooper's parents. What about Cooper's sister, Carleigh, and her new family?*

"Just you," he answered. "The Zeretti's are after *your* blood, *your* name. The others mean nothing to them." He cut a line through the air with his hand and turned his gaze to the darkened window.

"No!" I fumed. "I'm not leaving my family—my mother, Cooper—no way!" With arms folded across my chest, I threw myself back against the seat. No chance in hell he was changing my mind.

The Marshal pulled out a folder and handed it to me.

"What's this?" I asked, opening it to see the first picture. It was an older man, I assumed—grey hair and beard—his arms and legs bound to the wooden chair he was sitting in. His face was so swollen and bloody from the extreme amount of lacerations, it was hard to tell anything about his features . . . or lack thereof. "Why are you showing me this?"

"That's the latest victim of the Zeretti bunch. This is what seven hours of torture looks like." I heard him take a deep breath and let it out. "He worked for Zeretti. One of his top employees. Ran his mouth about Zeretti's niece, and this was the consequence." He took the folder back and shoved it into his briefcase on the seat next to him.

My stomach felt like it was filled with worms, making me queasy. "Why would you show me that?" I didn't recognize the voice that tried but failed to shout at him. It was weak and small.

His eyes narrowed on me again. "I'm having trouble getting through. You need to understand what these people are capable of."

Tears flowed freely as fear enveloped me like a straightjacket. After a moment, somehow I found the strength the break free and look at the Marshal. "I'm not leaving. I know you made a promise to my father, but I've made promises, too. I'm not leaving my fiancé or my mother. I couldn't live with myself if the Zeretti's did something to them, trying to find my location. Death I can handle. Someone hurting my family . . . I can't."

Twenty-Seven

Cooper

I came home to an empty house Monday evening, holding a bouquet of red roses for my girl. "Briley?" I called, searching the house and then the pool. "You home?" I looked in the garage to see her car parked in its spot.

With her number on speed dial, I called her cell. It rang twice before I heard it in the bedroom. Walking toward the sound, I found it plugged into her wall charger. Assuming she'd gone for a run, I grabbed a beer and flipped through the channels.

Ten minutes passed. Twenty. Forty.

Shit, B, where are you? I checked the living room window for the hundredth time. I was beside myself, worried she'd been injured, so I hopped in my truck and traced all the paths she usually took on a run. Covering new ground, even the ones I knew she wouldn't take, terrible thoughts ravaged my mind. Briley's crime shows fed me all kinds of ideas that had sweat trickling down my back.

No sign of her.

My phone buzzed with an incoming text. Two words that had my world spinning:

I'm home.

That was it. No explanation, no apology.

I sped down the road toward my house, eager to make sure she was okay. Rushing through the door, I saw her. She looked unharmed, but I had to see for myself.

"Are you all right? Where have you been?"

"I'm okay." She wrapped her arms around me, clinging to me like we hadn't seen each other in months.

I sensed something was off. "Where were you? I've been driving all over looking for you."

"I'm sorry. I should've taken my phone with me." Her arms remained clamped around my waist, raising my level of worry.

"Briley." I peeled her arms from around me, hooked a thumb under her chin, and lifted. "What happened? Where did you go?"

"You remember Sophie, from my office? We went for a drive. She needed to talk." She was lying. Her voice was high pitched, almost comical, and I could tell she'd been crying. It was obvious, but I let her continue. "You know what I'd really love? A walk. Loosen up these tense muscles. What do you say?"

"Sure, if that's what you want." I studied her odd expression. She seemed uncomfortable in her own skin, and I couldn't shake the feeling that something was really wrong.

Briley hiked across the grassy field at a fast pace, not stopping or saying a word until we were under a shade tree by the pond. The look on her face—eyebrows pinched together, sadness flashing in her eyes—confirmed something *was* wrong.

"What is it?" I pressed, stroking her arms with a pressure I hoped didn't reveal my fear. The way she was acting was throwing me off, and whatever she had to say couldn't be good.

Before she could explain, a whirlwind of possible scenarios bombarded my brain. I eliminated the most obvious ones. A few things I knew for sure: money issues wouldn't cause her this much grief. She wouldn't wait until we were in the middle of a park to tell me about a run-in she'd had with Madison or Blake. And after all we'd been through, the connection we had couldn't be tampered with by another man in the picture. So whatever she was about to say either had something to do with the Zeretti's or her family secrets.

"Let's take a trip," she said out of nowhere. "Life is too short not to do the things we've dreamed of. You still want to backpack all over Europe?"

I frowned at her. "I haven't thought of that since high school, B. What's going on?"

She turned away from me, facing the pond. "I need to get away, see the world. I'm not happy being stuck in this little town, Coop. Everyone does the same thing—work, save money, start a family, work some more. Let's be those people that live out of the box. We can be normal and boring later in life."

I took her arm and twirled her around to face me. "What is this really about? Why are you lying to me, B?"

She drew in a deep breath, and I could sense she was debating on telling me the truth or trying out more lies.

"I—I messed up." With shoulders slumped, she covered her face, tears spilling down her wrists.

My first thought was Blake. I knew she'd never go back to him, but maybe she'd said or done something to make him believe he had a chance. "Whatever it is, we'll get through it."

"We won't, Coop. We can't." She looked up, her face twisted in agony. "We have to go away." The way she whispered—looking around to see if anyone was near—I wondered if she'd lost her mind.

It had to be about her family and the secrets.

"Tell me why, B. Did they find you? Are they here?" I wondered if we even had time to get our passports and any money. I needed to get her to safety immediately. We definitely didn't have time to dance around the subject in the park, out in the open where they had a clear shot.

"No, but my searching may have raised some flags. It won't be long before they figure it out." She looked as if she'd pass out, wobbling on her feet. I guided her onto the grass, and we both sat down. "That cop from the warehouse took me for a drive today. He suggested I leave town. "

So that was where she'd gone. *Fuck, fuck, fuck!*

This was all my fault. If I hadn't dug around in the first place—

"We have to get you out of here," I raged. "Now!" Panic raced through my chest as we sat in the park like her life wasn't threatened. Why hadn't the cop taken her somewhere safe right then? I stood, offering her a hand. "What kind of moron cop would release you into the open with a target on your back?" I stammered.

"It's okay, Coop. We have time." She wrapped her arms around herself and dropped her head. "I know it's a lot to ask of you, and I'll understand if you don't want to come with me."

"What're you talking about? Of course I'm coming with you." I pulled her into my arms and held her trembling body against mine. "My life wouldn't be worth living without you in it."

"I want you with me, Coop, more than anything, but you have to understand . . ." She turned her back to me, whispering the next words. Her voice cracked occasionally as she tried to swallow back her grief. "You might not ever see your family again. Your mom, dad, sister, your new nieces—"

I hooked my hand through the crook of her arm and twirled her around to face me. "I'll have you. No one means more to me than you do, B. When I asked you to marry me and you said yes, it was a covenant. We started our own family at that moment. I'm coming with you."

She threw her arms around me, erasing any fear that she didn't want me to go. It was settled. We'd begin our lives. Somewhere—anywhere—together.

***

While Briley made arrangements for our impromptu trip, I drove to the bank to find out if and how I could transfer my funds into another account that we could access from anywhere in the world. I was met in the parking lot by the same car that we first met the Marshal in. *Are you serious?* How the hell did he always know our every move? He opened the back door and waited for me to climb in.

"Briley's already filled me in," I said, ducking my head and climbing into the seat across from him.

"Has she?" His eyes squinted as he analyzed me. "I'm going to go with my gut and assume she didn't tell you everything."

I sat back in the seat, arms folded, and gave him a sideways glance. "And what is it you assume she hasn't told me?"

"She told you the Zeretti's have tracked her scent?"

I thought his choice of wording was inappropriate, but I nodded. "She did, and I know she needs to get out of town. What I don't understand is why you didn't get her out of here as soon as you knew they were onto her, or why the hell we're wasting time sitting in this car when I need to protect her."

"That's what I thought." The Marshal leaned forward, shook his head, and sighed. "I tried to get her out, but she refused to leave. Said she didn't fear death and preferred it over a life without you."

If my heart hadn't been racing with urgency to get Briley somewhere safe, it would've warmed at the words she'd shared with the Marshal. "We've solved that issue. I'm going with her. As soon as I set up an account we can access or cash out, we're leaving." I started to get out of the car when he gripped my arm.

"That won't work. Listen to me." He waited for me to take a seat again. "If you empty your account or transfer funds, you're giving them a straight path to find you."

"What do you suggest we do then?" Goddamn, I felt helpless. "We need money to live on."

"There's only one way this'll work. This is my job, what I'm trained for. You have to trust me."

He explained the plan and, although I didn't like it, he was right—it was the only way to protect her.

Twenty-Eight

Briley

"We're all packed. I've got our passports, traveler's checks, phones, chargers . . ." I shook my head. "We can't bring the phones." I swiped at the tears that still flowed after telling my mom 'goodbye.'

"You okay?" Cooper asked.

"Yeah. It was so hard not to cry when I left my mom."

"You didn't tell her . . . ?"

"No. I told her I was going away for a couple weeks on business." I lifted a bag over my shoulder and gripped the handle of the smaller rolling suit case—Cooper's—the bigger one was filled to capacity with my things. "Ready?"

"No," he answered. His hands were shoved deep into his pockets as he leaned against the wall. He'd changed his mind and wasn't going with me. I could read it in his body language. My heart dropped, along with my bag, onto the floor.

"You're not coming."

"I'm not." He looked at me with wide eyes and reached up to cup my face in his palms. "But not for the reason you think. You know . . . surely you know if there was another way, I'd do it."

"I don't understand, Coop." My voice cracked around the lump of despair in my throat. "What about the plan?" It suddenly dawned on me what had happened. "That bastard got to you, didn't he? The Marshal talked you out of going."

"Listen, baby." He pulled me into his arms, but my body remained stiff. "I have to agree with him. If I empty my account, pack up, and we both leave, we'll give the Zeretti's a straight path to find us. It looks less suspicious if you go first. Let everyone believe you're going on a business trip. When the Zeretti's come looking for you, we'll be ready."

"We, who's we?" I pulled out of his arms and glared. "I'm not leaving you here to *take care of things.* I know you're strong, Coop, but this is way out of your league." I stalked over to the couch and planted myself there. "I'm not going without you, and there's nothing you can say to change my mind." But there was, and I had a feeling he would use it.

"You have to go. Trust me, it won't be for long. They'll come here looking for you but won't find you. What they will find is a trail, leading them on a wild goose chase. The Marshal has a plan to take them as soon as they take the bait." Cooper sat on the couch next to me and took my hands in his. He lifted my fingers to his mouth and kissed each knuckle. "Do this for me, B, please. A month tops, and then we'll have a lifetime together. No more running."

"Why would you coming with me change anything, Coop? The Zeretti's could still take the bait. Nothing—"

"This is the only way," he urged, his face full of the pain I felt so strongly. "I need you to go. I can't protect you here."

Just when I thought the tears had stopped, they started again, and this time with a vengeance. My shoulders shook with grief. "I can't leave you, Coop. I don't want to go without you. Please."

"I can't leave my family, B. My parents . . . and I have two infant nieces that need . . ." His voice broke and he looked away from me. "Surely you understand."

There it was. I knew he didn't mean it, and he couldn't even look at me when he said it, but I couldn't ask him to leave his family. This was my problem, and I'd deal with it. And I *could* deal with it, as long as I knew he'd be safe. I'd have to make sure the Zeretti's had no reason to question him or my mother about my whereabouts. It might screw up the plan, but I wouldn't let Cooper risk his life while I was off somewhere safe.

Unable to look at him for fear he'd see right through me, I agreed, "Of course I understand. It's only a month or so, and then we'll have a lifetime together. No more running." I nodded absently, trying to make myself believe it. Then I rested my head against Cooper's chest for a moment while we sat in silence. He stroked my back, smoothed his hand over the waves of my hair, and kissed the top of my head. I had no idea what was going through his mind, but I felt the need to give him peace about the situation.

Pulling away, I looked up at him. His forehead creased with worry and his green eyes were still pained. A slow, crooked smile graced his gorgeous face as he looked down at me.

"I'm not afraid, Coop."

"I don't believe you."

"I'm not," I insisted. "You make me brave." I lifted my hand to his face, trying to ease his worrisome expression. He'd done so much for me, always protecting me, never wavering in his love even when I pushed him away. His love had crashed over me like a massive wave, erasing all doubt and fear, leaving behind a new woman. Knowing what the future held for us and having something to fight for, I wasn't afraid. "I'm strong and brave and I know . . . I absolutely know that we're going to come out on top of this." I nodded with confidence then.

He pulled me to him, tighter this time. "You *are* strong and brave, Briley. I'm glad you finally realize it," he whispered, so low that I could barely make out the words, "I love you so damn much."

Twenty-Nine

Cooper

The most difficult thing I'd ever done to date was take Briley to the airport. It would've been hard enough thinking she was going to Ireland and by herself, but in reality I didn't know *where* she would end up.

We walked slowly toward the security gate as a frenzy of people, eager to get in line just to wait, passed us by. "Your ticket says Ireland, is that right?" I asked on a whisper, not sure if we were safe to talk freely.

"I don't know. I have a four hour layover in New York," she followed my lead, speaking in a low tone. "My instructions are to take a cab to Buon Cibo in Brooklyn. My next airline ticket will be waiting for me, if I understood correctly."

I gulped as I gripped her waist, my forehead resting against hers. How was I supposed to let her go? I had to remind myself that I wasn't enough to keep her safe. Given the choice of keeping her alive or holding her in my arms, I could endure letting her go for a time.

Not forever, just a month.

We waited until the last possible moment to say goodbye. Before wrapping her in my arms, I committed everything about her to memory. She was dressed casually in faded jeans and a fitted white V-neck. Her dark hair, pulled up into a pony tail, made it hard for her to hide the sadness in her eyes. It was time to make her laugh, but I was all out of jokes or reasons to smile. I looked down, searching for something to say.

"Flip flops?" I asked.

"Yeah. Makes it easier to go through security." She trained her eyes on the floor.

Hooking my fingers under her chin, I guided her to look up at me. "I love you, B. So much."

She rested her head on my chest, arms dangling down by her sides as if she didn't have the strength to lift them. Enveloping her, I could feel her back shaking and knew she was crying. She spoke into my chest, her words muffled but clear enough to etch themselves permanently into my soul.

"I hate this, Coop . . . I hate leaving you. This is the worst brand of torture."

As much as I needed her, I knew this was necessary. If she stayed, we might have a few days, maybe weeks together before they found her. I had to be strong for her and convince her it would be over soon.

It was crazy how everything had changed when all these secrets had come to light. Not so long ago, our lives had been pleasantly boring. Now I'd give anything to go back to that. The simplicity of enjoying her in a roomful of people we loved as we celebrated our engagement, or to have her beside me, her hand in mine as we walked along the beach under the moonlight. Even simply sitting next to her on the couch and eating takeout while we griped about whatever movie the other one chose. I'd take it.

As much as I wanted to break apart, I had to keep it together for her. *Not forever*, I reminded myself again.

"It's okay, baby. I'll see you soon." My hands circled her back and stroked over her arms. "Write to me, maybe a poem. I'll write to you, too, and the time will pass quickly." *Please.*

She pulled back and looked up with tear soaked eyes. "I can't write to you, Coop."

"I know." I cupped her face in my hands. "Don't send them, just write to me." My lips pressed against her forehead and refused to pull away. I trailed kisses over her eyelids, the tip of her nose, and finally rested on her lips. If I didn't let her go now, she'd miss her flight, but there was a force beyond my control pulling me to her.

A bump by a passing stranger with too much luggage broke our connection. After one more kiss, we said our goodbyes. I didn't take my eyes off her as she sadly headed down the aisle and through security. Every now and then she'd turn and blow me a kiss. Long after she was around the corner and out of my sight, I walked to my truck.

One month. I'd gotten through seventeen of them without seeing her at all, so thirty days shouldn't have been so fucking daunting. But the dynamics of our relationship were severely different now. During my time in prison, she really stepped up as my best friend. She was much more now. My best friend, lover, fiancée . . . Hell, she was my life, my everything. The only reason it didn't kill me to leave my family behind forever was her. The depth of our love was immeasurable. It was the kind of love that stories were built on. The kind that, if bottled, would solve world peace, cure disease, and most likely overpopulate the earth.

Crown Royal over iced Coke got me through that night. Nothing on television was strong enough to distract me from the fact that Briley was in NYC having dinner by herself. Was she alone? Was she afraid? But the thought that threatened to drive me insane was wondering where the next flight would take her. I had to remind myself they were protecting her and sending her to a dangerous third world country wouldn't be part of that plan.

***

I was thirteen when I experienced my first hangover. School had been near impossible to get through with blurred vision and a throbbing headache, but I'd made it and swore I'd never drink that much again. My freshman year in college I woke up on the front lawn in a pair of boxer shorts and a yellow duck float wrapped around my waist.

Those were memorable hangovers, unlike the one I was experiencing this morning. I hadn't drank for pleasure last night, I'd done it to numb the pain and erase the worrisome thoughts spinning through my mind. I was unsettled over Briley and this trip into the unknown. The look in her eyes when she asked me to love on her mom for the next month haunted my thoughts and reminded me that, soon, I'd be saying goodbye to my own family.

Colin was too full of life when he stepped into my office before I had the first sip of coffee.

"Dude, you look awful." He leaned against the frame of the door, studying me.

I couldn't remove the scowl on my face, knowing it would be fixed there for the duration of the hangover. "Shh." I held up a hand and closed my eyes until the throbbing eased. "Drank too much."

"What happened?" he asked, walking toward me. "You and Briley have a fight or something?"

"No, no." I shook my head—big mistake. "We're good. She's on a business trip. I was watching the game and drank too much." *Shit! There wasn't a game on last night. Don't go there, Colin.* I took a drink of strong, black coffee, waiting for him to ask but he didn't.

"Coffee's the worst thing for a hangover, man. I read it. You need water and a banana."

"You've got bananas in your office?" I asked, not daring to move my head in his direction.

"No."

"Then why mention . . ." I flicked my hand in the air, dismissing the idea. "I've gotta get that contract for Holden finished." Spilling a few tablets of Motrin into my hand, I grabbed a water bottle out of the mini fridge behind me and swallowed down the promise of relief.

"Why don't you go home? I'll take care of Holden," Colin offered.

"Nah, I've got it." I pressed my thumbs into the side of my head, massaging the ache.

"Go home, C. You're useless today," he grumbled, half joking, mostly serious. His chest puffed as he spoke and, although he was one of my best friends, I could've thrown a paperweight at his smug grin. "I can run this company myself."

"Sure, asshole." I stood, grabbing my keys and water bottle. "You can run this place."

I'm counting on it.

***

Tuesday and Wednesday night I ate with my parents. It would be hard leaving them behind, and even worse not telling them goodbye or why they'd never see me again. My heart tightened watching my mother's face as she talked about her new grand babies, Emma and Eden. Depending on how long Briley and I were in hiding, it was possible they wouldn't know me. Another ping to my already bruised heart, realizing my mother may never hold my future children.

"Have you heard from Briley?" My mother asked, passing a dish of roasted carrots my way. I hated carrots but took a small serving to avoid her frown.

"Yes," I lied. "She says Ireland is beautiful, the food is amazing, and she's gained ten pounds."

"I'm glad. Has she sent any pictures? I'd love to see—"

"No, she can't send any photos over until she turns in the article. Wants to surprise us." I needed to change the subject before they grew suspicious. My dad slid his fork into a piece of meatloaf and brought it to his mouth. His age was starting to show as he chewed carefully. "Dad, you up for a round of golf this weekend?"

"Sure. You still know how to play?" He flashed a crooked smile and took another bite.

"I'll manage." I wanted to smirk but the lump in my throat prevented it.

My parents never questioned why I lingered each night, watching reruns of *Gunsmoke* with my father. Briley's mom got regular visits, too. I'd planned on bringing her a fresh bouquet of flowers once a week as long as I was around. They all must've thought I was lonely for Briley—which I was—and that was the reason for my new behavior.

They'd never know or understand the real reason I was spending so much time with them. I was filling their memory banks—and mine—to last a lifetime.

***

"Keep busy, it'll make the time pass a little easier," my father said, giving my shoulder a firm pat. We never made eye contact when he wanted to talk seriously about something.

"I've got a lot going on at work." I leaned back in the old caramel-colored recliner, settling in for his words of wisdom.

"Have you and Briley set a wedding date?" My mother chimed in, drying her hands with a dish towel. It wasn't the first time they'd asked since we announced our engagement, but it rang a little louder in my ears this time, rattling me. We'd talked about a summer wedding, possibly on the beach. The plan was to have our family and closest friends join us for the entire weekend. As excited as my parents were to add Briley to our family, they wouldn't see the wedding.

I held out hope that the Zeretti clan would be wiped out, and we'd be able to come home, but I was alone in that optimism. Briley felt the large family would never die out and they would pass the vendetta on.

An answer for my mother could go one of two ways: I could tell her we'd set a date, at least let her have the thrill of making internal plans, giving her something to obsess over. Or, I could tell her we hadn't set a date.

"Next summer." I grinned at my mom when her hands clasped together. I could see the plans unfolding in her mind as she stood there.

It was the least I could do, giving my mother something to be happy about before I broke her heart.

Thirty

Briley

Walking away from Cooper—knowing it would be a month before I'd see him again—took second place as the most difficult moment in my life. Saying goodbye to my mother held a solid first. How was I supposed to casually say goodbye as if I were going on a business trip? Instead I'd wanted to wrap my arms her, tell her how much I loved her and appreciated all she'd done for me, and that I would never forget the love and friendship we shared.

I consoled myself by writing her a letter on the airplane to New York. When I knew it was safe, I'd find a way for her to get it. For fear of dropping it or someone reading over my shoulder, I kept it vague, listing the qualities I loved most about her. By the end of the flight I'd written a full length poem instead of the letter I'd planned. Once I reached my final destination I'd have more control over what I could write.

Stepping out of JFK airport, I was greeted by warm air and a sea of yellow taxi cabs. After waiting in line for my turn, the cabbie loaded my bag in the trunk while I climbed into the backseat. The ride to Brooklyn was adventurous. The cabbie didn't say a word to me as he created his own traffic rules, swerving around cars, driving between lanes, and finally screeching to a halt at my destination.

After paying him, I collected my bag and headed into the tiny Italian restaurant. A young hostess, blond and too perky for my mood, took my name and escorted me to a rustic wooden table in the back. Used to eating by myself—critiquing the

214

flavors and presentation of food, soaking in the atmosphere of different eateries—I should've felt at ease, but I didn't. This was different since I didn't know what was next. Would someone approach me and hand me a new itinerary or would they join me for lunch? And who would this person be? A woman my age that calmed the shakiness inside of me or a dark, brooding man that gave me the creeps?

When my server arrived to take my order, I asked for a glass of Chianti and whatever he recommended on the menu as long as it was light. My stomach couldn't handle anything heavy. I gladly would've skipped the meal but didn't know when I'd have a chance to eat again.

No one joined me as I sipped my wine and nervously pushed my fork around a plate of tomato and basil angel hair pasta. After two glasses of wine, I had swirled my utensil through the mound of pasta that reminded me of Mount Vesuvius and created a world of tiny Hobbit hills from the Shire in Middle Earth.

"You didn't like it? Can I bring you something else?" the server asked. Somehow I hadn't looked at him until now. He was about mid-thirties, dark hair, with a drastic side part and neatly trimmed beard. He wore the standard restaurant attire—white button down, black slacks, and an apron.

"Hmm? Oh, no, it's fine. I'm not as hungry as I thought."

He cleared my plate, offered dessert which I declined, then set a black wallet on the table, holding my bill. Not sure what to do next, I sat there, wondering where the stranger with my airline tickets was. Maybe I was supposed to stay in New York? Even so, I didn't have a place to stay or enough money with me for a decent hotel.

Without any other options, I started to feel panicked. Another glass of wine would've done a world of good in calming my frantic nerves, but if I was alone in Brooklyn—a city I knew nothing about—I'd need to save every penny. I opened the wallet to find that the bill was already paid for. Beneath the receipt was a paper sleeve holding my airline tickets. Before I could even read where they would take me, I inhaled a breath of relief.

***

My life had gone from perfect to train wreck in a matter of days, and it was about to get worse. Sitting on a bench a block from the restaurant, I pulled out the airline ticket and read the destination.

Detroit.

"Seriously?" I groaned. Usually northerners moved to Florida, not the reverse. I wouldn't survive a fall in Michigan, let alone their ghastly winters. Why the hell would they send me to Michigan other than to mess with me?

My cab driver on the return to JFK was just the opposite from the previous one. He talked incessantly and drove halfway decent. My only complaint was his topic of conversation— murder. Why he thought a woman alone in New York would be interested in hearing his tale was beyond me, but he made sure I was well informed about what had happened in Central Park only two days ago.

"Sure did. Cut that woman up so bad, they had to identify her through dental records." He kept looking in the rearview mirror for my reaction. "That's why you should get a carry permit and always have a gun on your person. My wife has one."

It wasn't that I didn't like guns. In fact, I agreed that every woman should take classes and earn a carry permit if they lived alone or worked in an unsafe environment. My face scrunched up as I thought about packing a pistol in my purse. No, I was definitely more a pepper spray type girl.

"You're one of those that want to ban guns?" he asked, his eyes staring me down from the mirror as he awaited my answer. If I didn't answer quick, he'd surely run into something.

"No, I'm okay with guns. All the criminals have them, and I think we have the right to protect ourselves." Now that I thought of it, I wished I had gotten my mother one before I'd left.

"Damn straight, they do." His eyes were back on the road as he spoke. Thank God. "Make guns illegal, they say. Sure, that worked just fine for drugs, didn't it? Hasn't been a single sighting of cocaine or meth since." He laughed and shook his head, the sarcasm evident in the way he rolled his eyes. "Am I right?"

"I hear you," I mumbled, lacking anything more intelligent. This was a subject I couldn't debate as I'd never been around guns or anyone that used them. The sole reason for this cab ride was to get as far away as possible from the threat of someone wanting to extinguish my life.

So I was going to Detroit—the mega center of crime.

Thirty-One
Cooper

Three weeks passed without a word about Briley. I was in hell and there wasn't a damn thing I could do about it. While flipping through the channels late Wednesday night, my doorbell rang. Thinking it might have something to do with Briley, I rushed to the front of the house and swung open the door.

"Colin," I deadpanned.

"Hey, dude. You busy?" He invited himself in, a bucket of fried chicken tucked under his arm.

"No, come on in." I waved a hand behind him and followed him to the living room.

"Where's Briley?"

"Business trip still." I sucked in a breath and diverted to the kitchen to retrieve a couple beers so he couldn't read my pained expression.

"You better get this place cleaned up before she gets back. She'll kill you," he shouted, no doubt taking in my piles of takeout boxes, empty beer bottles, clothes strewn about, and possibly the pair of heart print boxers that Briley got me on the arm of the couch.

Returning with two bottlenecks, I handed one to Colin, picked a drumstick out of the box, and tried to change the subject. "What's up? Why did you stop by?"

He looked at me sideways and then glanced around the room. "Is someone here?" He stood and got in my face. "You're not cheating on Briley, are you? Dude, listen to me—"

"Fuck, no, Colin!" I ran my hand through my hair, trying to calm down. "Shit, are you serious?"

"Sorry, man. But look at you, you're a mess, your place is a wreck, and you've been *off* lately. What's going on?"

It was nice of him to notice my *off*-ness, but I sure as hell didn't need him digging. No one else needed to be in danger.

After swiping a few food wrappers off the couch, I took a seat and a long drink of my beer. "Ah, you know, Briley's away and . . ." I trailed off. And what? I couldn't tell him anything, and I hadn't planned on explaining myself. I needed to get my shit together if I was serious about protecting her.

"You're lonely?" He folded his hands over his heart and batted his eyes, mocking me. "Pussy!"

We shared a laugh. Mine was not genuine.

"Are you and Claire coming to the show this weekend?" We had a repeat gig at Octane and, although I didn't want to do it, I had agreed. I was instructed to go on with normal life while Briley was gone to avoid suspicion. We had no idea whether the Zeretti's were watching my every move or not.

"Planning on it."

We sucked down two beers and polished off the bucket of chicken. I had to admit it was nice to have a distraction, even if only for an hour.

***

Saturday night's gig was uneventful other than rocking a full house. For two hours I was free from the weight of reality and could just be Cooper. Though I missed my girl being in the front row, I played well and covered our usual songs and a few new ones we'd recently added from The Black Keys, Wallflowers, and Cage the Elephant.

During intermission, I pushed the back door open and stepped out for some fresh air. Surrounded by dumpsters in an alley, there was no fresh air to be had so I turned to go back inside. The door was locked. *Fuck.* After banging on it with my fist for what seemed like ten minutes, I walked around to the front of the building. A small crowd was gathered, most of them leaning against the building with a cigarette or cell phone in hand. As I passed, someone grabbed my arm.

"Hey there," she crooned. The familiar voice had me gritting my teeth and closing my eyes. Maybe she'd be gone when I opened them. No such luck.

"Madison."

"Y'all are amazing tonight." She pushed herself off the wall, shoved her cell phone in her purse, and threaded her arm through mine. "You know there's an agent here tonight checking you guys out. I'd bet money you'll have an offer on the table soon."

"I've got a job—we all do. We play for fun." I pulled my arm loose and flashed a look that I hoped lacked any invitation to keep talking. "I've gotta get back."

"Me too," she agreed, catching up in no time. "My date is probably wondering what's taking me so long."

For a brief moment, I wondered if she was lying, then realized I didn't care about any aspect of her life.

"I noticed Briley's not here?" She waited for a response from me. When she didn't get one, she pushed again. "Did you two split already?"

I stopped too suddenly for her spike heels and she stumbled, catching herself against my body. "No," I ground out.

"Then why isn't she here, Cooper?" She blinked too innocent eyes at me. "This is a big night for you, she should be here."

I sure as fuck don't need to explain to you. Tucking away my rage, I said, "She's out of the country on business."

"If it were me, I wouldn't miss—"

"It's not you. It never will be." My night had been great until I had bumped into her. Now I was thinking about Briley, wondering where she was, how she was, and what she was doing. I had to believe she was safe, maybe doing some writing. Still, it pissed me off that she wasn't here. Not for the reasons Madison mentioned, but because of what she was going through and I couldn't protect her. I stalked off but turned after a few steps, just to make sure the psycho was clear on where things stood between us. "We're engaged. Briley and I are getting married."

"Great!" she called out, a faker than fake smile plastered on her face. "I'm in a serious relationship myself, and . . ." Her words trailed off as I took long strides toward the front door of the club and stepped inside.

"Where've you been, man?" Ryan asked.

"I went out back for some air and the door locked behind me. Had to go around. We ready?"

"Yup, just waiting on your ass." He slapped me on the back. "Thought you had the shits or something."

"Dude," I turned to him, curious to know how he felt, "would you sign with a label if a deal was ever on the table?"

"Hell, yes!" He rose up on tiptoes like he would shoot through the roof from excitement, his laugh lines sinking deep into the corners of his eyes as he grinned. "You heard about it? Who told you?"

"Overheard someone talking." I was afraid the entire band felt that way. I had to admit, it wasn't a bad way to make a living. We were all tight and always had a good time together. Maybe if things had worked out differently . . . but they hadn't. For me, the option didn't exist. I'd pretend to be excited about it and hope we didn't have to sign anything before I left. They'd easily find my replacement if that's the way they decided to go.

The second half of the show was meant to impress the agent. We agreed that our best genre was rock and jammed to Queen, Led Zeppelin, and AC/DC. My shirt was soaked so I stripped it off and flung it behind me. The crowd went wild, and I'll admit it felt good. I played hard, hitting every note and enjoying watching the crowd's response.

Ryan introduced the next song. "We're going to slow things down now with a classic. Sing along if you know the words."

Everyone cheered and then a rich silence fell over the room as the anguished and ethereal first notes were strummed. The crowd swayed and sang along to the words in unison. It was a moment I'd never forget. We ended with that song, took a bow, and exited the stage, ready to celebrate a successful night, but the crowd was wild and wouldn't settle down until we came back out for an encore.

"What do you want to end with?" Danny asked, beating his drumsticks against the sides of his legs.

"The song we played last night," I offered. "I'm in the mood for a little more AC/DC."

The best feeling in the world was hearing the crowd go from chanting *Encore! Encore! Encore!* to losing their shit when we came back out. *Remember this,* I told myself, in case I never got to experience it again.

I counted Danny's eighth note pattern on the cymbal, readying my fingers on the B string. When I went from the fourth and seventh fret to the fifth and eighth at the speed of light, the crowd went out of their fucking minds. Hands in the air, bodies jumping up and down, the sounds of cheering . . . *I agree, best damn song!*

My foot tapped to the beat, the crowd booming in unison, *thunder . . . thunder . . . thunder . . . thunder!*

It was a great song to end the night with.

As expected, the agent—Vincent J. Perry—left his business card for us to meet with him at the end of next week. We celebrated the news at the bar after the crowd was ushered out.

"What a night," Danny said, shaking his head, a foolish grin raising his cheekbones.

"Something I'll never forget," I mumbled beneath a smile that couldn't be contained. Most certainly.

"Thunder!" Ryan pounded his fist on the wooden counter of the bar and let out a whoop.

The bartender—a busty blonde that looked like she'd been around more than me, maybe because of her tat sleeves or the way her skin seemed overexposed and abused—slid two rounds of tequila shots in front of us with a ramekin of lime wedges. "On the house, boys. Great show tonight."

"How's it going with Joselyn?" I asked Ryan. My fingers wrapped around a longneck and tipped the bottle up, letting the crisp drink cool me off.

"You know." He shrugged. "She's cool." He paused to take a drink. "She works a lot, and I appreciate that she owns her own business and all, but I don't know. If I married this girl—" He paused to raise his eyebrows and cock his head to the side. "—and I'm not saying I will—but *I'm* the man."

"Fuck, man!" I nearly spit my beer. "Did you time travel from another generation?" I had never heard Ryan even speak the M word, let alone use it in an entire sentence. But 'the man'? Did he really think that girl would give up her business for him?

Danny, spinning his bottle between his palms on the bar, said, "You'd rather have a domesticated woman? One that'll be waiting for you with dinner and a glass of scotch when you get home?"

"Maybe." Ryan shrugged. "Doesn't sound like a bad life."

"No," Danny agreed. "Until she gets bored, wondering what to do all day. Sure, she can lay by the pool all summer, maybe even take up painting one winter. But what happens on a rainy day when she's had enough? She's walking through the grocery and some fucker shows her the least bit of attention . . . makes something like golf sound interesting enough and then next thing you know, they're fucking."

Danny's girlfriend of six years did that to him. He hadn't been in a serious relationship since. Ryan was smart enough to move the subject in a different direction.

"You're right, Dan. Sorry." He took a swig of his beer and turned the attention to me. "Heard from Briley? How's her trip?"

"Yeah, she's doing great. Busy." I struggled to find a few tales to tell. "She's drinking green beer and eating shepherd's pie and . . . would you believe she had to do an article on Haggis?"

"What's that?" Danny asked.

"It's a bunch of ingredients cooked in a sheep's stomach. Like a sausage." That got a lot of moans. Thankfully I'd just seen something on television about it. I tipped my head at Sloane the bartender. "Another round."

By the end of the night, we were wasted and I felt good about how we'd end our longtime friendship. My version of a goodbye hug—a strong slap on the shoulder—was given to Danny and then Ryan. They were good guys and I hoped they signed with that agent. Maybe one day I'd hear them on the radio from wherever Briley and I ended up.

Thirty-Two

Briley

"It's temporary," the two agents announced.

"It's freezing," I retorted. "Idaho? Really?" It was better than Detroit, what I had thought would be my final destination, but equally as cold.

Both agents had flashed their badges—out of habit, I guess—before leading me to the small house. One of them was a thin man with fragile, pale skin that looked like it would slip right off his bones if pulled with the slightest force. My other tour guide was a woman. I couldn't tell much about her features since she was wearing a ball cap pulled down low and refused to look me in the eye.

We walked through my temporary home—a place that would host me until it was safe to move again—examining each room. There were only four including the bathroom.

The place was dull and reminded me of a guy's first apartment. It was also backward from any space I'd ever been in. The kitchen was just inside the door, rather than the living room, so I dug through the drawers and cabinets. It was stocked with four of each in white melamine: coffee mugs, plates, and bowls. I also had four glasses to drink from and a set of silverware, but there were no pots, pans, or anything to bake with. I mean, I wasn't a baker, but what if I had been?

"No dishwasher?" I asked, surprised.

The male, *Mr. Thin Skin*, shook his head. *Okay, no dishwasher, but thank God there's a microwave!* My food choices were only non-perishables since I wasn't allowed to go out. The pantry was a teenager's dream, holding single servings of microwavable macaroni & cheese, chips, peanut butter, cokes, and hot chocolate. Not only would I dine on junk food for who knew how long, but they wouldn't let me go out for my daily runs. My diet—mimicking my life—was about to be turned upside down. I would be looking and feeling disgusting in no time.

After the bedroom and bathroom, we found the living room tucked away in the back of the house. An audible sigh escaped my lips when I saw the fireplace. I'd always wanted to experience the natural heat of a wood-burning fireplace. Other than the provider of my warmth, there wasn't much to the space—your standard couch, lamp, and TV. It wasn't home, but I was thankful all the same.

All alone I crawled onto the couch and flipped through the channels. There were four to be exact. And none were current. One carried rerun marathons of a crime show, while another ran sappy Lifetime movies. My other choices were a channel that taught you everything you ever wanted to know—or not know—about history, and finally, a home and gardening channel. Like everything the Marshal's did, I couldn't figure out why they blocked the public channels, but I'm sure they had a good reason.

After only three days of junk food and bad television, I was starting to wonder how teenagers survived. No wonder they were full of anger and angst—they were slowly being poisoned and brainwashed. I could already feel my face acting out with a few small zits ready to make an appearance.

By day seven of my stay, the female officer popped in to check on me. She came bearing gifts. "You said you wanted to go for a run?" She looked down at her arms that held a box with a DVD player and videos. I wondered if she knew the meaning of "run", or if she thought I'd been talking in code. "I thought since you couldn't go outside, maybe some exercise videos would keep you busy."

I gave her a weak smile. It was a nice gesture. "Thanks, I appreciate it." I took the box of DVD's from her and set them down. She squatted down and reached behind the television to plug in the DVD player. "I'm sorry, tell me your name again?"

"Tracie." She looked hard on the outside, someone who'd probably been bullied as a child and became a cop to rid the world of mean people. Her features were unexceptional—dirty blonde hair that reminded me of the dirt on an old country road, pale skin, a crooked front tooth that jutted out a little farther than the others—but I clung to her company like static on slacks. "I know it's lonely here all alone." She stood up. "But it'll be over before you know it."

"I miss my fiancé." I sighed. "I need to know if he's okay. And if my mom is safe."

"They're fine. We'd get word if something happened to any of them." She looked at her watch. "I'm off duty in ten minutes. Want me to stick around and see if this thing works?"

"Can you stay for a movie?" I tried but failed to keep the desperation out of my voice.

"Sure." She smiled, her fist lifting up beneath her nose to cover her mouth—a habit I assumed, formed because she hated her smile. Crooked teeth? Now I was curious.

Turned out Tracie was a lot of fun. She had a dry sense of humor and once she got going, she had me laughing until I could barely breathe.

***

It took me two weeks to convince Tracie to let me take a drive. I was going insane in this tiny one bedroom, and if I didn't see the outside world soon, I threatened to hang myself from the shower rod, so Tracie grudgingly relented.

When I heard the key turning in the lock, I jumped up and greeted Tracie at the door. "Did you bring it?"

She slid a large sack off her left arm and set it on the small kitchen table. "I still don't think it's a good idea. If we—"

"No one will know it's me." I pulled open the bag, reached in, and grabbed a small box. "Is this the wig?" Before she had a chance to answer, I opened it and lifted out a cropped blond wig. It felt like real hair, silky smooth. Apparently cops had the big budget.

"Now, you'll have to get it right." She took the wig out of my hands and reached into the bag, pulling out a wig cap.

I sat in the chair while she separated my hair into four sections, twisting and pinning it in place with bobby pins. Together, we fit the wig cap over my hair, tucking and adjusting until she was satisfied. Tracie picked up the wig, but I snatched it from her.

"Wait! Let me. I want to see your reaction." I bounded into the bedroom to change clothes and get the wig just right. I'd never had blond hair and was shocked to see myself in the mirror.

Tracie's expression was priceless when I came out of my bedroom.

"Ta da!" I threw my hands in the air and twirled around. "What do you think?"

"We did good." She grinned. "But you still need to be careful. Always assume you're being followed and watched like a hawk ready to be devoured."

"Okay," I huffed. "I got it." Zipping up my coat, I held out my hand for the keys. I was so giddy, I was bouncing. I hadn't seen the outside world in over two weeks and was more than eager to smell the fresh air . . . even if it was too cold.

I drove the few blocks she allowed, then came right back. Maybe tomorrow I'd venture out further, but I didn't want to break the rules and have my privilege revoked already. There wasn't much to look at on the drive. Small houses with fences in the front yards—I'd never seen that before—a few kids chalking the sidewalk and jumping rope, and a stray dog that I nearly hit while I gazed too long at the kids playing.

It was nice to get out, but it only made me crave my freedom more. I couldn't understand how people lived like this, always on the run, hiding, wearing disguises, and wondering who was watching you. If the people after my bloodline were so vicious and perseverant, would they ever stop looking? Was there a place on this earth the Marshals could hide us where they'd never find us? I doubted it. My stomach twisted with the thought of living in fear and dragging Cooper down with me.

Tracie and I hung out almost every evening, and I took the car out twice more. She was fun to be around off duty, letting her guard down and laughing. She eventually told me about her childhood, growing up with an alcoholic father and a mother too tired and beaten down to really care for her. I'd miss her when I was gone.

"You've never been married?" I asked, one leg curled beneath me on the couch. We'd been watching old episodes of Lost on DVD two or three at time. It was surprising how much

I'd forgotten, especially since Cooper and I had watched the entire show on DVD a few years back.

"No," she answered on a chuckle. "I like to play the field too much." There it was again, that dry sense of humor mixed with sarcasm. Her self-esteem was so low, I doubted she'd ever put herself out there to see if she could connect with someone. I would've given anything to take her out, show her that there was more to life than coming home every night to her dog—or in this instance, a stranger whose life was being threatened.

"Do you have friends that you go out with? You know, GNO?"

She watched me, waiting for an explanation.

"Seriously?" I heaved a sigh. "Girls night out."

"I don't have any G's for a GNO," she answered, mimicking a rapper.

I should've laughed, but it made me sad. "Yeah, me neither."

We were two odd ducks, sitting on that couch. Our connection was based on one of two things: our mutual social awkwardness or the fact that she was all I had and most likely vice versa.

"Since this is the last episode of the season, I brought something."

I guessed that was a hint to get the show started or maybe she was ready to move the subject onto something more comfortable. "Show me! What did you bring? Please tell me it's vanilla bean ice cream."

"If so, it's melted and filling my bag with a sticky mess." Tracie reached into her bag and pulled out a box of assorted chocolates. "Do you like chocolate?"

Um, is the earth round? "Are you kidding me?" I yanked the box from her hands and flipped it over to read the contents. "I'm a woman, of course I like chocolate. God, I need this!"

After two episodes of Lost and hint of a stomach ache later, Tracie was gone, and I was left alone again with nothing but empty wrappers and silence. Sitting on the couch, hugging my knees, I weighed the two feelings I was overcome with: fear and loneliness. Without question, I decided I'd rather live with fear than loneliness. I'd choose to look over my shoulder every now and then, living with the fear that one day someone was going to take me out. But I couldn't be alone, without someone beside me—without Cooper.

Late at night when I couldn't sleep, I penned letters to my mother. They'd never be sent, but it made me feel better. And as promised, I never missed a night of writing to Cooper. I'd spill my soul with pencil and paper each night, telling him my fears and hopes. He'd never get any of these letters either, but it was the closest thing I had to talking to him. A few times I tried to stay upbeat, telling him I was doing well, enjoying the sights of Ireland. But reality never failed to pull me down and make me pen what I really felt . . . scared, hopeless, lost.

I knew deep down that he wouldn't give up on me, but the mind is a tricky thing, always trying to convince you of untruths. Sometimes I'd fall asleep wondering if he'd decide this was all too difficult and change his mind. Would I reach my final destination, then spend the rest of my days waiting for him, watching for his silhouette to come through the door? What if he never did?

Shaking that thought from my mind, I wrote to him before falling asleep. I told him about the last episode of Lost, the chocolates, the drive I took earlier in the evening, and how the wig was scratchy, but I was starting to feel safer out in the open because of it.

My letters to Cooper always included dreams and plans of our future together and all ended the same way: *Stay with me, Cooper. I love you.*

***

Three weeks away from Cooper and my mother had been excruciating. I'd taken comfort in boxed Mac n' Cheese, frozen pizza, and all the chocolate I could get my hands on, thanks to Tracie. I didn't notice the added pounds since my new life consisted of wearing sweatpants—to keep warm, sure, but they were also comfortable, and I wasn't going to be seen anyway.

Sometime around six or so, Tracie bounded through the door with our Friday night chocolates and a new release to watch. I'd lost track of the time and her entrance startled me.

"You okay? What's wrong?" Her arm was around me, stroking my back. It was an affection she wouldn't have shown me even a week ago. Our friendship had been nurtured into something I'd never had with another female before. I'll admit, I liked it.

Wiping the moisture from under my eyes, I shook my head. There was no use telling her I was fine. I wasn't. "I miss Cooper. I don't think I've ever been this miserable. We've been separated before, and it was awful, but at least I could talk to him, write to him."

She glanced at the letter next to me. "You can't send that."

"I know. It helps to pretend that I can. It's the only way I can talk to him. They're not even addressed, but I go through the motions of putting them in an envelope and then I mail them to my nightstand drawer."

"That's sweet." She smiled. "You'll see him soon. I know it doesn't seem like it, but you will."

Chewing on the inside of my cheek, my brows drew together in worry. "I don't know. I have this feeling that I may never see him again." I repositioned myself on the couch so I could face her. "Promise me you'll give him all of my letters if I choose to let him go. I have a drawer full. Promise me."

She cocked her head to the side. "Let him go? Why would you do that? I've never seen someone so desperately in love. What's this crazy talk, hmm?"

I shook my head. "I can't ask him to give up everything. His family, friends, career. He's worked really hard to build up his business. And did I tell you about his band? He's good, really good. What kind of person would I be if I asked him to leave it all behind?"

She gave me a pointed look. "It should be his choice."

"No." I shook my head again. "He's a good man. I can't trust his choice. He'll do what's best for me, not him."

Tracie got up from the couch and went to the fridge. She held a plastic cup under the spigot of the boxed wine she'd brought over two nights ago, filled it and then filled another. I'd never had boxed wine before and laughed when she brought it over. I truly thought it was a gag. But it was good and apparently lasted a lot longer than bottled wine.

She handed me a cup and took her place on the couch. "When two people love each other, doing what's best for the other is doing what's best for themselves." After taking a sip of her wine, she said, "Change places for a minute. What would you do?"

"Of course I'd drop everything to be with him. But it's different."

"How?"

I frowned. "I don't know, it just is."

We were silent for a moment, sipping our boxed wine. I started a fire to knock the chill out of the air and give myself a distraction from the conversation. After watching the flames lick the logs for a moment, I returned to the couch. "I just have a feeling. Please, promise me you'll get the letters to him."

She held her hands up, careful not to spill her wine. "Fine. I promise. But it's going to be okay. You'll see. Besides, Frank Zeretti can't live forever. One day soon, you and Cooper will go back to Tampa, maybe with a little family, and have your happily ever after. And when you do . . ." She opened the box of chocolates, pulled one out, and pretended to toast me with it. "Bring me chocolates!"

After only one episode, she started on Cooper again. "Tell me about this Cooper. Something you haven't told me yet."

"You're the only person I talk to." I drew my legs up beside me and leaned my head against the back cushion of the sofa. "I'm sure I've told you everything."

"Tell me what makes you laugh. Does he have any funny quirks?"

I gulped as a few memories paraded through my mind. They caused as much pain as they did joy to recall. "Cooper loves to make me laugh. He tells the stupidest jokes, but they always crack me up." I paused to remember the last joke he'd told me. I wouldn't try to retell it to Tracie though, since I had a history of screwing up the punch line. "He sips his coffee really loud." She laughed and adjusted herself on the couch. "It's ridiculous the noise he makes over one sip of coffee." I held a pretend mug to my lips and mimicked the sound.

A moment later, I smirked to myself, realizing what she'd done. She distracted me from my misery and made me laugh.

Thirty-Three

Cooper

Tuesday evening I sat in my truck, engine running in the driveway. My house was a wreck—empty bottles, dirty dishes, and clutter everywhere—a depressing place to try and rest my head. Each day passed slower than the last, and all I had to look forward to was sleep. I hoped my liver could handle my alcohol sleep aid for a little longer. The month-long separation the Marshal promised had passed, but it wouldn't be long now before I'd see Briley. *Twelve more days.* I found myself repeating that assurance over and over again.

After shutting the engine off, I collected my things and started for the door when an unknown number came up on my cell. I thought about ignoring it, knowing it was local. Right before it went to voicemail, I answered, curious.

"Hello?" I was ready to pounce if it was a solicitor.

"Cooper?" A lady asked, uncertainty in her weak voice.

"Who's calling?" I leaned against the truck, debating on ending the call.

"I'm a friend of Nina's. Nina Sheff—"

My heart muscle shot straight to my throat. "Is she all right? Did something happen?" I hopped in my truck before she could answer. The lady sniffed into the phone, unable to form intelligible words. "Where is she?"

"She's home and—"

"I'm on my way." I threw the phone into the seat, not sure I'd finished my sentence before ending the call.

All I could think about on the way to her house was how upset Briley would be if something had happened to her mother. I didn't want to hit her with that news when I saw her, but even more I didn't want the Marshals to tell her anything while she was away, powerless.

I knew it was bad when I saw the cars parked in front of Mrs. Sheffield's house. Two police cruisers lined the curb in front while vehicles I didn't recognize filled the driveway. When I barged through the front door, I saw her. Sitting on the edge of her recliner in the living room, she didn't look hurt or ill.

Seconds felt like minutes as I stepped fully into the room. It was filled with bodies that watched me, their eyes boring into me like I was out of place. Mrs. Sheffield lifted her head as I approached. She seemed to have aged in the two days since I'd seen her last. I couldn't understand what was going on as I watched her swollen eyes clench together, shutting me out.

"What happened?" I knelt down before her, looking her over and wondering why no one was assessing her. "Are you hurt? What's happened?" I asked over and over. She wouldn't answer. Instead her body trembled as if she were in shock.

I turned to face the others and shouted. "Will someone tell me what the hell happened!"

"Cooper Sterling?" An officer asked, holding his hat by his side. His body language wasn't right.

"Yes." I followed him to the corner of the room where we could talk. "What happened to her?" I knew it had something to do with the Zeretti's, but I couldn't go first, unsure of what they knew.

"I'm very sorry . . ." I watched his lips move as he spoke but didn't hear the words.

None of this was happening, none of it was real. I'd been hitting the bottle too heavily. Still, as if it were reality, my heart plummeted to the ground, leaving me with a hole filled with a pain I couldn't begin to describe.

"Did you hear me, Mr. Sterling?" His hand was on my shoulder. I glanced at it and then him. Every one of his features stood out, from the muddy color of his eyes to the way a thin, twisty vein snaked across his left temple. I noticed every freckle and acne scar on his face, but I couldn't understand his jumbled words. "Briley was in an accident . . ."

"No, no, no, no." I shook my head. I had to get out of here. No one had a clue what was really going on. *They're wrong. All of them.*

"Mr. Sterling, are you with me?" He squeezed my shoulder until I looked at him.

I stared at that demon for what seemed like thirty minutes. His lips moved, but I couldn't hear anything he said. Nothing made sense. My surroundings were off and all sound was muted. I watched his lips as he spoke the words that clotted my blood and killed everything inside of me.

"She's gone."

I could feel my knees weakening, bile burning the base of my neck as it rose up in my throat, and the sting of my tear ducts filling. "You're wrong." I blinked away the tears, justifying my statement. *She's out of the country. You don't know . . . you don't even know what the hell's going on . . . you're wrong!*

I had to let Mrs. Sheffield know the truth. They were mistaken. It wasn't Briley. I rushed to her chair and squatted down in front of her. "Hey, don't cry. They're wrong." I stroked her arms. "This is all a mistake. Briley's in . . ." *Where is she supposed to be?* "Ireland. Remember? She's in Ireland on business. They made a mistake."

I heard wailing behind me. That wasn't helping. I snapped my head around and gave the woman a look that implied she should shut the hell up.

Mrs. Sheffield took my jaw in her hand and turned my face to look at her. "I know how much you loved my baby girl. She always loved you, too, you know. She just needed to work some things out, grow up a little. It's my fault for sheltering her too much. I just needed to keep her safe." She shook her head and brought a soaked wad of tissue to her nose. "In the end . . . I couldn't."

"You've done a great job, Mrs. Sheffield. Ask her when she gets back, she'll tell you. You mean the world to her. This is all a misunderstanding." I lowered my voice so only she could hear me. "They found her so she went into hiding. This is all part of the plan."

"Oh, Cooper," she sobbed, slapping her hand over her mouth. "I saw the report. Her dental records . . . confirmed . . . she's—" A sound came from her that sounded like a wounded animal. "She's not coming back, honey. She's gone."

There was no consoling her. I stood, looking around the room at each person. Some were weeping, some were shaking their heads in sorrow, and the two officers held onto their hats like security blankets, trying to avoid eye contact. With shoulders back, I stormed out of the house. None of them were on my side. They all believed Briley was dead. I knew she wasn't. They hadn't seen her body, they . . . *"dental records . . . confirmed . . . she's gone."*

Walking down the front porch steps, the words played over and over. *She's gone . . . she's gone . . . she's . . . gone?*

My girl was gone? The love of my life, my world . . . gone. Forever.

My brain wouldn't accept it, but my heart seemed to. The pain was too much, choking and poisoning my body until I was crazed. I didn't care that I had a mouthful of grass and dirt after I hit the ground, clenching the blades and ripping them out by the fistfuls.

Undiluted rage swam through my veins, pooling in my chest until it erupted like a fucking grenade, its shards penetrating everyone who dared to get close to me. My father tried to pull me up, help me stand.

"*No!*" I jerked my arm away.

"Son, let me take you home." Looking into my father's eyes, swollen and red from crying, undid me. I suddenly felt like a child, helpless and lost.

The last thing I remembered was standing in Mrs. Sheffield's front yard, gripping my hair with both hands while I turned in circles looking for something . . . answers, a place to hide, or maybe a way to ease the crushing pain.

Briley was gone.

***

I woke the next morning in my bed. When the memories of last night flooded in—reminding me why my head was still pounding and my heart felt like it had been shredded—so did the tears. Dragging myself out of bed, I walked mechanically toward the kitchen. My father was sitting on the couch.

"What're you doing here?" I asked. It was obvious he'd been here all night.

"I wanted to be here if you needed me." He stood, stretching his arms behind his back and rubbing a spot on the side of his neck. Neither of us spoke as we waited for the coffee to brew. I poured two mugs and gripped mine tightly, trying to keep it together. Maybe it was my body's defense, but I felt like I was in a dream state, my mind foggy and numb. The depth of exhaustion I felt was deep, as if I hadn't slept for days.

My father cleared his throat, took a sip of coffee, and said, "I talked to Colin, told him what was going on. He said to take as much time as you need."

"What happened?"

"Car accident."

"I know that, but how . . . ?" *God-fucking-dammit.* It was all crushing me again.

"I don't know the details, Son. All I know is that she didn't suffer. She died on impact."

"What're they going to do with . . . where's Briley's . . ." It was difficult to say the words. It felt like I was accepting her death, and I wasn't ready to do that. It was easier to believe that she was on a business trip, and I'd see her in a few weeks like we'd planned. But I had to know what the plans were for her funeral. She deserved a service worthy of her, something beautiful honoring who she was. "Are they going to bring her home?"

My father rested a hand on my shoulder, but I flinched and shook him off. Why did everyone feel the need to touch me? It brought no comfort. "After the autopsy, they'll send her body home, but . . ." He lowered his head, studying the liquid in his cup as he spoke. "They . . . I don't know how to tell you this, Son . . ."

"Just say it, Dad." My body stiffened, preparing me for what I already knew he was going to say.

"After the crash, the car caught fire. It'll be a closed casket ceremony."

I thought I could handle hearing anything. I knew what he was going to say, yet hearing him say it out loud, confirming my fear, it was too much. Without thinking, I threw my mug into the sink and stalked into the living room. My body quaked with grief for a few beats before the anger took over.

Why Briley? My sweet, beautiful Briley.

"Why!" I shouted.

Before I knew what I was doing, I'd grabbed a lamp and thrown it into the wall, kicked a chair across the room, and broken a few framed pictures. I was trying to flip the couch over when my father marched in and sat on the piece of furniture I was trying to destroy. He didn't say a word, he just sat there.

My father stayed with me for two more nights until I got through the first stage of grief, or maybe it was more than one stage. They seemed to all come at me at the same time, concocting a powerful potion that took me from denial to grief, anger to denial, grief to acceptance . . . back and forth, over and over again. But nothing ever changed the end result.

Thirty-Four

Cooper

Dressed in black, I chose Briley's favorite tie, black with a burgundy design. It seemed an appropriate torture to have something she loved choking the lump in my throat. I stepped inside the funeral home, in a fog. Nothing seemed real, nothing felt right. A large framed picture of Briley stood on an easel next to her casket. I didn't want to be here, didn't want to do this today, or ever. But I had to be here for Briley's mom. I promised I would take care of her.

Mrs. Sheffield insisted I stand next to her during visitation. People I'd never seen and ones I'd known all my life filed in, hugging me, sharing their stories about how wonderful Briley was. They all looked the same to me, whispering the same apologies, "So very sorry for your loss." But nothing they said or did would heal my pain or bring her back. I wished they'd all just shut up and leave me the fuck alone.

An older lady with haunting blue eyes made her way to me. She was small and feeble, using a cane to help her walk up the aisle. I'd never seen her before, but her words would be the only ones I'd remember. "I'm sorry. This will always hurt. It's like a broken leg . . . it eventually heals, but it will never be the same."

The funeral was everything Briley would've wanted. I stayed for the internment and watched them lower her into the ground. I thought it would give me closure when the last scoop of dirt was tamped down, but it didn't.

I felt pats on the back and my shoulders being rubbed as everyone slowly trickled away. Mrs. Sheffield held it together much better than I expected. About an hour later, we were the only ones left at the gravesite, and she came to stand beside me.

"Come by the house when you're ready. There's tons of food." She wrapped her arms around me, hugging me hard for a long while, and then she left.

Finally, I was alone.

Squatting down beside the fresh dirt that encased my girl, I started talking to her like I did at her father's grave that day, not so long ago. No tears fell. I was just numb, robotic. "What now?" I asked. "How the hell am I supposed to live without you, B? We had a plan!" There was no use hiding the fact that I was mad. Some say in order for a spirit to be freed, you have to let them go. I couldn't do that. "I can't do it, B. I'm not letting you go. Haunt me! There's nothing you could do to me to make my life more miserable than it is now. Try! Please, try. I'll take your anger, I'll take your pain, but I won't let you go." My fists pounded into the ground as I dropped to my knees.

Waiting for something, anything, I sat there on the ground next to her. "Where are you, B? Come to me or I'm coming to you." The air was still as I sat there, waiting. But unlike that day with her dad, Briley didn't offer me anything I could grasp as a sign that she was with me or could hear me. Nothing but silence.

***

Each day I waited for a sign, while every night I drank myself to sleep. She never came to me, not even in my dreams.

On a Friday afternoon, I went to the police station. It was the first time I'd walked in this place un-cuffed, on my own. It was strange walking up to the desk to ask a question instead of being forced down the hallway.

No one offered to help, so I spoke up. "Who can I talk to about my fiancé's accident?"

A petite woman looked up from her computer and waved me toward her. "Name?"

"Mine? Cooper Sterling. I want to know about my fiancée, Bri—Briley Sheffield." It was still hard to say her name. God, I missed her so damn much.

She clicked some keys, read the screen, looked at me, and then back at the computer. "Briley Sheffield . . . fatal car accident?"

"Yes. I'd like details."

"I'm sorry, I can't share any information with non-family members."

"I am family," I argued, my fists clenching at my sides. "We were engaged."

"Not married, though," she said sympathetically. "I'm sorry, I can't help you. Maybe—" Before she could finish her sentence, I turned and stalked out.

I drove by Mrs. Sheffield's house, tempted to ask her if she had any more details, but thought better of it and drove past. After stopping by the liquor store, I drove to the building where Briley and I had talked to the U.S. Marshals. They'd have answers. The back parking lot was empty, but I pulled into a spot and banged on the door. No one answered and my attempt at breaking in failed.

Pulling into the driveway, I noticed someone had mowed my front yard. If I had a heart I probably would've thought it was a nice thing to do. I had a bottle of Jack Daniels opened before I slammed the front door behind me. Throwing the cap on the floor, I took a swig, then walked into the kitchen. After filling a glass with ice, I added a splash of coke and filled it to the top with whiskey.

Early evening, I heard the doorbell and someone banging on the door.

"Fuck off!" I didn't want company and sure as hell didn't want to buy Girl Scout cookies. I never heard the lock being worked, so when Colin nudged a knee into my side, it got my attention. "How'd yew get'n?" My words were slurred and sloppy.

I felt my bottle of Jack being tugged from my grasp. "I need that, motherfucckk—"

"I'm sorry, dude. I thought you could use a few days alone, but I see that wasn't the best idea."

"I don't want you here. I don't want . . . anyone here." I grabbed for the bottle, but I was no match for his sober ass speed.

"What're you trying to do, kill yourself? I think you've had enough."

"Give me the fucking bottle, Colin!" I was sobering fast and not happy about it.

"Do you think this is what Briley would want? I know it's hard, man, but—"

You know it's hard? "The fuck do you know? You think this *hurts?* Like I'm just a little down over a breakup? We didn't break up, Colin. She's dead. You have no fucking clue what this feels like." I could feel the creases in my forehead creating deep crevices, revealing a rage that was begging to be released. "You're gonna go home tonight, walk through the door, and see Claire. I'll never see Briley again. Never!" With both hands fisting my hair, I paced the room. "You have no fucking clue, and I hope you never do." My pulse slowed along with the rage, and it was replaced with the empty sadness I had been trying to deaden. "But if something like this ever happened to you, I wouldn't ask you to suck it up and get on with your life. I'd tell you to numb the pain any way you could." I was about to lose my shit and cry in front of him, something I'd kick myself for later. Swallowing back the sorrow, I channeled the remnants of rage and hissed, "Give me the fucking bottle and get the hell out!"

"I'm sorry, man. Really sorry." He handed me the bottle. "You're right, I have no idea what you're going through." He picked up a chair off the ground, sat it upright, and took a seat. "What can I do?"

"Unless you can bring her back, there's nothing you can do or say, Colin." I sank back down into the couch and tilted the bottle, eager to regain the numbness.

Colin didn't leave, and I didn't force him out. Maybe one day I'd appreciate his sacrifice in sitting with me as I pushed my liver closer to death and flipped through the channels with no intention of landing on anything.

***

A gurgling sound woke me the next morning. My eyelids felt like they'd been glued shut, but I eventually blinked them open and wiped a string of drool off my chin. A bottle rolled on the concrete next to me as I started to move. I was next to the pool, close to the edge. I must've fallen asleep out here. Studying the water, I noticed how the algae clung to the sides, turning the neglected pool a dark shade of green. The thought wasn't lost on me that soon the poison I was filling my body with would take over and I'd be dead. *If you're lucky. With your luck you'll just be a filthy drunk, reeking of piss and alcohol.*

The gurgling sound got my attention again so I followed the sound with my eyes to the skimmer. Something was blocking the circulation. Once I sat up, letting the floaters swimming around my head settle, I felt okay to stand. Whatever was blocking the intake valve on the skimmer was big enough to cause a problem. I lifted the lid to find a dead bird suctioned into the bottom. It wasn't the first time it had happened. Small birds often got trapped inside the screened-in pool, eventually got thirsty, and drank. What I didn't understand was how or why they drowned.

I studied the soaked creature for a long time, its lifeless body peaceful at the bottom of my skimmer basket. Death was a mystery. Life was a mystery. It seemed backward, life and death. Peace came with death. There was nothing after, no more pain. The dead didn't grieve the living.

After removing the bird, I looked around my place. Empty bottles and trash covered every surface. Hours had turned into days, and I'd lost track of time. Standing in the doorframe between the pool deck and the living room, I contemplated my next move. For now it was leaning against the frame, listening to the silence.

The doorbell chimed, bringing back the anger I was beginning to cling to for comfort. It felt better than sadness. Stalking to the door, I swung it open, ready to spew vile words to the solicitor on the other side.

"Mr. Sterling, I don't know if you remember—"

"I remember you." I thought of how good it would feel to punch him in the throat, watching him sputter and gasp for air. Then I thought of being back in that cell with nothing to numb the pain, only time and silence to dwell on my thoughts and heartache. "You're the reason she's gone." I strode away, leaving the door open.

The U.S. Marshall I had met, the one that had encouraged Briley to flee, followed me inside. "We need to talk." He looked for a place to sit, then settled for the arm of the sofa.

"It's too late. You fucked up. She's gone. The end." God, I wanted to slam my fist into him until the pain eased. But I knew it wouldn't end there. This was going to hurt forever.

"You went to the cops." Something flickered in his eyes, raising a flag for me to question him. He knew something.

"Tell me what happened to her." I towered over him, my jaw clenched as tightly as my fists. Instinctively, he stood to face me.

"It was a freak accident."

Freak, my ass. "Details! I want to know exactly what happened. Fill in the blanks for me." My head pounded in response to my increased pulse. "Start from the beginning. When I dropped her off at the airport. Tell me everything."

His hands were on his hips, probably ready to pull a taser on me if needed. "Have a seat and I'll tell you what I know."

I conceded and grabbed a chair, setting it down across from him and straddling it so I could rest my forearms on the back. He sat back down on the arm of the sofa and began telling me about Briley's course from New York to Detroit to Idaho. "She was in a safe house in Idaho until we felt it would be safe to move her out of the country."

"She never left the country? I thought . . . the report said she died in Ireland."

"You know why we had to alter that report." Again I saw something in his eyes.

"What aren't you telling me?" My eyebrows drew together. This guy had better start giving me answers if he knew what was good for him. "Dammit, I deserve to know the truth! She was my fiancée. I was ready to give up everything to go into hiding with her. I *did* give up everything." I slammed my fist into my thigh.

"I'm not convinced you're ready for the truth, Sterling." He stood, taking a defensive stance and cracking his neck to the side.

"Bullshit answer!"

His eyes flared, and I realized then that I needed to calm down or this asshole would shut down on me.

"Please," I said, calmer. "Sit back down. Give me some answers."

The Marshal hesitantly took his seat, his narrowed eyes locked on mine. "She befriended one of the female agents on duty. Miss Sheffield wasn't admitted outside of the safe house, but she convinced the agent to let her out incognito." He sighed, disappointment creasing his forehead. "We assume she lost control of the vehicle going down a steep hill over by Union Hill—a row of warehouse-type clothing stores. She crashed into the side of a brick building at the bottom."

I narrowed my eyes at him. "You expect me to buy that load of crap? Briley's never wrecked a vehicle in her life, but you want me to believe she crashed into a building? C'mon, you can do better than that." And he'd better. I was about to go fucking caveman on his ass.

He sucked in a deep breath, rested his palms on his knees, and finally told me, "The brakes were no good."

My blood turned to ice. "Someone tampered with them?" I couldn't sit still. Jerking out of the chair, I stood and ran a hand through my hair—greasy, unwashed hair that stayed in the position I left it when I released my grip.

"There was no evidence of tampering," he admitted carefully. "It was an older car and—"

"Was there brake fluid in the lines or not?" I demanded. *Stop fucking around with me!*

"No. But like I said, there was no evidence to question foul play. The case was dismissed as an accident." He was careful to keep a straight face, but had trouble maintaining eye contact. *Why the fuck are you lying to me?*

"Of course they didn't find evidence," I growled. "You're dealing with professionals, not a teen gang. You know it was the fucking Zeretti's! They found her." I scrubbed my hands over my face, my heartbeat now pulsing furiously behind sore eyes. "I trusted you to protect her better than I could. I was wrong."

"We have no reason to believe they had anything to do with it." He looked around the room, lifting an eyebrow. I assumed he was trying to tell me to watch what I said in case the house was bugged.

"I don't give a fuck if they're listening." My knuckles whitened from gripping the back of the chair. "I hope you *are* listening to me, motherfuckers." I tossed the chair across the room, knocking over one of the vases of flowers from Briley's funeral. "I'm coming for you. Briley had nothing to do with your mess. But I do. You hear me?" I turned wildly in every direction, raising my voice so they could hear. "I'll kill every one of you. Everyone you've ever cared about. Do you hear me?"

The Marshal hissed through gritted teeth. "It's over, Sterling. It wasn't the Zeretti's. Be careful with your threats, and consider your present company. I know you're going through hell. You look like hell. Don't give me a reason to take you in."

I knew the Zeretti's had gotten to her. I also knew I would kill every one of them. The only thing I didn't know was how or when I'd find them, but I would.

I never heard the Marshal leave or shut the door behind him. I was too deep in plotting my revenge and letting the red haze of rage take over the all-consuming grief.

***

Chinese takeout wasn't the smartest choice. It reminded me of Briley and how she stubbornly tried every time to use the chopsticks. But Mrs. Sheffield seemed surprised and happy to see me, although we mostly ate in silence, picking at the food containers while Wheel of Fortune played on the television in the background. It was too soon to talk about Briley, and she was the only thing we had in common. I excused myself to the restroom mid-meal and slipped unnoticed into her late husband's office to lift the Smith & Wesson pistol I'd seen before.

After dinner, I hugged her, trying to find words but falling short. Not only did I not know what to say to the woman that was almost my mother-in-law, but I had just stolen from her and felt the knot of guilt twisting my gut. I couldn't wait to get out of here.

"Thank you for stopping by. It was nice to . . . it was a needed distraction . . ." She trailed off, her eyes returning to the sad emptiness.

I made a promise to come by next week, though I knew I wouldn't be around to keep that pledge.

With a new bottle of Makers Mark and the gun concealed in a backpack, I got out of my truck, checked the mail, and headed inside my house. I kept the gun in the backpack and stuffed it into the back of a closet before uncapping the liquor bottle and going through the stack of mail that had gathered over the last few days.

A package, addressed to me in handwriting I didn't recognize, caught my attention. Ripping it open, I found a stack of envelopes tied together with a rubber band. The one on top was labeled with a fancy C, decorated with girly swirls . . . something Briley did when she was bored.

My heart skipped a few beats and then resumed in a fast, chaotic rhythm. I stared at the stack of envelopes in my hand, not able to move a muscle. I searched the box for a return address, a note explaining something—anything—but all I had was a stack of letters from Briley.

It took a while for the alcohol to have any affect. My body was becoming tolerant and needed more now to reach the desired outcome—numbness usually. This time for the courage to face the words Briley had written after she left . . . before she died.

Gripping the now half-full bottle of Makers, I opened the envelope, careful not to tear it, and read the first letter in the stack.

Coop,

It's midnight and I can't sleep. I miss having your arms around me. I know you'll never read these, but it feels good to talk to you and this is the only way I can do that.

I read it several times, my heart aching with a new, different feeling of loss, before opening the next.

My love,

God, this is awful! Sometimes I wake up in the middle of the night and try to snuggle into your side. Once I realize you're not there, I can't go back to sleep.

A sob got lodged in my throat, wishing I had gone with her. *I'm sorry, B. So fucking sorry.*

Coop,

I wonder what you're doing right this minute. I imagine you pouring coffee into your travel mug, checking your email on the way to that monstrous truck of yours, and listening to talk radio as you drive into work. Did I miss anything?

I don't tell you enough how much you mean to me. You're my hero, Coop. Do you know that? I can't imagine my life without you.

I love you. So much.

P.S. I ate chocolate for breakfast. Can you imagine? I'm kind of glad you'll never read these.

For the most part the letters seemed to be in order, detailing what she ate or watched on television. She talked about finding friendship with the female Marshal on duty—Tracie—who brought a disguise so she could get a few minutes of fresh air and take a drive.

You killed her, Tracie. Maybe the angry thought was misplaced, but it helped. For now.

I opened the next one and read it.

Cooper,

It won't be long now. It's so hard to be away from you, but we've survived worse. How are you? How is my mom? I was thinking about our new location. I'm pushing for something tropical. I told the Marshal I had a rare disease that flared up in cold weather. I think he bought it! Can't you see us now, sipping cocktails on the sand while our babies play in the surf?

I know we said we would wait, but I can't help picturing two little boys with green eyes. And maybe a few years later, a girl. It's so easy to talk to you about my dreams, Coop. You've always been a good listener, but your silence is killing me now. I need to hear your voice and feel your touch. It's so lonely without you. I'm not really afraid here, but I feel safer in your arms.

The way the next one was written, I had to assume it was a poem.

It hurts to think of you.

An ache radiates through my chest,

bouncing off the empty walls within.

Sometimes I pretend that you don't miss me.

I imagine you outside, soaking up the sun, and enjoying life rather than feeling the way I do.

I don't know what hurts more—the phantom pain of my missing heart—or knowing

that you're feeling the same.

Selfishly I want you here, but I know it's not the way.

I can't ask you to leave all you have and live with me in disarray.

If I let you go, will you understand? Will hate darken your heart, so bountiful and generous?

Knowing that your life is good eases the unbearable severance.

Worst poem ever written! And it didn't do shit to make me feel better. I wish I could read your mind or see a billboard telling me what to do.

The letter ended with a circular pattern of scribbles that ripped through the paper. Had she been coming unhinged? Guilt eating away at her over asking me to leave the life I had here to be with her? *Don't be ridiculous, B. Where else would I want to be? If you were in my shoes . . .*

If she had been in my shoes, she'd still be alive.

I had to take a break after the ninth letter. They were getting more emotional, more detailed. She never thought I'd see them so she didn't hold back. *I'm sorry I didn't protect you, B.* I sucked down the last drops from the bottle and threw it across the room, sending shards of broken glass everywhere.

With blurry eyes that wouldn't stop leaking, I pulled another letter from the stack. This one started out differently from the rest. This one destroyed me.

Thirty-Five
Cooper

Coop,

If you're reading this, it means they got to me. If that's the case, it's finally over, no more running. No more hiding. No more fear.

I need to you to move on, Coop. Get on with your life. I know without a doubt that Madison would be perfect for you. You have so much in common.

You've always been such a great friend to me, Coop. I'm glad we didn't go through with the plan to elope. You can start fresh, have the family you've always wanted.

You and I were never meant to be more than friends. We both knew that deep down.

I'm sorry, Coop. So sorry.

Briley

P.S. My favorite memory of you was the $9^{th}/10^{th}$ grade class trip. The note we passed back and forth that Mrs. Marsh took up to the front and read aloud. Remember? Don't forget me, Coop.

"What the fuck?" I threw the letter down, hearing a clank when the envelope hit the floor. Inside was a gold key.

I squeezed the key in my hand, feeling its jagged edges cutting into my palm. The pain was nothing compared to the black death-grip her words had on me. How could she have left me with that? None of it made sense. She wanted me to move on with the woman she hated the most? She was a terrible liar, and her words made no sense. *"I'm glad we didn't go through with the plan to elope."* What the fuck, B? I was drunk, but not so drunk that I couldn't remember the truth. We'd never planned to elope.

Slamming the key down on the coffee table, I rubbed the back of my neck. It was too much for any man to take. I spotted a half empty bottle of Jack Daniels across the room on a small table. Next to it sat a photo of Briley and me on the beach. She was on my back, her chin near my shoulder, her face lit up with a wide grin. I remembered making her laugh right before the self timer went off and took the picture. She had it framed in silver to match the lamp. Her feminine touches were scattered throughout our home and, although I wouldn't change it, being surrounded by her memory now was hard.

Making my way to the table, I picked up the picture and the bottle of Jack. I unscrewed the cap, pressed it to my lips, and gulped the liquid that would soon take the edge off my pain. Holding the picture tightly against my chest, I took another long swig.

When the numbness took over, I crashed down onto the couch, going over her last written words to me. Not a poem, not a confirmation of how much she loved me, but a fucking *move on* letter. Had I not known her as well as I thought? Darkness finally enveloped me and I gave in to it, slipping in and out of consciousness.

When I was awake, I talked to her as if she were in the room with me.

"Mrs. Marsh? *That's* your favorite memory, B?" My emotions battled, tears pooling but not spilling over due to the rage that reined them in. I thought she loved me as much as I loved her? *She did. No one could fake that.* "What waz-zo special about being hu-mil-i-ated . . . in front of . . . everyone when she read that letter . . . out loud?" My words slurred as I talked to Briley's ghost. Not that I could feel her presence, but I believed she could hear me. Maybe she'd eventually haunt me if I talked to her enough, taunted her.

"Come at me, B! Tell me what the hell you're trying to say!"

Unable to keep the room from spinning, I closed my eyes and passed out.

***

Just like my other alcohol binges, I woke up in an odd place, my body contorted in an uncomfortable position. My head throbbed as expected, but the pain in my neck needed attention first. I'd fallen asleep on the couch with my head dangling over the side. It took a while to sit up and steady myself before I could walk to the kitchen for Motrin.

"Damn!" I yelled when a sharp pain gripped my right foot. Hopping to the wall, I leaned against it and searched for the source of discomfort. A shard of glass, now covered in blood, was stuck in my heel. *What the hell?*

It was too slippery with blood to get a grip, so I pulled off my shirt and used the material to yank it out. I looked around the living room. Broken glass and trash were everywhere. I followed a trail of empty liquor bottles and sheets of paper to the coffee table where a stack of unopened envelopes waited. I remembered reading Briley's letters but hadn't remembered what they said, only that one of them had upset me.

Hobbling toward the couch, I found the last letter I'd read. She had suggested that Madison and I were perfect for each other and recalled a memory from her freshman year in high school. None of it made any fucking sense. Had they made her write those words? Why? Blood dripped from my heel onto the floor. I'd had my leg crossed over my knee so the blood made a faint splattering noise when it hit the tile. I watched, fascinated for a moment until I noticed the key peeking out from under the coffee table.

Like a tingling sensation in your head just before lightning hit, I got it. A jumble of things happened at once. Thoughts rushed to my fuzzy, intoxicated brain, trudging through the thick-with-poison ducts to get information where it needed to go. My heart raced with urgency to get up—sober up—enough to think straight.

Carefully stepping through the broken glass to the kitchen, I ran the tap on cold and stuck my head under the faucet, gulping at the stream to flush out my system. It felt good on my face, so I let the water flow over my hair and the back of my neck. I was still drunk, but I felt more alert and able to think a little more clearly. Before leaving the kitchen, I started a pot of coffee and led my mind back to my tenth grade year.

I was on a bus headed to Boston with the ninth and tenth grade class. Briley and I were bored out of our minds, sitting together in the back row. We'd listened to each song on our iPods twice and needed something else to pass the time. Mrs. Marsh was in the middle of laying down the rules of the trip for the second time.

I watched Mrs. Marsh's lips form around each word as Briley scribbled something in her notebook. It was better than concentrating on the round, black mole next to her right eye or the puffy, dark half-moons under her eyes. She had the typical old school teacher hair, short and dull brown. But the worst part was her voice. Monotone with a screech, if that was possible. With every word, she sounded as if she'd die before she took in another breath. She hated teens and they hated her.

Briley never made fun of anyone. She felt sorry for heavy kids, envied the nerds for their bright futures, and even felt pity for the cheerleaders. Said they had to live their lives for others every single day, never figuring out who they really were. So it surprised me when she had ugly things to say about Mrs. Marsh. Once she said, "Mrs. Marsh is mean. Truly wicked. I overheard her telling a student teacher, 'why did you choose this career? You're going to hate these kids and this job. These kids will age you before your time. It's not too late to choose another path.' And when she called out Tina Cagle in front of the class yesterday, I knew I hated her."

Ripping the sheet of paper out, Briley handed it to me. "Write in opposites in case she takes it up," she said.

Dammit, that's it! Briley mentioned Mrs. Marsh so I would remember the way we'd written such ugly things about her. Briley had written that Mrs. Marsh had a hidden beauty and that she was her favorite teacher.

I limped to the living room—water dripping down the sides of my face and back of my neck—and snatched up Briley's letter. This time, I read it slowly, translating it the way she'd meant for me to. For once in my life I was grateful for her silly games.

Coop,

If you're reading this, it means they got to me. If that's the case, it's finally over, no more running. No more hiding. No more fear. (Be careful?)

I need to you to move on, Coop. Get on with your life. (Don't give up.) *I know without a doubt that Madison would be perfect for you. You have so much in common.* (I knew she hated Madison. She picked her as a trigger, but I was too drunk, too depressed to catch it.)

You've always been such a great friend to me, Coop. I'm glad we didn't go through with the plan to elope so now you can start fresh. (We never planned to elope. Another trigger for the dumb ass just in case.) Smart move, B.

You and I were never meant to be more than friends. We both knew that. (She loves me . . . loved me.)

I'm sorry Coop. So sorry. I know "You-Loved-Me"
Briley

Why did she go through all the trouble to write the note in opposites? It's not like the mob had anything against *me*. They got what they wanted, wiping out the entire Paciello name. And the woman I loved. My tears dripped down onto the paper, smearing the ink that spelled out her name. I set it down so I wouldn't destroy one of the last things I had from her.

I had no bad blood with those monsters and since Briley and I never married, I wasn't connected to her in any way that would make them come after me. So why was she being so secretive? Why couldn't she just tell me she loved me? Maybe they were after me and wanted to wipe out anyone close to her or anyone who knew about them. Too bad they wouldn't get any pleasure out of killing me. I didn't have anything to lose or anything left to live for.

I poured a cup of strong, black coffee, sipping the brew too quickly and scalding the roof of my mouth. Appreciating the burn, I took another sip, feeling it torture my throat and insides. I was becoming addicted to pain—anything to mask the heartache.

"Fuck, B!" I set the cup down and fisted my wet hair. "What were you trying to tell me? Why wouldn't you let me come with you? I could've protected you. I—" My words came out in sobs as I hit the floor on my knees, begging her to give me answers or to change what had happened. "I can't do this. Where the hell am I supposed to go from here? Come back to me! Talk to me. I'd go to the depths of hell if it meant one more touch, one last glimpse of you."

Sliding the key out of my pocket, I turned it over in my hand, finding the flawed, sharp edge that had cut into my palm earlier. Leaning against the cabinets, I dug into the wood, carving the numbers as I repeated our childish phrase, "One-four-three."

Just as I finished, the key slipped from my grip and dropped to the floor next to the last letter I had read. Tear-soaked eyes blurred my vision, but I was able to see what I was searching for. *"You-Loved-Me"* The opposite would've been "I-loved-you."

There was nothing left for me here and I'd get revenge, ending the lives of every one of the bastards that took Briley away from me . . . as soon as I found out what this key was for. I had to know if there was something else she had left behind.

There was no number on the key indicating which safe deposit box it opened. Since we'd just been on a similar journey, I hoped she'd make it easier on me. I assumed she would've used one of the two banks that held the uncovered secrets we'd found. I'd have to start there. But which box? I'd have to try each one.

***

As soon as L & M Bank & Trust opened, I stalked through the doors and convinced the bank manager to let me in the vault. I'd been prepared to choke her on the spot and break in myself. Surprisingly, she didn't fight me or ask questions. It was as if she expected my visit.

"Thanks," I hissed as she opened the door. She stepped out, leaving me alone in the room to wonder which box the key opened. My eyes grazed over each box, the numbers descending from left to right, top to bottom. First I tried her favorite number with no luck. Next I tried her high school basketball number without success. Finally I tried one-forty-three.

Damn it!

"I love you. You love me. You loved me," I chanted under my breath. "You loved me . . ." *If I love you is 1-4-3, you loved me would be,* "Three- five . . . TWO," I shouted the last number into the empty room. It was a long shot, but I found box number three-fifty-two and slid the key in, slowly turning it to the left. Inch by inch it turned until the tiny door swung open.

I pulled the long box out of its chamber and set it on the table. It took forever to open, though. I knew that whatever was inside was the last of Briley Sheffield. The last of everything. A lone manila envelope rested inside. What was it with these stupid manila envelopes? I had hoped it would be something of hers I could hold, something that carried her scent, or a voice recording I could listen to over and over again.

Unfolding the gold tabs, I spilled the contents of the envelope onto the table. Inside was a passport and a small piece of paper with a phone number. I opened the passport to see my own mug in the front flap. My picture but not my name. It was similar, but not mine.

Connor Stermann.

Thirty-Six
Cooper

Dialing a number repeatedly was something I hadn't done in years. It was similar to trying your hand at winning concert tickets on the radio, but substitute the excitement with frustration. No one answered and the voice mailbox apparently hadn't been set up, according to the automated response system.

Pacing the floor, I dialed again and again, wondering why Briley would leave this number for me to find. Nothing made sense anymore. Had she planned a trip for us? *No, so why the name change on the passport?* Maybe she had planned for me to join her all along? I was too late. I'd missed a clue somewhere along the way. I was too late and now she was gone.

This time I had to search for something to throw across the room. I'd broken every empty liquor bottle, so I picked up a framed picture and readied my arm to hurl it at the wall. But something stopped me. It was empty.

Racking my brain, I couldn't remember what had been inside, but it sure as hell hadn't been empty. I set it back down amongst the trio of pewter frames and tried to imagine what had been in its place. One frame held a picture of Briley and I on the beach at sunset, and the other was the two of us—sitting on a porch swing with popsicles—we were kids. I remembered then, Briley framing one of our engagement photos. Of all the perfect poses, she'd picked a candid to frame.

The photographer had been changing her lens when one of us had said something—I couldn't remember what now—that made us laugh. We were lying down on a blanket in the grass, under a tree. Briley's head had been on my stomach and, when I started to laugh, her head bounced. It was a comedy of events, her laughing from the effect, me laughing at her laughter.

Instead of lobbing the empty frame across the room, I held it, enjoying the memory of that day, despite the agonizing pain it caused. But I wouldn't let Briley's memory die. I'd rather be gutted, remembering her than forget and feel nothing. Only one thing interfered with my moment . . . who the hell had gotten into my house and taken the picture?

***

On Tuesday night, Madison brought dinner. I had no intention of letting her in or eating her food, but I decided to be polite.

"Thank you," I deadpanned.

She placed the dish in my hands and I took it, keeping my gaze fixed on a piece of lint that was clinging to her left shoulder. *Might want to leave while you still can, little bastard.*

"I can understand that." I lost track of how long I'd been standing there, zoning out while she'd been rambling on and on about something. "It's so sad what happened to Briley. I know things weren't good with us in the end, but she didn't deserve to die like that. I just wish—"

When she mentioned Briley's name and how sad she was, I snapped. Madison must've seen the rage in my eyes as her own widened and she took a step back. I couldn't say I was sorry that I scared her. If that was what it took to make her go away, then so be it. I wasn't in the mood for company anyway, and I sure as fuck wasn't in the mood for her crap. I growled and slammed the door. Realizing I was still holding her dish, I stomped it to the kitchen and found a spot in the fridge amongst the others. It would probably grow mold in there, though. I wasn't eating it.

***

An hour later the doorbell rang. *Fucking hell.* I'd had enough liquor to calm down but not enough to deal with Madison again. Hell, there wasn't enough liquor on the planet to make her tolerable. It was too bad, really. She was a beautiful woman and nice enough when I'd first gotten to know her. But the way she'd treated Briley, and her obsessive behavior, had me wanting to hide behind the sofa.

I peeked around the corner so I could see who was at the door without being spotted. Satisfied it wasn't Madison, I opened the door.

My sister, Carleigh, reached up and placed her palm on my cheek. No words were spoken as we stood there. Just when I thought it was too much to handle, she pushed past me and walked into the living room. Her gait wasn't sassy as if she thought she was all that and a bag of chips, but no one ever doubted she was a take charge kind of woman.

"Mom was right," she sighed, picking up all the trash she could fit in her arms before heading to the kitchen. "This place is filthy."

I made my way to the couch, settled myself in, and lifted a bottle of Jack Daniels to my lips. Before the liquid reached my tongue, though, Carleigh jerked it from my grasp, some of it sloshing out onto my shirt.

I bit my tongue, trying not to unleash the hell I wanted to verbally dump on her, but there was no hiding the anger in my eyes.

"I'll give it back to you in a minute." She perched herself on the coffee table in front of me and rested her hand on my knee. "I wanted to come by and see how you were holding up." She shook her head as if she'd said something stupid. "I know you're in pain, Coop, and you will be for a long time. But you can't live like this. You're going to kill yourself. Have you eaten anything today?"

I didn't speak. Since Briley's death, a heavy fog clouded my vision and made the air so thick I found it difficult to breathe at times. I noticed how everyone else went along with life while I was trapped in a nightmare. My sister's eyes revealed the sorrow she felt for me, but they still sparked with life. While for me, nothing made sense. It never would again.

"Coop, did you hear me?" she asked. "When's the last time you've had anything to eat?" She looked around the room, not missing a beat when she noticed the empty chip bags. "And I mean *real* food."

I watched her face, then lowered my gaze to her hand that was now annoyingly rubbing over my knee in a circular pattern. Over and over again, she made the circle. I attempted to move her hand, but she gripped both of mine in her firm grasp.

I tried without much effort to pull away. "Car, stop. I'm fine."

"You stop," she argued. "You're obviously not fine, and I doubt you've eaten anything substantial in who knows when." She popped up from her spot on the coffee table and stalked into the kitchen. When she returned, she handed me a sandwich and demanded I take a bite.

The bite was an effort and the mouthful rested inside of my cheek like a stubborn kid refusing to swallow a dreaded vegetable. I didn't have enough energy to chew or entertain my sister's need to care for me. But I did chew, and eventually swallow because, dammit, I wanted my liquor bottle back.

Carleigh flipped the channels until she found a game on ESPN. It was a repeat of this season's opener, Los Angeles Lakers and Boston Celtics. She zipped through the house, picking up after me and wiping things down as she went. I never understood how girls did that, looking like tornadoes when they cleaned. Around halftime, I heard the hum of the dishwasher. Then my sister sat beside me and glanced at the bottle of Jack, still in the spot where she had left it for me after I'd finished my sandwich.

Of all the times to break down, this had to be the most inopportune. Sitting next to my older sister, watching the game, it started with a wet film slipping over my eyes. That film turned to moisture and moisture turned to flooding.

In total silence, she pulled me into her tiny frame and let me release some of the pain, not offering a single awkward word that wouldn't have helped anyway.

"She's gone, sis. Briley's . . . gone."

"I know, Coop. I'm sorry. I'm so sorry."

My father had never been the kind of man to tell me, "Suck it up, kid. Real men don't cry." In fact, he probably would've encouraged it if he thought it would help. But it didn't. Briley wasn't coming back, no matter how many tears I shed. The pressure of pain wasn't relieved by ridding my body of salt water. The only thing that came with the tears was a pounding headache.

Scrubbing my eyes with the softer part of my fists, I straightened.

"Did you take the photo out of that frame?" I nodded to the trio on the end table next to her.

She frowned. "No."

"Did Mom? Who made the slideshow for the funeral? Maybe she pulled it for that? I want it back."

"I made the slideshow, but I didn't remove any of your framed pictures, Coop. Maybe she never put one in there. Maybe she was saving it for your wedding photo?"

"You can say her name, Car." I rubbed my palms along the thigh of my jeans. "Briley. There was a picture. It was one of our engagement photos. Now it's gone."

Thirty-Seven

Cooper

It happened again. In the middle of the night I rolled over and reached for Briley. This time I felt her back to me, so I scooted up against her and wrapped my arm around her waist. Her fingers were cool—they always were—as she rubbed them along my forearm and drifted back to sleep.

When I tried to kiss the top of her head, my lips met her pillow instead. This happened every time I fell asleep in our bed, which was why I hardly slept here.

It didn't matter what time it was, there was no use trying to get back to sleep. Sometimes I woke up at two and sometimes it was closer to six. No matter, the routine was always the same. First I'd rummage through the fridge and decide there wasn't anything to satisfy me there. Next, I'd flip through the channels and curse the television for not considering the insomniacs. And finally, I'd walk to the backyard and listen to the sounds of night.

On this night—or early morning rather—I'd gotten up just in time to hear the newspaper hit the front of my door. It was usually at the end of the driveway, and I would leave it there until it weathered away enough to collect it for the trash. Since it was at the door, a look at the sports page seemed like a good idea.

But as I spilled the rolled paper out of its plastic sleeve, something fell onto my lap—an airline ticket to Atlanta, Georgia. *What the hell?* The ticket was by itself, nothing written on it, not one clue as to why someone was sending me to

Georgia. It didn't take long for me to realize what was going on. I was part of a game. A pawn, playing right into the hands of the Zerettis. Pushing the thought of a drink out of my mind, I pulled out a notepad and started making notes. For this game, I'd need to be sober, smart, and careful.

***

After a shower and a handful of pills to ease my headache, I contemplated my situation. The Zerettis weren't stupid. They had a plan. And any way I looked at it, I would be walking straight into their trap. No way in hell could I get through security packing a gun. Even if I followed protocol and checked it, there was a fifty-fifty chance I'd get caught. As a convicted felon, I'd lost my right to bear arms. Instead of avenging Briley's death as planned, the Zeretti's would make sure I rotted in prison. On the other hand, if I met them unarmed, my death would be easy and guaranteed.

A few months ago I remembered seeing something on the internet about 3D print weapons being undetectable by airport scanners. With the help of my buddy from prison, it was my best shot.

He picked up the phone on the fourth ring.

"Roland, I need a favor."

A heavy sigh preceded his answer. "Sure."

"I know, I owe you . . . double." Seemed like he owed me a few, too, but I was asking for something way out of both our leagues here.

"Shoot."

"Actually, that's what I need your help with. You heard about these new 3D print guns?"

"Sure." His pitch picked up, excitement evident in his voice. "Military's thinking about using them."

"I heard a rumor they're passing through security undetected. That true?"

"It is, but not for long," he warned. "They've already got new scanners in half a dozen major airports. Got some kinks to work out, but—"

"What're the chances of me getting through?"

"Why? What kind of mess have you gotten into this time, bro?"

Time was not on my side. As much as I appreciated all Roland had done, I couldn't trust him with my plan. Any small threat on his life and . . . hell, he'd probably spill everything for a large pepperoni pizza. No, he'd have to settle with as little information as possible. "If you get me through this, when I get back, I'll fill you in on every detail."

"Okay. Here's the deal." He spoke quickly, telling me more than I needed or wanted to know about how the 3D printer worked, who already had them, and the future of 3D printing.

"Can I get through security?" That was all I really cared about.

"With the gun, yes. Bullets, no. There are a few people making 3D bullets . . . cost about twenty-seven cents to make one, but it's difficult and takes a while. I know a guy. If you can get your hands on 3D ammo, great. If not, check them in your bag. Scatter them so they don't stand out. Maybe one in a shoe, one in a shaving kit . . ."

"Got it."

***

The gun maker wasn't what I had expected. He was tall and thin with thick black-framed glasses that didn't fit his face. He reminded me of the typical gamer sitting in front of the Xbox with a bag of Fritos and an unlimited supply of Dr. Pepper. But I had complete respect for him when he showed me the pistol.

"This is plastic?" I held the pistol, felt the weight of it—or lack thereof—in my hand, and studied the silver and black details. It was an exact replica of one I'd seen on television recently.

"Yep. It's a good one, too."

"Got any 3D ammo to go with it?"

"Nope. You won't find any either. But I've tested these and you can get at least twenty shots out of it before you see any damage."

Twenty shots. That didn't seem like enough, and what if he was exaggerating and I only got five shots before it fell apart in my hands? Or I missed. Target shooting wasn't one of my hobbies and I didn't expect to be amazing. I also didn't know how many of Zeretti's henchmen I'd be up against. "Got anything else?"

He removed another gun out of a metal case, pulled back the slide, checking for ammunition, and handed it to me. "This is the best I've got, but it'll cost ya. Browning 1911 .45. It can take six hundred shots minimum."

The gun felt good in my hands as I gripped it, then turned it over in my palm to study the details. It was heavier, even though it was made from the same materials. It wasn't as pretty as the smaller gun, but it gave me more confidence about being able to blow the heads off the bastards I was about to face. The reality hit me and my voice cracked when I asked, "It's powerful?"

He looked at me like I had three heads before leading me through the back door behind his warehouse. There was a target set up against a wooden post, and he instructed me to take aim for the orange circle in the middle. I almost dropped the gun after it fired, and my ears were wrecked from the sound of the massive blast. The single shot shook my body as if a bomb had gone off next to me.

"What the hell?" I asked, pissed that he hadn't warned me about the kick.

He grinned. "Powerful enough for ya?"

Walking to the target, I saw that I had shot north of the bull's-eye, but the hole was substantial. Guess you didn't have to have good aim with one of these. *Good thing.* I could target the person next to Zeretti and drop them both with one shot. My chest vibrated as blood pumped too rapidly to the heart muscle. The weight of what was about to happen had finally gotten to me. Holding the weapon, I thought about facing my enemy for the first time. Would it be like the movies, the main dude sitting in a chair smoking a cigar while his cronies surrounded him, guns ready to take me out? I'd seen every action movie out, but not knowing what to expect, what I was walking into, I was more than freaked out.

If I arrived at a house, like I'd pictured, I'd go in at night and sneak around the back. Maybe take a day or two to feel the place out and learn all I could. But if they met me at the airport—and I assumed they would—blind folding me and shoving me into the back of a van, I'd have to be ready.

"I'll take it." He hadn't even named his price, but I was eager to get out of here. "And a box of ammo."

***

With a small bag packed, I drove to the airport, eager to get to Atlanta and find out what was going on. The most obvious scenario was the mob waiting for me. No one I knew lived in Georgia. And the way the ticket was delivered had trouble written all over it. I was ready to die, but I wasn't going out without a fight. I'd take out as many as I could first. I would make them pay for taking Briley. Having never killed anything besides a fish, I wondered how it would feel taking a man's life. At the moment the idea felt good. Vengeance wouldn't bring her back to me or take away any of the pain, but knowing I was doing anything felt like something.

Sweat beaded along my forehead as I checked a too-large suitcase packed with nonsense to help conceal the ammo scattered throughout. It was stupid, really, thinking I could hide it. If my bag was tagged and they found the ammo, they would naturally search it thoroughly and find the gun. Once they checked my record, I'd be arrested. My only hope was the assurance that it would make it through the scanner undetected as promised from some punk kid making guns out of a metal warehouse.

Walking through security, I felt like a criminal. My back was soaked with perspiration and I probably wiped my forehead too many times, a clear and very public indication of how nervous I was. Finally I made it through security with my ticket and false passport, then boarded the plane. I took an aisle seat and pushed my ear buds in so the businessman next to me wasn't tempted to start a conversation. I needed to think, plan, even though my mind raced in every direction, unable to focus on anything realistic. The truth hovered at the edge, taunting me to accept the fact . . . I was a dead man.

Once we were in the air, the flight attendant took drink orders. I slipped her a bill, and she set me up with four mini bottles of Jack Daniels and a coke over ice. I drank down enough of the coke to fit two of the bottles in. Draining the drink in one gulp, I poured the remaining two bottles over ice and sipped on it until we were descending in Georgia.

Before I had left Tampa, I purchased a disposable phone to make the call. I hadn't given a lot of thought as to why I needed one, but wanted to cover my bases in case this was some kind of set up that landed me back in the slammer. Pulling out the cheap flip phone, I dialed the number that was left for me.

After two rings, a modified voice—male?—answered. "Connor Stermann?"

"Yes," I answered, my voice flat.

"Terminal D. Gate 22." Then the line went dead.

I made the trek to Terminal D, watching each face that looked my way, wondering how many eyes were on me without my knowledge. Funny how a dose of fear will make you appreciate your life. My world was shit without Briley, but I still had to fight. I knew they wouldn't take me out in plain sight, but I couldn't shake the nerves. Fuck, why had I agreed to this? I should've demanded answers instead of letting someone control my every move. The only thing that kept me moving forward, walking straight into their trap was thinking about what they took from me and letting that rage brew.

Once in the gate, I waited for my phone to ring or for someone to approach me with what to do next. Glancing around, I noticed couples holding hands, suits typing away on their iPads, and families busying their kids with handheld games, but no one looked at me suspiciously or said a word to me.

Finally, I approached the counter. A female attendant with cropped black hair peeked up from her computer screen. "Can I help you?"

"I'm not sure. Do you have anything here for me? Coop— Connor Ster . . ." Shit, what was it? I pulled out my passport and handed it to her.

"Connor Stermann," she said, reading the name. She smiled condescendingly. Probably thought I was mental. "I do." She fished around and pulled out a boarding pass. After looking it over, she handed it to me. "We'll be boarding in about twenty minutes."

I took the ticket and looked at the screen behind her. *Flight 2310 departing to Dallas. On Time.* "Thanks."

Two more Jack and Coke's and a bag of peanuts got me through the flight to Dallas. My hands were shaky from the lack of protein—and I was man enough to admit—also from fear of what, or who, I'd meet when I stepped off the plane.

I was the last one to exit, my heart rate picking up speed as I came out of the jet way and rounded the corner. The lobby was empty except for two female flight attendants arguing over something. Another dead end. I pulled out my phone, growing frustrated by this game, and dialed the number.

As soon as I heard the line click, I growled, "What the fuck is going on, coward. Take me—"

A loud beep interrupted my rant. "C10," the robotic voice said before ending the call.

"Sure. Another gate, another flight. Why not, motherfucker. " I mumbled to no one before walking toward the designated gate. It was the same game at C10. The flight attendant had another ticket for me behind the counter and it was all I could do not to take out all my frustrations on her.

A ditzy blonde who dropped everything she touched gave me a quirky smile, apologizing for her state. "I'm sorry, it's one of those days, you know?" She giggled and bobbed her head from side to side. "Like when you go to grab a pen and fling it across the room."

It took everything in me not to suck in an exasperated breath and close my eyes, hoping she'd disappear. "Yep. It's one of those days." *You have no idea.*

"Here it is." She flashed a quirky grin and handed me the ticket. Business or pleasure?" she asked.

"Business." *But hopefully a little pleasure if God is on my side.*

She shifted her weight to one hip and smirked. "Well, it's beautiful there. I hope you have *some* time to enjoy it."

Looking down at the ticket I saw that I was headed to Mexico. *Perfect.*

I had twenty-five minutes to sit and contemplate whether or not to get on the flight. Nothing good would come out of me going to Mexico. I might take out a few of them before they killed me, but the crime rate was so high, I had no doubt they could get away with murder . . . my murder. My only hope was that I'd go out fighting, and go quickly.

At the last minute I made the choice to get on the plane. Exhausted, hungry, and terrified of what I was walking into served up a jumble of emotions. I thought about my parents and how they'd react when they saw the story on the news. I wondered how my sister would take it and if she would tell my little nieces about me or if by the time they were grown I would be a distant memory. The whole thing made my stomach churn and the flight seemed to last forever.

The airport in Mexico was a nightmare. Being jerked around by the Zerettis—catching plane after plane—was bad enough. Now I was in a Godforsaken airport, standing in line amongst a sea of people trying to get through customs and retrieve their baggage. *Motherfuck.* As if I wasn't out of my mind already, I had to worry about the 3D gun again. If they searched my bag I was fucked. The only thing worse than getting busted in the states would be spending the rest of my life in a Mexican prison. I couldn't spend the rest of my life locked up. It was too quiet and there were too many demons waiting to devour my sanity. Taking stock of my surroundings, I wondered how I could get out of it. I hadn't come all this way to not to get the revenge due me. God may not care what happened to me, but Briley deserved justice and if God was who everyone said he was, he was in agreement with me. *If you can hear me,* I offered a silent prayer. *Get me through this. Let me avenge Briley's death.*

Two steps forward in the line with a screaming toddler in front of me, staring me down like he was begging me to help him escape his mother's grip. The room was too warm, too loud, too stale. I rubbed the back of my neck and took another step forward. Why had the Zerettis gone to so much trouble to get me here? It seemed to me like it would've been easier to rig my truck with a bomb or throw a sack over my head, chain bricks to my feet, and throw me in the water. Wasn't that classic mob? Flying me from city to city until I was finally out of the country seemed like a lot of hassle. And why would Italians send me to Mexico?

"Excuse me, sir?" Someone tapped on my shoulder and I jumped before turning to see a squatty little man in a Hawaiian shirt. "The line is moving."

Shit. I'd been so deep in thought, there was a large gap between me and mom-with-screaming-toddler. I closed the space, realizing I was now third in line. I tried not to look as nervous as I felt, finding a teenagers backpack to focus on. She must've had twenty different pins with angsty comments.

It was my turn. I stepped up to the counter and a petite woman lacking any personality stuck out her hand. I placed my passport in her palm and waited. No smile, no greeting. The lady glanced at my passport, studied my face longer than was comfortable, and then looked at her computer. My stomach knotted, and I fought the urge to wipe the sweat from my brow.

Keep cool.

Heart slamming against my chest, I waited for her to alert security. Instead, she scribbled something in my passport, slid it across the counter, and called for the next in line. Just like that, I was through and in the clear. Now I could concentrate on what would happen when I faced my enemy. If I could get into a cab, I could get to my gun and load it. I dialed the number, wanting to get the next set of instructions, but the call wouldn't go through. Frustrated, I clenched my fists and sucked in slow, deep breaths of the warm, stale air.

My bag was at the end of the row of lined up suitcases. Gripping the handle, it rolled behind me as I strode forward, following a sea of people with destinations. Personally, I had no clue where I was headed. With no instructions, my only objective was getting to my weapon and finding a drink.

Several people stood in front of the doors leading outside, holding signs. They were grouped together according to which resort they worked for and had matching uniforms. I read each sign until I found the name Connor Stermann written neatly on a square white sign. The man holding it wore white pants and a teal shirt. He was a big dude with dark skin and a scar along his chin. He had to be one of Zerettis men. Maybe he had a picture of me, or maybe it was the way I stopped and studied my alias on his sign. Either way, he knew it was me when I made eye contact. He looked rough, but if I could keep him from getting to a weapon, I could take him. Before I could unzip my bag and retrieve my gun, he was beside me.

"Señor Ster-man?" He had trouble pronouncing the name. I wondered if it was because he knew it wasn't my real name.

"That's me." I gripped the handle of my bag tighter as he reached for it. "I've got it."

"With me, señor." He turned and walked toward the line of cars and busses, never looking back to see if I was following. He kept a fast pace, and I bumped into a few people trying keep up. Finally, he stopped at a black car with tinted windows and popped the trunk.

"Just a minute." I held up a finger, squatted down, and began to unzip my suitcase.

"No. No." He shook his head and gestured to the trunk.

I only had time to pocket three bullets before he began tugging at my bag. At the last minute, I gripped the handle of the gun and moved it from the luggage to my backpack. While he loaded the suitcase into the trunk, I managed to get the ammunition loaded, but I kept my hand on the gun inside the bag.

This was it. I'd slide in next to the bastard that took Briley from me. I could only imagine what he had planned. He sure as hell went through a lot of trouble to make sure no one would know where I was. Part of me wanted to question him before I blew his head off, try to figure out what kind of monster would take the life of an innocent just to check it off his list. The larger part didn't give a fuck about his sick mind. The only thing I cared about was being face to face with the motherfucker that ended Briley's life and seeing the fear in his eyes before I took his.

My nostrils flared as I gulped a few breaths of courage before gripping the handle of the car door and swinging it open. There was no one inside. A cool blast of air laced heavily with the smell of air freshener assaulted me. The driver slipped in behind the wheel and didn't say a word as he pulled away from the curb. I'd taken Spanish four years in high school but didn't remember much. I knew how to ask his name and where he lived, but couldn't remember how to ask where we were going. I tried anyway.

"Donde es?" I was pretty sure that meant "where is it," but hopefully he'd give me a break.

He shrugged his shoulder, kept his eyes forward, and swerved through traffic. We passed through a poverty stricken part of town where the houses were falling apart, roofs caving in. Children, filthy with layers of dirt, were sitting on front porches or drawing in the dirt with sticks. I'd never seen anything like it before.

Forty minutes later, the driver pulled onto a dirt road. Overgrown foliage hugged each side of the road, which made me assume we were going somewhere very secluded. A place so far from the public that no one would find the large mansion, paid for by drugs probably sold to children. The bitch of it was, it was also far enough away that no one would ever find my body. *Or his. Fuck, find your balls.* My nerves were getting the best of me. I'd never killed anyone before. Hell, I'd never killed much more than a spider. And although I had nothing left to live for, the fear of death was present and all consuming.

The air in the car was arctic, yet sweat dripped beaded my forehead and trickled down my back. My heart raced as I chewed on my bottom lip. What was I thinking? I could take anyone in a fist fight, but I felt sure they hadn't gone this far to put me in the cage with someone. This wasn't the movies. I'd be outnumbered and shot to death. If I was lucky. More likely, they'd cut me up just for fun. It was the kind of monsters they were. Who else would take the life of an innocent girl?

I couldn't do this sober. Searching through my bag, I prayed I was smart enough to stash one from the plane. No such luck. I got the driver's attention and made a drinking motion. "Drink?"

His blank eyes glanced at me through the rearview mirror.

I rubbed my throat. "Bar. Saloon." He shook his head, clearly not understanding what I was after. "Tequila?"

His eyes lit then. "Ah, Tequila!" He pulled a bottle from under the seat and reached back to hand it to me.

Seriously? Normally I would've hesitated drinking from a mystery bottle, given by a stranger who didn't speak my language. But I was desperate. I half smiled and took the bottle. There wasn't much left.

"Gracias," I breathed, unscrewing the cap and swallowing the contents.

The car finally stopped in front of a small stucco villa. Not at all what the movies portrayed of a mobster or drug lord's home. The front porch was absent of the security guards I'd expected, but the small cameras on each corner of the house didn't go unnoticed. Through the trees, I saw a glimpse of turquoise water behind the villa. Briley would've loved that view.

Briley's not here, I reminded myself. And it was because of these bastards. The anger brewed to a full boil inside my chest and I let the lust of killing the old man and his shitty sheep consume me.

Not wanting to waste any more time, I sucked in a deep breath, palmed the .45, and swung the car door open. I didn't bother shutting it behind me, instead I concentrated on keeping my finger on the metal guard around the trigger so I wouldn't shoot the first lizard that skidded across the walkway. Heart pumping, nerve endings sizzling on high alert, I made my way to the door.

"Señor!" The driver shouted, scaring the hell out of me. He had pulled my bag from the trunk and was jogging toward me. Thank God I hadn't rested my finger on the trigger. My finger jerked on the metal rim at least four times in panic before I realized who he was and what he was doing. *Fuck, man, I nearly shot you to shit.*

"Gracias." I nodded for him to drop the bag. His eyes widened when he saw the gun in my hand. He dropped the bag onto the dirt road where he stood and backed up slowly, his hands in the air until he reached the driver's side. I hoped he wouldn't peel away, making too much noise, but of course he did. Not that the Zerettis hadn't already seen me on camera. They were expecting me after all. In hindsight I wished that I had kept the gun concealed and kept my element of surprise. But like I said, this was my first mission of revenge. My first time using a gun on something other than a cardboard target.

Sucking in a deep breath, I reached for the doorbell but pulled my hand away at the last minute. There was no need for formalities. They were inside waiting to kill me. I was here to destroy them.

Get it done.

Another dose of oxygen and a crack of my neck on the right side, and I was as ready as I would ever be. Once I double checked that the safety was off, I pulled the slide back to engage a bullet. Wishing I had loaded more than three, I gripped the doorknob, turned it until it clicked, and swung the door open. A cross breeze was the only thing that greeted me.

I'd seen enough movies to know they were playing on my fear. It was a game where every move was calculated, pushing and playing with my sanity as they inched me closer to death. By the time I was face to face with one of the Zerettis, they'd have me so shaken with fear, it would be no trouble to gain complete control over me.

What they didn't take into account was the big ass gun I'd gotten past security and the fact that I had nothing to lose.

Stepping inside, I didn't see anyone at first. Movement from the sheer fabric covering the windows drew my attention, but it was only the breeze blowing from the open windows. Before moving forward, I took in the simple surroundings. I'm not sure what I expected—framed pictures of victims or an assortment of weapons hanging on the walls—but this place didn't live up to my imagination at all. Cream walls, large wooden beams across the ceiling, and a few colorful paintings along the wall suggested a vacation home rather than a place of torture.

Suddenly, I caught a glimpse of someone coming toward me from another room, and I readied my weapon. But when my eyes finally focused on the person closing in, my legs buckled and I went down on my knees.

Thirty-Eight

Briley

I wasn't sure how Cooper would react to seeing me . . . alive and well. I'd planned our reunion over and over in my head. Sometimes he was glad to see me, and other times I imagined him so mad he couldn't stand the sight of me. I couldn't blame him, but prayed he would forgive me in time. In my mind, the way I was determined for that moment to go down, we would stand perfectly still, frozen in the moment as we took each other in. But now that the time was here and he stood in front of me, I crumbled. Words wouldn't form, space and time ceased to exist, and a force beyond my control pulled me toward him. Never in my life had I needed to feel his arms around me as much as I did in that moment.

Before I reached him, he dropped to his knees. I followed his movement and wrapped my arms around his neck at the same time he closed his arms around my body. Finally, my dream became reality and I felt him. *Strong.* Smelled him. *Fall.* Heard him. *Shaky Breath.* His scent and the way his arms felt snaked around me was like medication for my dying soul. In that moment I felt my heart begin to heal and the tears wash away the pain clouding my vision.

"Briley?" He seemed to be choking on his words. The sound of his broken voice shattered me. "How? I don't understand." I felt his breath on my neck as he spoke. "Are you okay?" He stroked my hair and tried with little effort to pull back, but I tightened my grip. I couldn't let him go. Not yet. I knew for a fact I'd lose my mind if he let me go. I needed more nourishment to survive the heartache of breaking his.

"Are you alone?" He pulled back with force this time, gripping my shoulders while he looked at me and then around the room. "Are you safe?" His eyes were filled with a crazed rage I'd never seen before. "How much time do we have?"

"No one else is here, Coop. It's just us. We're safe here." My hands reached up to cup his face. It was obvious he hadn't shaved in days and he looked run down. His bloodshot eyes belonged to an older version of Cooper. *What have I done?* His blue T-shirt was soaked with sweat and clung to him like I needed to.

Forgetting his strength, he pulled me to him again, my body slamming into his like a ragdoll. I buried my face in his neck. Although he smelled divine to my Cooper starved senses, he reeked of alcohol. "Are you sure?"

"Yes." I nodded, burying my face in his neck.

We repeated the same actions again and again until I thought he was satisfied. He'd pull away to study me, making sure the moment was real and check me for injuries, then he'd wrap me up in his arms whispering my name and stroking my hair, arms, and back. On the third round I noticed the gun.

"What's that?" Panic rose in my chest as my mind raced with all the possible reasons he had a gun. Neither of us had ever held a weapon, let alone fired one. My eyes fixated on the gun, refusing to move.

"I bought it. I thought I was walking into a trap."

"Trap?"

"I was going to kill the bastard that took you from me. I thought Zeretti mur—" He looked at the ground between us, his shoulders slumped. It was easy to see he'd been through hell and I was the reason. "We buried you." He rubbed his hands down the front of his thighs. "I mourned you."

"I'm so sorry." The tears began to fall again, my heart breaking for what I'd done to him. It was a cruel thing to fake my death, but the decision hadn't been mine. Knowing that any contact with him would've put his life in danger, it was out of my control.

"How're you alive?" He glanced up, his eyes glassy with the threat of tears.

"I didn't want to participate, Coop." My shoulders shook with grief. "I begged the Marshal to find another way. You know I would never hurt you on purpose."

He nodded, dazed and in shock. Probably that I was here, that he was here, that we were here together.

"He said I had no other options. If I wanted to be with you and save my mother, I had to do it this way."

His head tipped up slightly as if urging me to go on.

"One of the cops covering the safe house was a woman. She was nice and helped me get out of the house a few times with a disguise. It was a really good disguise, and I felt safe. Once I had been out a couple of times, I got cocky and drove farther than I was supposed to. She panicked and got Mr. No-Fun Marshal involved, telling him what we did. They took away my disguise and wouldn't let me out of the house again."

I shifted off of my knees and sat on the floor, stealing a glance at the gun next to Cooper.

"I thought I'd go crazy, Coop. At first, I thought writing to you, like you suggested, would help. But it only made me miss you more. It made me realize I couldn't live like that." I blew out a long breath, wishing that statement hadn't just come out of my mouth. Cooper was in hell thinking I was dead and I had the gall to complain about boredom. I tried to fix it. "I couldn't live without *you*." My hands were still in Cooper's. I focused on his thumbs circling my knuckles and continued, "I sunk into a depression and said something stupid to the Marshal. It was a flippant comment, but he took it seriously."

He squeezed my fingers. "What did you say?"

"I asked him to give me the car keys so I could take a drive, and maybe something about not giving a damn anymore." I couldn't lift my gaze from Cooper's hands. I didn't want to face the hurt or anger in his eyes. "I told him life wasn't worth living if it had to be this way. The Marshal stormed out, pissed. And I couldn't blame him." I shook my head, recalling the ordeal. "He's worked so hard to keep my family safe and I was an ungrateful ass."

"Baby." His voice was soft, absent of the anger I'd assumed he would possess. He lifted my chin to look in his eyes. Mine were blurry with tears, but I could see the love and gentleness in his expression. He stood and offered a hand to help me up. We made our way to the sofa, and he pulled me into his lap. "You were in a difficult situation—in hell—all alone. I can't imagine that anyone else would've reacted differently."

The position of sitting in Cooper's lap made it difficult to look at him while we talked, but I loved the feeling of being so close to him so I didn't budge. "The next day, the Marshal brought doughnuts and coffee. The first thing he said when I opened the door was, 'you don't like it here? I guess it's time to die.' He scared the hell out of me, so I guess I valued my life more than I thought." I let out a nervous chuckle.

Cooper smiled with only half of his mouth. It was clear he needed answers before he could fully relax. Thankfully, he wasn't angry like I had anticipated. Maybe more nervous or curious. Either way, neither of us could keep our hands off each other. I felt two of his fingers slide across my cheek, chin, and down my throat. I held his fingers with one hand while I traced each of his knuckles, making my way to his hand and forearm.

"He—the Marshal—came up with a plan to fake my death. He said it was the only way besides my actual death to finally close this case." I risked a glance at Cooper, who seemed to be reliving the events of my death.

"I—" He worked his bottom lip between his teeth. On a heavy sigh, he turned his face away from me and studied something on the floor.

"I can't imagine what you went through, Coop." I reached up and rested a hand on his cheek. When he looked at me—his eyes bloodshot and vacant, the vibrant green now muted—I realized how much this whole scheme had damaged him. My stomach knotted. "I'm sorry. I'm so very sorry."

I pulled my legs up and curled into a ball on his lap, resting my head against his chest. His heartbeat was chaotic, and I wondered what he was thinking and feeling. He had to be furious with me after such a betrayal.

It was a great effort to speak, my words forced out around the huge lump in my throat. "Please say something . . . anything." I pulled my head off his chest, ready to face his anger. It was better than silence. "I know you're mad at me, and it's completely justified. But you have to understand, I only had two options: never see you again or go along with the Marshal's plan and . . ." My fingers wrapped around the hem of my shirt, squeezing tight to distract myself from sobbing the rest of my plea. "I didn't know what to do. They were never going to stop looking for me. The Marshal said this would be the best way. If they think I'm dead, it's over. Done."

"I love you, B, and I'm not mad at *you*. It's just a lot to process. When they told me you were dead, I didn't believe it. I knew it was part of the Marshal's plan. But he had dental records, he had so much proof." He faded into a whisper, and I had to strain to make out the words. "I talked to your ghost every day . . . and your mom . . ."

When I heard the word *mom* and thought about the fragile, sweet lady who'd raised me with more love than I deserved, I lost it. Head in hands, I cried that ugly, loud, sobbing, snot-and-hiccups-included cry. Cooper held me as I grieved the woman I may never see again and wept over the pain I'd caused her.

"You can—go back," I said between gulps of air and with shoulders shaking. "Your tracks were covered. No one will know you were here. You don't have to leave your family."

Although I'd imagined every negative scenario, every reaction possible, I hadn't allowed myself to indulge the thought of him staying with me. I had perfected the art of building walls and protecting myself, so it was easier to assume he would leave and go back to his family, friends, the company he'd worked so hard to grow . . . home. In the evenings, I had rehearsed how the reunion would go.

"You're alive?" His eyes wide, incredulous.

"Yes. It was the only way, Cooper. I couldn't live without you, and this way I don't have to."

"I mourned you and then I moved on." His hands up in the air. *"I can't do this."*

He would grab a chunk of his hair and act like he was conflicted, but the outcome was always the same: he left.

He squeezed me so tightly to his body, the little air I was getting between sobs now completely extinguished. My lungs burned for more air. He released me seconds before I would have been forced to push away from him.

"I'm staying." His eyes locked on mine as if to solidify his statement. His strong hands cupped my face as he repeated, "I'm staying." My eyelids slowly closed as he leaned in and pressed his lips against my forehead. His breath whispered against my skin, "This was the plan, B. Remember?" He lowered his forehead to mine. "I never should've let you go alone."

A final tear slipped down my cheek, leaving its mark on Cooper's jeans. He was staying, and I was soaring. My body didn't know how to deal with the news. The love of my life was willing to give up everything to be with me. Everything hurt inside. My heart was so full from the amount of love between us, but I could also feel the fractures forking through my chest knowing he was giving up so much. In the end though, I was needy and it consumed the guilt like a wildfire.

Cooper's gentle strokes on the back of my head ceased, and he pressed his lips firmly to my forehead, holding me there for a few beats. My hands wanted to be everywhere at once, greedily covering every inch of the man I'd been deprived of for too long. Cooper seemed to be in the same state of mind—desperation, all-consuming.

He kissed my face in small pecks. Not romantically, but the way a parent kisses a child—or the way someone would kiss after finding out they were alive—covering every inch to make sure they were real. But every touch received sent an erotic signal to my nerve endings. By the time he reached my throat—his soft lips now gentle on my skin, seducing every fiber of my being—I felt like a block of silver being held at the hottest point, molten and shimmering in the heat.

With a lift of his head, Cooper's eyes, dark with desire, locked with mine. The manic rhythm of my heartbeat caught up with my hunger and pumped loudly in my ears. I had to remind myself to breathe as his fingers, pushing a strand of hair away, brushed across my shoulder.

He tracked the movement as I licked my lips, then his gaze lifted to my eyes for a moment before falling to my lips again. The anticipation was grueling, almost more than I could handle. I had to have his mouth, his hands, his anything—everything. *Now.*

Feather soft touches stroked my arms as he searched my eyes. He seemed to be asking for permission to take what already belonged to him. A slight nod was all it took. At the same time his fingers speared into my hair, his mouth crushed down on mine. Our tongues met in a duel, in which both of us won. His lips were punishing and desperate and I moaned in pleasure.

I had already covered every inch of him that I could reach in my awkward position on his lap and wanted more. I tried to reach between us to lift up his shirt. Wrong angle. Our bodies were physically too close, but not close enough in the ways we both craved.

"Can . . . we . . ." I tried to get the words out between kisses.

Cooper scooped me into his arms, refusing to let our lips part as he carried me. "Bedroom." It was more of a statement than a question, even though I knew he didn't know the layout of the tiny villa.

I lifted my arm and pointed down the hall. There were only two doors, the bedroom and a small hall bathroom. Both were open and he had no trouble finding the space. He was careful not to toss me onto the bed, instead depositing me so my head rested just below the pillows. He crawled over me and cupped my face in his hands as he deepened the kiss. He slipped his arms under my shoulders and I gripped his biceps. Both of us held on tightly, trying to pull our bodies closer. Every touch, every kiss, felt like the first, yet it was familiar and as necessary as electricity feeding a light bulb.

"I missed you . . . so much," I tried and failed to say without moaning.

"God, B, you have no idea." Cooper's hands were urgent on my sensitive flesh. He shoved the fabric of my tank top up along with my bra and brought his mouth down over a peaked nipple. A delicious current soared through my body. Goosebumps broke over my skin, another moan escaped my lips, and my back arched to ensure he wouldn't stop.

Reaching between us, I worked the button and zipper of his jeans, and wondered why he'd chosen something so hot in this climate, and so difficult to remove. "Shorts would've been a better choice." This wasn't the time to talk, but I was nervous and couldn't control it. "Aren't you hot? What—"

"Shh." His mouth covered mine before moving to my jaw and down my throat. "I missed your lips, your taste, your neck."

"Jeans," I panted. "Off."

"Done." Cooper stood, grasped the hem of his shirt, and pulled it over his head, tossing it to the floor. Next he lowered his jeans and boxers in one swoop, faster than I'd ever witnessed him perform the task before.

He crawled back onto the bed and helped me sit up. "I thought I lost you," he whispered as he lifted my shirt and bra over my head.

"You'll never lose me." The sadness in his eyes balanced the heady ache inside of me with reality. I hadn't been able to live without him for the short time I was away and he thought I was gone forever. Concentrating on his touch, I realized his movements were unhurried. He seemed to be savoring every moment.

As much as I wanted him to hurry, we both needed to take it slow and let the heartache mingle with the emotions of elation and desire.

"I'm never leaving you again," he whispered against my throat.

For a moment, we ignored the hunger and held each other in a firm embrace. "I love you so much, Cooper."

"I love you, too, baby." His hands began to move again. At my waist, down my hip, thigh, and back up again.

"God, I missed your hands on me." Truth was, I also missed his warmth and the weight of him on top of me. Or at least the weight he allowed. With that consent, his hands were everywhere, driving me crazy with need.

Sitting back on his knees, he scooted my shorts down my legs, tossed them aside, and sat there for a moment, admiring my body.

"So damn perfect." He hovered over me for a moment, his lustful eyes contradicting soft features and the slight pull of a smile in the corners of his mouth. It was as if he was considering whether to kiss me or say something. We had so much catching up to do, so many things to talk about, but right now I needed to be as close to him as humanly possible and I sensed he needed it too. Not just for the sex, but the healing that came with coming together in such an intimate way. Lifting up enough to slide my hand around the back of his head, I tugged him down. His lips pressed to mine softly at first, then urgent, hungry, and appreciative.

I reached between us and took his hardness in my hand, stroking until he hissed a curse word.

"I need you, B."

"I'm yours." Lifting my hips, I encouraged him to fill me. I needed it, needed him more than anything. The time we were apart was so long and torturous, I wondered if the persistent ache would ever be stilled. It was the oddest feeling of hunger and desperation mixed with sadness and happiness at the same time.

He settled between my legs and pushed in slowly but deliberately. My eyes drifted shut, back arched off the bed, and we both sucked in a sharp breath from the ecstasy. *Heaven.* My fingers dug into his shoulders, partly in pleasure, mostly to hold on to the moment. He pulled back and pushed in again, just as slowly as the first time so I felt everything. Once he picked up the pace, our bodies rocked together in a perfect rhythm. All I wanted to concentrate on was the way his skin felt as his stomach slid against mine, but my entire body was on fire, burning up from the meteor shower igniting inside. With every press of Cooper's body into mine, I needed more. Needed to be closer.

My hips came up in counterpoint to meet his every thrust. His triceps bulged as he held himself up with one arm, his other hand gliding over my breasts, down the curve of my waist, over my hip, and back up. Shivers moved along my spine as we moved together. I tried to keep my eyes open, focusing on his expression as I was pushed closer to the edge. It was a look of awe, appreciation, and raw lust.

Whispered curses and panting moans meant we were on the same wavelength, sinking together, drowning in a sea I didn't want to be saved from. Looking into his eyes as the inferno brewed to a boiling point, I knew I'd never felt more safe, treasured, and loved. He was my everything, and I'd do everything in my power to be his. I tried to breathe through the powerful shockwaves racking my body, wrapping my legs around his back as every muscle in my body clenched in ecstasy. Cooper was right behind me, burying his head in my neck as he came undone. His breath puffed against my neck as he whispered, "Briley, Briley, Briley."

He didn't move for a long time, but kept his weight from crushing me. Finally, he rolled onto his back and pulled me against his chest. Hearing his heartbeat, feeling it beneath my head felt so good, so right. I had so much to say, but the silence was good. His eyes told me everything I needed to hear at that moment.

When we were finally ready for words, Cooper spoke first. "I still can't believe this is real."

Without lifting my head from its place of comfort, I stroked a thumb across his bristly cheek. "Me either."

Thirty-Nine
Cooper

We didn't get any sleep the first night, so my body finally revolted and took ten hours from me last night. When I realized Briley wasn't next to me, I panicked. From the smell of bacon wafting through the house, I calmed and made my way to the kitchen. Briley was standing over the stove, making breakfast. It was easy to sneak up on her in this tiny house, the sound of the waves outside drowning out any other noise. Leaning against the doorframe, I watched her work in a handmade apron she must've picked up locally. Her backside was bare except for the red fabric tied around her waist and a tiny pair of white panties that barely covered her exquisite ass.

She seemed happy. Happier than I'd ever seen her actually, moving her body to a song playing on the radio. It was a sight I would've gladly watched all day if she hadn't turned around and spotted me.

"Gah!" She slapped a hand over her heart. "How long have you been standing there?"

"Not long." I chuckled.

She held the spatula in the air as I pulled her in for a good morning greeting. We ate breakfast at the small kitchen table for two and talked about trivial things like the difference in American eggs versus the ones in Mexico. Honestly, I couldn't tell the difference. We had more important things to talk about, like where were the Zerettis and would we be on the run forever, but for now we needed this time to pretend everything was normal. I don't think either of us could take the stress right now.

During our morning walk on the beach, after Briley gushed over the beauty surrounding us, the sounds of the ocean, and the aroma of the sea—both sweet and salty—she decided it was time to discuss the more pressing issues.

"A lot of things have been set up, but it's going to take some getting used to." She glanced at me quickly as if she was nervous. "Money, for example." She paused and squinted one eye as if feeling me out. "There's not much of it."

"Can I access my bank account?" I knew the answer before the question completely left my lips. How would we live off what little money Briley had collected or been given? It couldn't have been much. After I'd asked, I realized how it sounded, and I didn't want there to be a shred of doubt in her mind as to my intentions. My place was with Briley, no matter where we were or where we went. But there was no way to take it back or backpedal to make it sound better without sounding like a pushover. She needed strength behind her, not a maybe guy.

Briley shook her head but didn't turn to face me. She squatted down next to the shoreline, digging her fingers into the wet sand. What she was looking for, I had no idea.

I walked up behind her, peering over her shoulder to watch her movements. "What're you doing?"

"Watch." She waited for the water to wash over her fingers, then she dug down deep before it receded. Tiny white sand crabs scurried to bury themselves as soon as they were uncovered. "Aren't they sweet?"

"Sure." Sweet wasn't the way I would've described them. Maybe creepy. I never cared for a grouping of tiny objects crawling over each other. Ants, baby spiders, anything that showed up in a horror flick to terrorize the victim was not sweet.

"I'll find work." What could I do in Mexico? I had a vocabulary of maybe ten words. "Hell, I've always wanted to scoop ice cream. We'll open a little shop and get fat sampling all the product."

Briley rinsed her hands in the water, then stood and faced me. The smile gripping her entire face made all my worries fade away.

"I want to show you something." She took my hand in hers and hurried down the beach toward the house.

Once inside, she grabbed a jacket and car keys. I knew she was eager to get going, but the money situation was eating me up, and I needed to get some things lined up. Briley deserved a good life, even if it was in Mexico. They say *love is all you need,* but that's bullshit. I'd die happy, but we'd definitely starve to death. No, I needed to get something lined up. Surely there was manual labor opportunities out there.

"B," I smoothed my palm across her lower back, "If we plan on making a life here, I need to find work."

"I know." She gave me a soft smile, one that was meant to reassure me. She pressed a hand on my cheek, still unshaven. I was starting to look like Ryan with a man beard. The thought of him and the band stabbed at my heart.

"I've got enough to last until we find something." She perched on the edge of a chair in the living room. "Before you came here, I was alone." She lifted a hand to stop me from comforting her. "Tracie, the other Marshal was here at the beginning, but after she left I was alone. It was so quiet. My only companion was the sea, so every morning I'd walk to the edge and think. It's remarkable how freeing the quiet is. With no noise to distract, your mind is free to think clearly." She drew in a deep breath as if savoring the feeling. "Sometimes, when the tide is low, I like to go for a swim. I take my snorkeling gear and just float and watch. You'd be amazed at all I've seen in those waters!"

The pitch of her voice rose with the excitement. "The most brilliant fish and creatures, turtles, and there's a huge coral reef out there." Her arms traced a big circle. "I haven't braved swimming out to it, but once when the tide was really low, I could see the tops of it sticking out of the water, and the shadow of how wide and long it traveled."

How she thought she was relieving me of money stress was beyond me, but I loved seeing her so happy. If we could find a way to live off of that happiness, we'd be golden.

"So, here's my idea." She sucked in a gulp of air. "Snorkeling tours."

Snorkling tours?

I pursed my lips, pretending to think about it. There were so many reasons that wouldn't work, but I wasn't about to squash her excitement. So I went along with her and we drove to the marina to look at boats, Briley gushing about her plans.

The thing about Mexico, everything was a lot cheaper. Apparently the Marshal had found a way to access and close out Briley's savings account. He made it look like her mother had done it, but Mrs. Sheffield didn't even know about the account. She only knew about the checking account. We had just enough to buy a cheap boat, a license, and the necessary snorkeling gear to get started.

But my first priority, as always, was keeping Briley safe. That meant keeping her hidden. Taking tourists out to sea seemed like the worst possible way to do that.

"Baby," I took her hands in mine. "This doesn't seem to be very safe, bringing people into our lives, close to where we live."

"Cooper, there are coral reefs all over. We wouldn't take them to the ones by our place." She smirked as if I'd missed an important part of the conversation. "Those reefs are tiny compared to the others. We have aliases and we'll run the business at the marinas to get started." She shifted her weight to her right hip. "Scooping ice cream on the corner does sound wonderful, but I think this will bring more money . . . and we'll be as brown and bleached as the lovers on *The Blue Lagoon.*"

It did sound fun, and maybe she was right about the aliases. I thought back to the maze I was put through to get here. The devil himself couldn't find us. With Briley's charm and my business sense, maybe we could make it work. Then after the business took off, we would add deep sea fishing. And maybe, if Briley was interested, we'd get certified to take people scuba diving. I couldn't help following her excitement.

***

We spent our days snorkeling and making plans for the future and our nights making love. Briley's hair lightened and her skin darkened from the sun and sea. She was a goddess, and she made me feel like her hero.

As the days turned to weeks and the weeks rolled into months, the snorkeling idea grew on me. There was no reason we couldn't pull it off with our new identities.

I couldn't think of a scenario where vacationers wanting a snorkeling experience would question who we were or where we came from. The Marshals made contact once a month to check in, so I'd run the idea past them before we dove in. A silent chuckle shook my shoulders as I considered the pun.

Overall, we seemed to be living the life. A life vacationer's lust after and retiree's dream of. But two things were still keeping Briley in a funk. With our lives no longer caught up in developing careers, we had decided to go ahead and try for a child.

I didn't need to see the stick in her hand to know the results. Her expression twisted, trying to hold back the emotion and hide her pain from me. As soon as she reached my arms, any control she thought she had was lost. Her tiny frame shook in my arms as I held her, rubbing her back and trying to ease her sorrow.

"It'll happen, B. It takes time."

I felt her head shake against my chest. "There's something wrong."

"Nothing's wrong, B." I gripped her biceps, pulling her away from me enough to look into her eyes. "It's just stress. Give it time."

It was obviously stress. Her body knew she wasn't in the safe zone yet and bringing a child into that chaos wouldn't be ideal. Or maybe it was me—my seed not taking purchase because I needed to protect her and our future children. There was no consoling her about it. She was determined something was wrong, and once her mind was set, there was no changing it.

Her hands slid up between us and with palms flat on my chest, she pushed away. Her brows pulled together, forming that infamous V in her forehead that let me know a shit storm was brewing. "I'm gonna take a walk."

Before I could process what I was going to do or say, I gripped her wrist and twirled her around. "Not this time, B. We're talking about this now and settling it."

A mix of anger and shock pinched the corners of her mouth as she stood before me. "I just need to walk it off alone, Coop."

"You mean marinate in sadness. I know you too well, babe. You'll walk along the beach, thinking about how your life sucks and letting all the bad weigh you down. Maybe you'll construct a new poem while you stroll about dark clouds and how the waves crashing against the shore are full of rage." My hands moved to her shoulders and rested gently once I knew she wasn't going to budge. "You've got to balance the sadness with the good, baby. Think. You have life. You have me. We have time." I cupped the back of my neck and blew out a frustrated breath.

"I know, you're right." She sighed and blinked back unshed tears.

"Excuse me? Can you repeat that?" I huffed out a laugh. Bad timing.

"You're right. Honestly, Coop, I think it's just something to focus on right now. A way to hang on to the sadness, even though I don't want to. All of this," She waved her hand from her chest to mine. "Seems too good to be true. I want to trust this happiness, but my mind is revolting." She chuckled nervously. "They have loony bins here in Mexico, right?"

"If they do, I think I've found our new careers. We could run the place, screwball." I pulled her into my chest and held her there, letting the feel of her giggles vibrating against my body consume me.

"Yes we could, you big kook."

***

The second thing that sucked the joy from Briley was not being able to see her mother and tell her that she was alive. I could understand this one, as the thought of my parents crazy with grief threatened to take my sanity. Often I'd wake before the sun came up and find Briley standing on the lanai in the back of the house. The last time it happened—two nights ago—when I asked her to come back to bed, she cried herself to sleep in my arms. So I took a risk, maybe one that I shouldn't have, but I felt like I had no choice. When I let Briley in on the plan, there was no going back.

"It's dangerous." I shook my head. "I wish I hadn't said anything."

"It's brilliant, C." She cupped my face in her hands, stood on tiptoes, and kissed me hard on the mouth. "*You're* brilliant. Thank you so much. We'll do the same thing for your parents, okay?"

"The Marshal still has to agree to it. Don't get your hopes up yet."

The smile faded from her lips and her expression grew serious. "No matter what, you're always there for me. Always my hero. You've given up so much for me. Don't think for one second I don't know just how much." Unshed tears shimmered in her eyes as she spoke. "One of these days I'm going to prove my love to you. I'll do something over-the-top awesome for you. Not a payback—I could never compete—just something to show you that you're my everything, and I love you more than I could ever express in words."

Pay me back? Briley and her silly notions. I chuckled and shook my head.

She was beside me on the sand, drawing infinity symbols with her finger. Snaking my arm around her waist, I scooted her closer to my side, dragging a line across the sand with her rear. "Every morning when I wake up to you beside me, your sweet smile, the way you take care of me physically, mentally, emotionally. Every single day you give me a gift, B—a priceless gift. Don't ever think you owe me, B. You do more for me than I can ever do for you."

She started to protest, but I covered her mouth with mine. A giggle erupted, her body vibrating beneath me as I eased her onto the sand and devoured her lips. We could've easily made love on the beach—not a soul in either direction—but it wasn't as romantic as the movies made it seem. We'd attempted it one night, candles all around, a blanket to keep the sand out of places it didn't belong. But the movies never mentioned bugs, and no matter how careful you were, sand was a tricky adversary that managed to make its way into those very places you didn't want it.

Instead, we walked hand in hand back to the house, going over the plan again. It was the same routine but I never tired of it. Knocking as much sand off of our legs and feet as possible before heading to the bathroom inside our bedroom. The shower stall barely accommodated one person, let alone two, but we managed. Scrubbing sand off each other in the small space, our bodies sliding against each other as we moved, quickly turned into foreplay. With one arm snaking around my waist, Briley stroked a soap-filled sponge over my body in long, erotic strokes with her free hand. She lowered her wet, slippery body all the way down as she washed one leg and then the other. She arched her back, ensuring our connection wasn't lost and slowly drew her body back up.

I was fully turned on but wanted to make her wait. Taking the sponge from her, I rinsed and re-soaped it. I washed each granule of sand off her back, starting at the shoulders and working my way down. My fingers deliberately left the sponge and traced the curve of her waist, over the dimples in her lower back, and around her hips until I was cupping her fine ass.

She slid her hands up and planted them on the shower wall in front of her. Bending at the waist, she let me know she was ready. Instead, I turned her around. She huffed but let me sponge her arms, waist, stomach, and finally her breasts. I couldn't wait another moment to be inside of her, but I wanted to bring her pleasure another way first.

Lowering myself without breaking through the shower wall was difficult, but possible if we were positioned just right. She was so ready, it didn't take long to bring her over the edge, my name spilling from her lips as she gripped my hair in one hand and held herself up by white-knuckling the tiled wall with the other.

Giving her a few moments to recover, I held her in my arms and kissed her lips, her moans vibrating on my tongue. "I need you now, baby."

"Take me." She turned away from me, planting her palms on the wall and bending at the waist. I knew I wouldn't last long after hearing her soft moans and I needed to pound into her fast and hard. Just before the blinding sparks of bliss consumed me, I bit down on the tendon between her neck and shoulder, careful not to let my lust-induced aggression take me too far. It worked every time. She cried out as her core clenched around me.

Neither of us moved. Steam billowed around us as I wrapped my arms around her and rested my forehead on her back. Fucking outstanding.

Forty

Cooper

Connor Stermann married Brandi Sharpe on a Thursday morning in a small catholic church two hours from our little house by the sea. Even though our real names weren't used, the vows were true and accepted in God's eyes.

I couldn't get used to calling her Brandi in public, so I continued to call her B and I was either C, babe, darling, or—and this one made me laugh—lovey.

Briley was happy with the ceremony, but I still wanted something more meaningful for her. So, I went to work, stealing a few moments here and there in secret. It was a lot of work and took me over two weeks to get it all together, but totally worth it to see the sparkle in my girl's eyes. God gifted us with a full moon on December sixth, which was nice since I didn't have enough candles to light the path to the beach.

She looked stunning in the strapless white dress I'd picked up for her in town. The flowers were the most difficult to acquire. Even if my Spanish didn't suck, I still wouldn't have known the names of the flowers I knew I wanted her to have, especially the white flowers that smelled like a candle she liked to burn back in Tampa.

"I need flowers, por favor." Sliding a list of flower names across the counter, I added, "I don't know all the names. Can I look around?"

"Sí," she nodded as she looked at my list.

I'd finally gotten what I wanted across to the florist, after a comedy of errors.

"I'd like berries mixed with the orange and white flowers."

The florist gave me a funny look. "Fruit?"

"No, berries. Decoration." Looking through a book, I found what I was looking for.

"Ah, sí, sí."

I thought the hardest would be trying to get *birds-of-paradise*. I couldn't remember the name so I asked for flowers with pointy noses. Somehow she knew exactly what I was talking about.

Once everything was set up, I made a list of clues for Briley. She drove me crazy trying to get me to spill, but I held strong.

"C'mon, what did you do? Cook? Are we eating down there?" She gripped my biceps and tried to lock eyes.

"Just do what the notes say."

"Notes? It's a scavenger hunt?" Her eyes lit. "Wait, I have to hunt for my food?"

"Give up, B, and go get dressed." I turned, hiding my grin, and faced the window in the living room overlooking the ocean. "If you don't hurry, the birds will eat all the food." I chuckled to myself.

"I knew it!" With a skip in her step, she headed for the bedroom and I raced outside to make sure everything was set.

The first note was attached to the bag holding her dress. It read, *"Put this on and find your next clue in the guest bathroom."*

Her bouquet, along with the next note, sat on the bathroom counter. *"Take this down to the beach and follow the signs."*

There were no signs, only candles and shells to guide her toward me. She was already my wife in the eyes of God, but when I saw her walking toward me, the bouquet in her hands and the shimmer of tears flooding her eyes, I felt like the luckiest man on earth. It was just the two of us on the beach that night to witness the promises we made to each other and only our memories to capture the beauty.

"What have you done?" Briley whispered as one of the tears slipped from the pool and traveled down her cheek.

"I wanted something more meaningful for us." I took her free hand in mine. "Conner and Brandi are married, and I'm good with that, but I wanted Cooper and Briley to have their own thing, you know." I shrugged a shoulder and hoped she didn't think my idea was foolish.

"You never cease to amaze me, Cooper. I'm the luckiest girl in the world."

We stared at each other for a long moment before I huffed out a chuckle that turned to a full on belly laugh. "I have no idea what to do next. I only got this far with the plans."

"Vows. We should do those," she said on a giggle.

With a nod, I agreed. "I'll go first." Clearing my throat and straightening my shoulders, I attempted the impossible task of telling Briley exactly how I felt about her and trying to voice all the promises I had every intention of keeping. "Baby . . . Briley," Pausing, I took both of her hands in mine, my left fingers hooking around the bouquet in her hand. "I've loved you since we were kids. You're my best friend. You make me laugh, you challenge me, you make me want to be a better man." The words were coming out of my mouth, but the voice didn't sound like mine. After a humorless chuckle, I continued. "You're the love of my life. I promise to love you with all that I have, in good times and bad. When you're stubborn, out of control, and even when you're a smart ass—especially when you're a smart ass—I'll love you and take care of you to the best of my ability." I chose not to mention *until death do we part*, for obvious reasons.

Briley wiped the tears under her eyes, swallowed hard, and took her turn. I'd wanted to make this night special for her, but instead she imbedded an unforgettable memory into my heart. "Cooper, you're the love of my life. You're my hero, my protector, my best friend. I promise to do everything in my power to be all those things to you. I never want to be apart from you again. As your wife, your life mate, half of your soul, I will be your biggest fan and give you more love than you can stand. But you promised to deal with it, remember?" She smirked and I laughed with a nod. "I love you so much, Coop, and I thank God for choosing me to walk by your side. We've been through a lot, and we almost didn't make it. But in the end we were blessed with a love so rare . . . a gift that I'll treasure as long as I live."

I winced at her last words. I couldn't and wouldn't think of her life ending. My mind refused to revisit that hell. Kissing her to seal our vows was next and I savored the moment. Releasing her hands, I lifted my palm to her face, gently cupping her cheek as my other arm snaked around her waist. Dipping down, my lips a hairsbreadth from hers, I whispered, "Now my life begins."

Lips pressed together, eyes closed, I gripped her and pulled her tightly to me. As the kiss deepened, so did the promise of what was and what would be. We danced to our favorite song— the sound of the waves rolling onto the sand—until the desperation and longing were too much.

Briley pulled away, cupped my face in her hands, and tilted my head down. "Make love to me, husband."

Without a word, I scooped her into my arms, her hands locking around the back of my neck as she squealed. "It's too far to carry me all the way."

"I could carry you to the next town knowing what awaits me at the finish line." With long strides I carried her down the beach and up the hill to our place, enjoying her lips and tongue across my jaw, playful nips at my neck and ear, and especially the feel of her hand slipping into my pants, gripping my dick as it hardened at her touch.

Making love to Briley was always amazing. Each time seemed as good if not better than the last. But there was something deeper after we shared our personal vows on the beach. We connected in a way I didn't know existed. Each sensation was intensified, like we'd paid extra for the premium package. There was no explanation for it, no way to understand it, but Briley felt it too and was fascinated.

Forty-One
Briley

Cooper and I sat at the bar in the kitchen, waiting for his brilliant plan to unfold. Shifting from side to side, I tried to contain the storm inside of me. Excitement took my breath, worry that it wouldn't work creased my brows, and my bottom lip was raw from nervous biting. The Marshal finally agreed to help us, as long as he felt it was safe, but the small chance that he didn't consumed me. He'd done so much for us already—I'd never understand why—and for some reason I couldn't make myself believe he'd so more.

My heart rate spiked when Cooper pulled up the site and my father's tombstone filled the computer screen. On the ground in front of the stone was a single poinsettia bloom—silk since you couldn't get fresh ones this time of year, especially in Tampa.

"He did it." My grip on the side of my chair tightened. "Think she'll see it? Will she get it?"

Cooper rested his hand on mine, curling his fingers over my locked knuckles. "Of course she will. That was your thing."

My free hand instinctively unlatched from the chair and slapped over my mouth. The threadbare hold on my emotions gave way, unleashing a flood of warm tears as my mother's frame came into view.

"She looks good, right?" I muffled through my hand that wouldn't move away from my mouth.

"She does." Cooper's arm snaked around my shoulder and tightened around me, helping to hold all the pieces of me together.

Afraid to move, I remained still, watching my mother pick up the flower and study it. She looked around the cemetery for the source, and I hoped she would understand what it meant. My mother and I had created things only the two of us knew about. The same way best friends made up their own language, we had totems that only meant something to us.

When I was at that terrible age—thirteen—I hated to hear her say 'I love you' in public. So she said 'poinsettia.' The ridiculousness of it made me laugh, and that was a difficult task for a teen girl. She'd smirk and retort, "It's so far out, no one would ever guess what we were talking about."

It stuck, like so many other things she came up with to bond the two of us. We also used the word poinsettia instead of an apology that was too difficult to give. One night, after a knock-down, drag-out fight we had over something we couldn't agree on, she put a silk poinsettia on my pillow. I brought it to her room that night and asked what it meant.

"Since it works for everything else, I thought it would work for an apology, too. We don't have to agree on everything, baby girl. We can agree to disagree. But I always want to you to know that I love you and things are okay between us even when we disagree."

She had to understand my message now. She had to.

From the computer screen, I watched my mother as she held the flower, her chest heaving from the sobs.

"She's upset." My eyes wide with worry and regret, I hopped off the stool and turned away from the screen. "Oh God, I made a mistake. She doesn't get it."

Cooper stood in front of me and hooked a finger under my chin. "Just wait. Give her a chance."

He climbed back onto his stool and pulled me between his legs. With one arm draped over my shoulder, and the other hand stroking the length of my arm, we continued to watch my mother on screen.

She cried for a long time, resting against my father's tombstone and hugging that damn silk flower to her chest. When she finally stood and gathered herself, she brought her hand to her mouth and blew a kiss into the air. The smile on her lips lit up her entire face. I couldn't tell if she was laughing or crying—probably both, as was I—but it was clear she'd gotten the message. Her baby girl was alive and safe.

And one day, when this mess was over, I'd embrace her again, and we'd laugh and cry. But until then, every year on January tenth—the anniversary of my father's death and the day we had always visited his grave—I'd have a poinsettia waiting there for her. Maybe one day soon, I'd surprise her with two.

THE END

ABOUT THE AUTHOR

Eleanor Green writes New Adult and Contemporary Romance swirled with mystery.

She currently lives just outside of Nashville, Tennessee with her husband and two children.

CONTACT ELEANOR

Email: contact@authoreleanorgreen.com

Website: http://authoreleanorgreen.com

Twitter: @AuthorEGreen

Newsletter http://bit.ly/1kPrTZ8

FB: https://www.facebook.com/AuthorEGreen

Instagram: eleanorgreen10

I'd love for you to be a part of a fun group where I share exclusive giveaways and we talk books! Just search Facebook for:

The Green Room

OTHER BOOKS BY ELEANOR GREEN

Torn

Wait for Me

Eleanor Green